Would she ever forgive him? Caine wondered as he watched her sleep.

He wasn't sure, but he knew he couldn't let it matter. He'd walked around Limores for a couple of hours, trying to decide what to do, but in the end he'd had no choice. Her life and her baby's were the pawns in a deadly game, and he didn't even know the rules. He had to protect them. Even if Lexie never forgave him.

Finally she opened her eyes. "Is everything set for tonight?"

He saw the sudden tenseness in her hands, and for a moment he thought she knew. He hated himself for forcing her to do this. But he shut his mind to everything except what would happen if El Cuchillo caught them.

If he thought about what he was going to make her do, he wouldn't be able to go through with it.

Dear Reader,

Our lead title this month hardly needs an introduction, nor does the author. Nora Roberts is a multiple *New York Times* bestseller, and *Megan's Mate* follows her extremely popular cross-line miniseries THE CALHOUN WOMEN. Megan O'Riley isn't a Calhoun by birth, but they consider her and her young son family just the same. And who better to teach her how to love again than longtime family friend Nate Fury?

Our newest cross-line miniseries is DADDY KNOWS LAST, and this month it reaches its irresistible climax right here in Intimate Moments. In *Discovered: Daddy*, bestselling author Marilyn Pappano finally lets everyone know who's the father of Faith Harper's baby. Everyone, that is, except dad-to-be Nick Russo. Seems there's something Nick doesn't remember about that night nine months ago!

The rest of the month is terrific, too, with new books by Marion Smith Collins, Elane Osborn, Vella Munn and Margaret Watson. You'll want to read them all, then come back next month for more of the best books in the business—right here at Silhouette Intimate Moments.

Enjoy!

Leslie Wainger
Senior Editor and Editorial Coordinator

Please address questions and book requests to:
Silhouette Reader Service
U.S.: 3010 Walden Ave., P.O. Box 1325, Buffalo, NY 14269
Canadian: P.O. Box 609, Fort Erie, Ont. L2A 5X3

TO SAVE HIS CHILD

MARGARET WATSON

Silhouette®

INTIMATE™ MOMENTS®

Published by Silhouette Books

America's Publisher of Contemporary Romance

SILHOUETTE BOOKS

ISBN 0-373-07750-5

TO SAVE HIS CHILD

Copyright © 1996 by Margaret Watson

This edition published by arrangement with Harlequin Books S.A.

Printed in U.S.A.

Books by Margaret Watson

Silhouette Intimate Moments

An Innocent Man #636
An Honorable Man #708
To Save His Child #750

MARGARET WATSON

From the time she learned to read, Margaret could usually be found with her nose in a book. Her lifelong passion for reading led to her interest in writing, and now she's happily writing exactly the kind of stories she likes to read. Margaret is a veterinarian who lives in the Chicago suburbs with her husband and their three daughters. In her spare time she enjoys roller blading, birding and spending time with her family. Readers can write to Margaret at P.O. Box 2333, Naperville, IL 60567-2333.

For all my friends in Chicago North.
Thanks for your help, your support and,
most of all, your friendship.

Chapter 1

"You're the only one I trust to get her out of that godforsaken country, O'Roarke. Dammit, I'd go there myself if I could."

Caine O'Roarke watched as James Hollister pushed himself away from the desk and stood slowly and painfully, turning to look out the window.

"She's all I have left," the older man muttered. "I don't want to lose her in some senseless revolution."

"You should have thought of that before you let her go down there in the first place." Caine leaned back in his chair and rested his boots on the polished walnut surface of Hollister's desk.

James turned around and scowled at him. "You should know as well as anyone that you don't 'let' Lexie do anything. She's done what she damn well pleased since she was fifteen years old."

Caine raised his eyebrows. "And whose fault is that? You're going to have to learn to control your daughter, James."

Instead of blowing up at him, the older man smiled wearily. "Wait until you have a daughter, O'Roarke. Then you can lecture me on child rearing. Until then, keep your opinions to yourself.''

Caine shifted in his chair, restless and edgy. ''Those weren't opinions—just pointing out the facts.'' Sliding down farther into the soft leather, he continued, ''You still haven't told me why I should risk my butt yanking your daughter out of San Rafael.''

James eased himself down into his chair again and fixed Caine with a piercing look. ''Before you left on that assignment eleven months ago, you were dating her. I would think that would be reason enough.''

Caine sat up slowly, his heart suddenly pounding. His feet hit the expensive Oriental carpet with a muffled thud. ''Did Lexie tell you that things were serious between us?''

''Of course not.'' James sighed. ''Lexie's never been serious about anything in her life. I just thought you might have a vested interest in getting her safely back to Washington.''

''Why? We never had any future. Lexie and I came from two different worlds. We had about as much in common as a poodle and a pit bull.'' Caine heard the hint of pain and longing in his voice and struggled to control it. It had taken a long time, but he'd thought he'd finally managed to banish his useless fantasies about Lexie Hollister. He didn't want to examine his reaction to her father's request.

James ignored his outburst. ''You've been a lone wolf for too long, Caine. You and Lexie could be good for each other,'' he said quietly. ''I thought so a year ago, and I still do.''

''You're dreaming, old man.'' Caine's voice was brutal. ''The only thing Lexie and I were good at was fighting.'' There *was* one other thing, he acknowledged silently, struggling to control his body's response to the sudden memories. It just wasn't the kind of thing you mentioned to a woman's father.

''Maybe she's grown up down there in San Rafael.'' Her father sounded wistful.

''Yeah, and maybe cows will start climbing trees, too.'' Caine propped his feet on the desk again, ignoring James's withering look. ''She's probably down there visiting all the nightclubs in Limores and hanging out with the rich planters' kids.''

"What did she do to you, Caine?" Hollister's voice was quiet.

"Not a thing. We only 'dated' for a month, remember?"

No, Lexie hadn't done anything to him. And that was the problem. In one short month he'd come to hate her world—the world of parties every night and shopping and lunches every day. He'd raged at her for her useless life, and she'd coolly told him that no one was forcing him to participate.

But he couldn't stay away from her. In spite of his determination not to get involved with anyone, in spite of the way he felt about her friends and her life-style, he'd become damn near obsessive about Lexie Hollister. Underneath the social butterfly he'd sensed an intelligent, caring woman, and it had infuriated him that she wouldn't grow up. He'd told James the truth. In the short month that he'd known her, they'd spent most of the time fighting.

Except for the two times they'd made love. There had been no hostility between them then. Even now, almost a year later, the memories of those two nights could get him harder faster than any other woman in the flesh.

"Maybe it was a mistake, encouraging you to take Lexie out." James Hollister suddenly looked old and defeated.

Caine shook his head and stood. "No, James, it wasn't a mistake. Lexie taught me a lot. She taught me how the other half lives, and made me damn glad I'm not one of them. I'll always be grateful to her for that."

As he started for the door, the other man spoke behind him. He sounded utterly weary. "I shouldn't have asked, Caine. I'm sorry."

Caine slowly turned around, knowing he couldn't refuse his mentor's request. "I'll go get her for you, old man. I owe you." He smiled without humor. "If I recall, that's how I got involved with her last time. It's a good thing I'm getting out of this business. I can't afford to owe you anything else."

Lexie Hollister tucked a strand of damp, limp hair behind her ear and took a deep breath. Squatting down onto the dirt floor, she took one of the boy's trembling hands into her own and spoke soothingly to him.

"Now, Luis, I know you're scared. Seeing a big needle like that is frightening. Why, it's almost as big as one of the mosquitoes that come out at night, isn't it?"

Luis gave her a watery chuckle, and she felt him relax a bit. At five years of age, he was old enough to realize that getting a vaccination was going to hurt. And he was stubborn enough to refuse to lift his shirtsleeve, in spite of the pleas and threats from his mother. The other woman rolled her eyes when Lexie glanced up at her.

It was time to try another tack.

"Maybe you think that a man such as yourself should receive his vaccination by himself. Should I ask your mother to leave?"

Lexie could see the boy was torn. The idea that he was a man was enormously appealing, but he was still afraid of that needle. She would have to help him make up his mind.

"Consuela, why don't you wait outside while I give Luis his shot? A man likes to be alone at times like these." Lexie could see that the boy's mother was going to protest, so she hurried her out the door. Turning to Luis, she rolled up his sleeve and swabbed his arm with alcohol.

"It will only hurt for a moment, Luis," she said gently. "Then you can go and tell the other boys how brave you were." While the child was contemplating his coming glory, she quickly and efficiently injected the vaccine. By the time he yelped, it was all over.

Lexie leaned back against the wooden table and watched as the dark-haired boy and his mother walked away from her tiny house. One more child vaccinated, she thought wearily, and only about a million more to go. But as long as the government of San Rafael was able to get vaccine to her, the children of the village of Santa Ysabel would be protected.

Glancing at her watch, she calculated that she would have time to see at least one more patient, maybe two, before she had to take a break. Picking up the cup of lukewarm coffee that stood on a small table, she drank it down and willed the caffeine to kick in. Weariness had been her constant companion lately, and she got through most days with a combination of coffee and stubbornness.

Stepping to the door, she opened it and called out, "Whoever's next can come on in." Without waiting to see who followed her back into the house, she walked over to her most important possession—the small refrigerator—and squatted down to remove another dose of the precious vaccine.

"Your Spanish has improved since the last time I saw you, Lexie."

The tiny vial of vaccine fell from her hand and rolled across the dirt floor, disappearing under the refrigerator. Shock held her frozen in place. *It couldn't be.*

Gripping the edge of the refrigerator door with one hand, she slowly got up and turned around. *It was.*

Caine O'Roarke stood in her house, not more than three feet away from her. If possible, his face looked even harder than it had eleven months ago. It could have been carved from granite, and his blue eyes were devoid of expression as he stared down at her.

"Caine. What are you doing here?" Her tongue felt thick and clumsy as she stumbled over the words.

"I'm staying at the resort right up the road," he retorted. "Hell, Lexie, what do you think I'm doing here? Your father sent me to bring you home."

"So you're still doing what my father tells you to do, Caine?" Just saying the words made her tremble inside. She told herself it was rage and not pain that caused it.

"This time he's right." He ignored the reference to their past history. "The political situation in San Rafael is critically unstable, and he doesn't want you caught in the middle of it. Whoever's in charge of these rebels seems to be virulently anti-American. It's not a good time for you to be hanging around in a South American village at the back of nowhere. Especially with a name like Hollister. Your father is well-known in this country."

"My father is several thousand miles away. He has nothing to do with this. And I'm not simply 'hanging around,' as you so quaintly put it," she said coldly. She fed the anger, hoping to keep other, more dangerous emotions at bay. "I have a job to do here. So while I appreciate your concern, I'm afraid I'll have to decline your generous offer."

"What's your job that's so important, Lexie?" he asked scornfully. "Organizing the weekly luncheon for the ladies of Santa Ysabel?"

In spite of the fact that it had been almost a year since she'd last seen him, his barbed comments about her life-style still hurt. Even though they were no longer valid. Turning away from him, she searched under the refrigerator until her hand closed around the smooth glass vial she'd dropped. She carefully placed it back in the refrigerator.

"I'm the only nurse in this village," she said quietly. "If I leave, there won't be any medical care for the people here. And if a civil war is coming, it's even more important that I stay."

He didn't answer, and she turned around slowly to find him watching her with stunned astonishment. Finally his eyes narrowed. "Since when are you a nurse, Lexie?"

"Since I graduated from nursing school five years ago." Congratulating herself on her even voice, she began methodically straightening the contents of the tiny table that sat next to the refrigerator.

"I never heard anything about your being a nurse."

His voice was tinged with disbelief, and Lexie let her anger bubble to the surface, willing it to bury the pain of his scornful words. Spinning around to face him, she said, "There were a lot of things you never heard about, Caine. You didn't stick around long enough to ask. But then I guess when James Hollister says 'Jump,' you only ask how high."

A tiny voice told her to stop. But she couldn't. "Since we're on the subject, there's something I've always wondered about. Did you sleep with me on my father's orders, too? Was that another way he thought he could control me?"

She'd finally managed to remove that remote, unreadable expression from his face. Something blazed to life in his eyes for a moment, quickly replaced by a look that was half fury, half pain. "Nobody tells me to do anything, Lexie," he said softly. "I thought you'd figured that out by now."

"I never figured out anything about you, Caine," she whispered. "Nothing at all."

"You'll have plenty of time to learn on our way out of here," he said, ignoring her words and looking around. "Take as much as you can carry on your back, and we'll leave in the morning.''

"Didn't you hear me? I'm not going anywhere.''

"Don't be a fool. If half of the stories I've heard about this guy are true, you don't want to be within five hundred miles of this country. What is it that they call him?''

"El Cuchillo," she answered reluctantly.

"And they don't call him The Knife for nothing, I'm damn sure of that. So what's the problem, Lexie?'' he asked, his voice impatient. "Believe me, it'll be easier to get out of here now, with me, than in a couple of months when all hell's broken loose.''

"I'm not going anywhere, Caine, not with you or anyone else. Haven't you heard me? This is where I belong. I've made a life for myself here, and I'm happy. I don't need rescuing.''

"You need your head examined, that's what you need.''

His deep voice began to rise, the sound echoing off the mud-brick walls. Lexie looked anxiously toward the next room, her ears straining to hear and her palms beginning to sweat. She had to get him out of here.

"Look, I have patients waiting to see me," she said, speaking too quickly. "Could we continue this conversation later?''

"I don't care when we discuss it as long as you're ready to go tomorrow morning.'' He looked around the small room one more time, then back at her. His gaze was hard and determined. "I'm staying in the inn at the other end of the village. I'll be back at daybreak.''

He turned and walked out her door, and she watched him through the window as he strode down the narrow street. His dark blond hair was too long, as it had been a year earlier, and he'd tied it back with a rolled-up bandanna. His smooth, fluid walk hadn't changed, either, and she couldn't tear her gaze away from him. Sensual memories stirred as she watched the way his faded jeans hugged his taut rear end.

This is the man who walked away from you eleven months ago, she reminded herself as she moved back from the window. A fragment of remembered pain stirred in her heart, but she pushed it ruthlessly away. She couldn't afford to wallow in self-pity. She had to figure out what to do. If she knew Caine

O'Roarke, and she was afraid she did, he wasn't going to disappear just because she'd told him no.

Caine had always moved through life as if he owned the world, and it didn't look as if that had changed, either. He was still the same arrogant, autocratic man he'd been a year ago, making demands instead of requests. He'd wanted her to change her life back then, too.

This time she wouldn't come close to succumbing to him, she vowed. She was stronger now. She had grown up down here in San Rafael, and Caine O'Roarke had no power over her anymore. Sooner or later he would have to realize that she couldn't be persuaded to leave. Then he would go away and leave her alone.

Her gaze strayed back to the window, but he had disappeared. It was just as well, she told herself. She had things to do, and she couldn't afford to be distracted by him. Moving to the door of her tiny house, she looked at the silent women and children who waited outside.

"Whoever's next can come on in," she said, suddenly feeling bone tired. As she turned and walked back to the refrigerator for a dose of vaccine, she ruthlessly tamped down the emotions that Caine had freed from their burial place deep inside her. There was no place in her heart or her life for him. Any possibility of that had ended eleven months ago. His unexpected appearance in her life was simply a brief diversion from her usual routine.

Turning around, she forced a smile onto her face and crouched down next to the frightened little girl. "I know you're scared, Pilar. But it will only hurt for a minute."

Caine lounged against a tree across the street from Lexie's house and watched a steady stream of women and children go into the small building and emerge a few minutes later. The children were invariably crying when they came out, their mothers trying to comfort them. What was Lexie doing in there?

Finally he saw the last family leave. Pushing away from the tree trunk, he strolled over to the hut, identical to the others in the village. Before he knocked on the door he looked at the tiny building Lexie now called home.

It was a far cry from the house where she'd grown up and lived until eleven months ago. That stately Colonial stood on several acres in one of Washington, D.C.'s, most exclusive suburbs. Furnished with antiques and priceless heirlooms, it reeked of old money, privilege and influence. It was a setting that had seemed to fit her perfectly.

The last place he'd expected to find Lexie Hollister, spoiled debutante and member of the idle rich, was a mud-brick hovel in a tiny South American village. The only thing more surprising was finding her giving medical care to the people who lived in that village.

Lexie was a nurse. He still couldn't believe that. But then, nothing about what he'd seen today jibed with the woman he'd known.

Then which was the real Lexie? The question prodded at him, made him slightly uneasy, until he dismissed it. She was playing at nurse this week, the way she'd played at everything else in her life. No doubt she would have come to her senses by now. In fact, she was probably all packed up and eager to leave. Raising his hand, he knocked on her door.

"Come on in."

He heard the weary resignation in her voice as he pushed open the door. She sat on a rickety chair next to a tiny table, a half-eaten tortilla on a crude plate in front of her. The first expression that crossed her face when she saw him was surprise. Then she looked down at her plate to hide her face, but not before he'd seen the unwilling softening in her eyes.

"What are you doing here, Caine?" She didn't look up at him as she spoke.

"You told me we could talk after all your patients left. I didn't see anyone waiting for you."

Pushing the plate away, she finally looked up at him. "I'm busy, Caine." Her gaze darted toward the next room, and when she looked back at him he saw desperation in her eyes. "Why don't you come back tonight, after dinner? Anything we need to talk about can wait until then."

Leaning back against the hip-high refrigerator, he crossed his ankles and folded his arms across his chest. He'd never seen Lexie rattled like this, ever. Except for two times, he reminded himself, and she'd done her best to hide it then. His body tightened in response to the memories, and he struggled to suppress them. Now was not the time to be thinking of how Lexie tasted and felt.

"What is it that you wanted to talk about, anyway?" he drawled. "Did you have questions about what to bring with you?"

She pushed away from the table so fast that the chair almost tipped over. "I told you, I'm not going with you. You're not going to change my mind, and you're not going to browbeat me into agreeing with you, either."

"I don't recall ever browbeating you into anything." He raised his eyebrows. "I thought everything that happened between us was by mutual agreement. Or am I forgetting something?"

She looked away, but not before he'd seen the sudden flare of sensual awareness in her eyes. "You were always good at convincing people to do what you wanted them to do, Caine," she muttered. "That's why you got along so well with my father. He appreciated someone with the same qualities he had."

He straightened, startled by her perception. To the rest of the world, his relationship with James Hollister was one of opposites attracting. Few people had seen below the surface of either of them to find the essential similarities.

"Lexie, your father doesn't have anything to do with this. It's a matter of common sense. The government is warning all Americans to get out of San Rafael while they have a chance." He struggled to keep his voice calm and unemotional, when what he wanted to do was shake her until she saw sense.

Walking over to the small stove, she scraped the remainder of her lunch into a small bowl and carefully covered it, then waited for him to move so she could slide it into the refrigerator. Straightening, she looked up at him and instinctively moved back a step.

It was a good thing, he told himself grimly. Her formerly long, streaked blond hair had been inexpertly cut short and now curled around her face. The strands of lighter blond hair that he was sure used to come out of a bottle were now completely natural, put there by the sun. No makeup enhanced her bright blue eyes or her flawless skin, and there were lines around her eyes that he'd never seen before. Instead of designer clothes she wore baggy shorts and an equally baggy blouse. Both were scrupulously clean, but far from new.

In short, she was the complete antithesis of the fashionable, perfectly made-up and coifed woman he'd known a year ago. And he found that he suddenly ached to kiss her. It had been eleven long months since he'd seen her, and the woman he'd known had disappeared almost completely. In her place was a woman he hardly recognized, but desire for the new Lexie hit him like a fist in the gut.

He saw an answering awareness in her eyes before she took another step backward and turned away. She fiddled with something on the table, carefully keeping her back turned to him. "I'll be fine, Caine," she said. "You can go home and tell my father that you did your best but I was as stubborn as ever. I've grown up, and I'm taking responsibility for myself."

The flash of approval surprised him. He'd felt a lot of emotions for Lexie Hollister, but admiration of her character had never been one of them. "Your father would be proud of you, Lexie." His voice was low. "But I don't think you completely understand the situation here in San Rafael. Nobody knows much about this El Cuchillo, but what we've heard isn't good. The guy is brutal, and he doesn't like Americans. If he gets control of this part of the country, you'll be in danger."

She turned around, and he saw that she'd managed to shutter her face. That surprised him, too. In the past, Lexie had been an open book. "I'll be safe here, Caine. The people in Santa Ysabel are my friends. They'll take care of me."

"You don't owe these people anything, Lexie." He tried to keep his voice level. "I'm sure they appreciate all you've done for them, but they would be the first to tell you to go. If they're your friends, they wouldn't want you to stay and put yourself in danger."

"First of all, Caine, you're wrong. I owe these people everything. They saved my life," she said quietly. "And **you're** right, they would tell me to go. But I can't. This is where I belong."

Her casual words about people saving her life evoked a shiver of panic that was disturbing. He heard himself asking, "What in God's name happened? How did they save your life?"

"They took me in," she said simply. "They had no reason to help me, and precious little to spare, but they gave it anyway. They showed me what 'Love thy neighbor' really means."

The relief he felt was equally disturbing. "Then you weren't actually in any danger."

She smiled, and he felt as if he'd been struck. It was a smile of such genuine sweetness and caring that he wanted to grab on to it and let it fill the dark corners of his life.

But it wasn't for him, he realized, as she looked out the window. It was as if someone had yanked a rug out from under him. "It depends on your definition of danger," she said. "No, I wasn't in any physical jeopardy. But they made me realize what a worthless waste my life had been up to that point. I had training in a profession that would have allowed me to do a lot of good, but I'd never used it. All I'd done was spend money and fill empty hours."

It was what he'd told her, more than once, in their past life. He should have been glad, should have rejoiced that she'd finally grown up. Instead, it made him uneasy. The new Lexie had backbone that he'd never even suspected. The steady resolve in her eyes told him that she'd refined her stubbornness, redirected it toward what she thought was the right thing to do. This Lexie had decided she needed to stay in this village, and it was going to be damn hard to convince her otherwise.

"If you won't think of yourself, what about your father?" Maybe he could appeal to her newfound sense of responsibility. "He's worried about you, Lexie. He wants to make sure you're all right."

"Now you can tell him, can't you?" Her gaze was cool as she looked at him. As he stared at her, wondering what would convince her to go, he saw her eyes flicker toward the other room again. Before he could ask her why, she looked back at him. "And that brings up another question. How did you find me?"

Shrugging, he said, "I have some connections down here in San Rafael. I asked a few questions and found out where you were."

Now her attention was fully on him. She seemed to have forgotten whatever had distracted her in that other room. "Who could know who I am, much less where I am? Nobody knows I'm here."

He nodded toward the refrigerator. "I saw what looked like medicine in there. Where are you getting that?"

"From the government," she said slowly. "But they think they're sending it to the doctor who used to live here."

"Maybe he told them otherwise."

"I don't think so. He died two years ago."

"So maybe they know about that." He shrugged again. "Does it really matter? Your father has connections in this country and someone in the government of San Rafael knows you're here in this village. That's how I found out."

"I suppose it doesn't matter," she said slowly. "As long as I get the vaccines and medicine I need, I don't care. I just can't figure out how they know."

"This is a small place, even compared to Washington, D.C. Word gets around."

"I suppose," she replied, doubt in her voice. "I guess the isolation is just an illusion, even here."

She actually sounded regretful. He watched her, puzzled by the complete change in her personality. Something had happened to her down here in San Rafael; something a lot more profound than what she'd told him. A bunch of villagers making her welcome couldn't be the life-altering experience she'd led him to believe.

"This makes it even more imperative that you leave with me, Lexie. If I found out about you so easily, anyone else could, too."

"Nothing's going to happen to me, Caine." Her face softened again as she looked at him. "But I appreciate the trouble you've gone to in order to find me. Even if it was only because my father asked you to do it."

"It wasn't just for your father." He took a step closer, and she didn't move. "He's the one who told me that you were here, and he did ask me to come and find you. But I think I would have done it anyway.''

He didn't know why the sadness appeared in her eyes. ''Would you? I'm not so sure. But thank you for saying so.''

He opened his mouth to answer her, when she jerked her head sideways. A small sound came from the other room, but he couldn't place it.

''You need to go now,'' she said, her voice trembling. She stepped closer to him, as if to herd him out the door. ''I have something to do.''

''I'm not leaving until we get this settled. I won't leave Santa Ysabel without you. I couldn't have that on my conscience.''

''You left once before and didn't seem to have any trouble with your conscience that time.'' Her eyes flashed at him.

''That was different, and you knew it. I had a job to do. I couldn't stay.''

''You didn't have to leave the way you did.'' She clamped her mouth shut, but not before he'd seen her lips trembling.

''Lexie, I've regretted that more times than I can tell you.''

Another sound came from the other room, louder this time, and she looked over again. When she turned to him, he thought he saw fear in her eyes. ''It doesn't matter now,'' she said, her words quiet and rushed. ''That happened a long time ago. In another lifetime, in fact. Please, just leave, Caine. Come back later if you have to, but go now.''

He stood watching her, wondering why she was so frantic for him to leave. Before he could ask her, another sound came from the other room. This time it was louder, and he finally figured out what it was. It was the sound of a baby crying.

When she saw that he wasn't going to budge, weary resignation filled her eyes. ''Excuse me. She needs to be fed.''

He watched her walk away, wondering why she'd been so worried that he would find out she had a patient in the other room. Maybe she remembered his complete indifference to kids, his impatience with anything connected with them.

The sound of her crooning voice drifted past the curtain hanging in the doorway, the words murmured so softly that he couldn't distinguish them. But he couldn't mistake the tenderness and love in her voice. For just a moment he felt a fierce jealousy of the child in the other room. He couldn't remember anyone ever feeling that tenderness toward him.

The baby abruptly stopped crying, and he heard the faint rustling of cloth from the other room. A chair creaked, and he assumed she was feeding her patient.

He turned and headed toward the door. The love he'd felt coming from her when she was talking to the baby made him uncomfortable, and suddenly he didn't want to stay here any longer. He would leave her with her patient and come back later.

He was almost out the door when he realized he hadn't told her what to bring when they left in the morning. Walking back into the house, he brushed the curtain aside and stepped into the dimly lit room. She sat facing the window, and all he could see was the nape of her neck over the top of the chair as she bent over the child in her arms.

The sight of her holding a child evoked a feeling close to panic in his chest, and he struggled to ignore the sensation. What Lexie did with her patients was no concern of his, after all. He walked around the chair, determined to tell her what she needed, then leave. As he looked down at Lexie, holding the baby close, he began to speak and then stopped, shocked.

He'd been expecting to see her holding a bottle. Instead, the soft skin in the shadowed curve of her breast seemed to glow in the dim room, and the child's tiny rosebud mouth suckled at her nipple.

Chapter 2

Lexie felt the heat creeping up her cheeks as Caine watched her nurse. Keeping her head bent, she tried to focus on Ana as the baby ate greedily.

"Why are you nursing that baby?"

His voice was ominously quiet, and she pulled the blanket closer around herself and her child. "Because she's hungry."

"Dammit, Lexie, that's not what I mean and you know it. Whose baby is that?"

She looked up at him, surprised. She was sure he'd figured it out the minute the baby had started crying. "She's mine, of course. Why else would I be nursing her?"

A coldness began to gather in Caine's eyes—a wintry, desolate look she'd never seen there before. "How old is she?"

"Two months old," she said quietly. "Don't bother counting, Caine. She's yours."

He went oddly still in front of her, his face shuttered and impossible to read. "You're saying this is my child?"

"I'm saying you're her biological father, yes." Ana sucked harder and began to wriggle restlessly in her arms. Staring at the red fuzz on the top of her daughter's head, she unfastened the other side of her nursing bra and deftly transferred Ana to her other arm. Trying to keep herself covered with the baby blanket, she waited until the child was happily nursing again before she looked back at Caine.

He was staring at the back of Ana's head, which was all he could see. Lexie watched as a mixture of pain, bewilderment and anger flickered across his face.

"How the hell did that happen?" he finally asked.

She wasn't sure what she had expected, but it wasn't this. Somehow, in her daydreams of this moment, Caine had always professed regret for the way they'd parted and eager, unconditional acceptance of his daughter. That was the trouble with dreams, she thought, trying to keep her lip from quivering. They usually bore no resemblance to reality.

Swallowing hard, she managed to keep her voice level. "I believe it's called a failure of protection."

Caine finally tore his gaze from the back of Ana's head and looked at her. "Just when did you plan on telling me about this?"

"First of all, she's not a 'this.' Her name is Ana," she said fiercely. "And I didn't tell you because I wasn't sure you'd even care. You couldn't have made your feelings about me more clear the morning I woke up alone in your apartment and found you'd gone out of the country on an assignment." The lump in her throat suddenly seemed as big as a boulder. She looked down at Ana, blinking hard. "I suppose I would have written to you when she was older."

"That's damn generous of you."

She felt his gaze on her, but refused to look up.

Finally he spoke again. "I never intended to leave you that way, you know. I thought I would be back by the time you woke up."

The unexpected tenderness in his voice made her eyes burn and her throat constrict. "That's ancient history now," she muttered. "I got over it a long time ago."

"Maybe I didn't." His voice was as quiet as hers.

She looked at him sharply then, but he'd moved away to stare out the window. "This complicates things," he said, almost as if he was speaking to himself. "It's going to be harder to slip out of the country with a baby."

"It doesn't change anything." Ana jerked in her arms, startled, as Lexie's voice rose, and she soothed her daughter with one hand as she spoke. "Nothing has changed. I'm not going with you."

"Yes, you are, Lexie." He didn't even bother to turn around. His gaze fixed on something outside, he continued, "It was idiocy to imagine you could stay when it was just you. Now that you have a baby to consider, how can you even begin to think you can stay in San Rafael?"

"I'll be safe here. No one in the village would let anything happen to me."

He turned around to look at her, and his eyes were as closed off and unreadable as a dead man's. "What makes you think they could keep you safe?"

"What makes you think *you* could?" she retorted. "Are you telling me it's safer to be on the roads, where the rebels are probably patrolling, than here in an isolated village?"

"That's exactly what I'm telling you. And as far as whether or not I could keep you safe, that's what I do for a living." He smiled at her, and she didn't think she'd ever seen anything colder in her life. "Or have you forgotten that?"

She hadn't forgotten anything about him, but she wasn't about to tell him that. "I thought your specialty was the same as my father's—stirring up trouble," she said coolly. "Not rescuing people from that trouble."

"Dammit, Lexie!" he exploded. "We don't have time to play word games. Once we're back in the States we can trade insults all day long, if that's what you want. Right now, I just want you to make sure you and your baby are ready to leave in the morning. I'm not going to argue with you about this."

He leaned against the wall, his arms folded across his chest, and stared at her. She tried to look away, but she couldn't. *Your* baby. She couldn't believe his choice of words was deliberate—that somehow made it even worse. The scorn and disdain in his eyes stabbed into her soul, but she lifted her chin as she watched him. This was reality, and she would deal with it. She'd had a lot of practice at that lately. Never would she let him see how much his words had hurt.

The bundle in her arms started wriggling, and she realized she was holding Ana much too tightly. Making sure the blanket covered her exposed breasts, she bent her head and kissed her daughter, nuzzling her soft cheek and whispering reassurances to her.

Standing, she turned her back to Caine and refastened her bra. Then, holding Ana carefully, she rebuttoned her blouse. Laying the child over her shoulder, she gently patted her back until she heard a soft burp.

There was a sound from over by the window, and when she looked at Caine she found he'd turned away again. His back was ramrod straight, and the hot, heavy air seemed suddenly thicker in the small room.

Giving Ana another kiss, Lexie carefully placed the baby in the carved wooden infant seat that had been lined with soft, woven blankets. Then she faced Caine again, her hands clasped behind her back to hide their trembling.

"Intimidation isn't going to make me change my mind, Caine."

He turned around slowly to face her. "I'm not trying to intimidate you." His eyes were still devoid of expression. "I don't have to. You're an intelligent woman, Lexie. I don't have to spell out to you what could happen if this El Cuchillo gets hold of you and that baby."

She began to shake even more. "That's not going to happen. He'd have no reason to look for an American in this village." Who was she trying to convince? She pushed the traitorous thought out of her mind.

"You don't think so?" His gaze hardened. "Don't be such an idealistic little fool. I told you how easy it was for me to find you. How much reward money do you think it would take for one of the people in this village to turn you in? A few hundred dollars? A thousand? That's a drop in the bucket for this guy. Whatever else he is, he's apparently well-financed."

"I've lived here for ten months. I take care of their children. These people wouldn't turn me in for money."

A flicker of expression crossed his face. It might have been pain, but it was gone too quickly to tell. "Get real, Lexie. A thousand dollars would make anyone in this village rich. Do you really think that if it was a choice between you and making sure their family was taken care of that there would be any choice at all? However much you think you're their friend, in the end you're a stranger here.''

"You always were such an idealist. I see that hasn't changed,'' she said, hoping the sarcasm hid her pain at his words.

He shrugged. "I'm just telling you the way it is. But if you don't care about what happens to you, maybe you should think about the kid.''

Involuntarily she looked over at Ana. The baby sat watching the two adults, her face solemn. It was almost as if she understood what they were talking about, Lexie thought. As much to comfort herself as her child, she picked Ana up and held her close.

"The most I can promise you is that I'll think about it. You can't expect me to abandon my life here without a backward glance.''

He watched her and Ana for a moment, and that strange flicker passed over his face again. She was almost sure it was pain.

"You do all the thinking you want, as long as you're ready to leave in the morning.''

Without a backward glance he strode out of the hut, closing the door carefully behind him. She couldn't resist going to the window and watching him leave. Not once did he look back at them.

Caine walked down the main street of Santa Ysabel, his head spinning. He was a father. He had a daughter named Ana. Remembering the tiny bundle with the fuzzy, bright red hair, he realized his hands were trembling and shoved them into his pockets.

He and Lexie were parents. His mind was still numb with shock, but not so numb that he didn't feel the pain. He had a daughter who was two months old, and Lexie hadn't even bothered to tell him. If James hadn't asked him to come down here and bring her home, he might never have known.

James. His step faltered as he walked down the narrow dirt street. James hadn't said a word to him about Lexie having a baby. Remembering their conversation, he wondered if he even knew.

It didn't matter, he told himself. *He* was the one who'd had a right to know. Remembering the seven long months when he'd done nothing but dream of Lexie—when memories of the two nights they'd shared were all that kept him going—a red mist of anger rose in front of his eyes. Obviously, what had happened between them hadn't been nearly as important to her. She hadn't even bothered to tell him she was pregnant with his child.

The pain of her betrayal burned hotter, searing into his soul. It ripped open the place, deep in his heart, where he'd buried the remains of another betrayal. Once exposed to the light, the ancient memories spilled over him like a corrosive, eating away at his heart and soul.

Trying to obliterate the pain, he let his anger flame higher. It didn't matter that he wouldn't have been able to be there even if she had written to him. It didn't matter that the thought of being a father filled him with a bottomless terror. It didn't even matter that he'd always sworn he would never subject a child to his legacy of pain and anger; would never repeat the mistakes his father had made.

None of that mattered anymore. It was his child, and his responsibility. Lexie should have told him.

But Lexie hadn't wanted him to know, hadn't thought it would be important to him that he had a child. He'd had the right idea all along, he told himself savagely. Relationships caused nothing but anguish. The faint wisp of hope he'd been clinging to—the one that had whispered so seductively to him eleven months ago and had beckoned like a siren again at her father's request a week ago—shriveled up and died. She couldn't have made her feelings about him any clearer.

And she would never find out about those absurd dreams, he vowed. His first instinct, stubbornly clung to for most of his thirty-two years, was right, after all. If you relied only on yourself, no one could ever let you down. If no one got close, it didn't matter what they did, because it couldn't touch you.

He and Lexie together was the most absurd idea of all. In spite of his dreams, they were from two different worlds, worlds that could never intersect. He'd come here to do a job, he thought grimly, and he would finish it. It was a job he was damned good at, and part of his job had always been hiding his true feelings. He would get her and the baby back to Washington, then he would fade out of her life as quickly and silently as he could fade into the jungle that surrounded them now.

The trees of the forest crowded close to the houses as he reached the slightly larger building that served as the only inn for Santa Ysabel, and he forced himself to put Lexie out of his mind. Something about this town had made the hair on the back of his neck stand up from the moment he'd arrived in his rented Jeep earlier in the day. He needed to pay attention to what was going on. His life—all of their lives—might depend on it.

He approached the inn warily. In reality it was nothing more than a larger house with a few extra rooms for rent. Pausing to knock on the door, he waited until a voice invited him inside before he entered.

The woman who had taken his money for the room earlier was gone. Instead there was an older man in the kitchen, stirring something on the stove. He turned to Caine.

"May I help you?"

"I'm Phillip East. I rented a room earlier," Caine answered easily.

The man nodded and smiled. "Of course." He waved his hand in the direction of the rooms. "Make yourself at home."

Caine's instincts went on alert. The smile didn't reach the man's eyes, and he was studying Caine much too carefully. Turning his face away as if looking around the room, Caine nodded. "I thought I'd rest in my room for a while. It was a long trip."

"But of course, Señor East. Everyone rests during the afternoon in Santa Ysabel." The man took another hard look at him, then turned back to the stove. Caine watched him for a moment, then walked to the room he'd been given and closed the door quietly.

Nothing looked out of place, but the hair on his neck rose again. Checking the tiny traps he'd left behind, he found them all disturbed. Someone had been in his room and searched his belongings.

Grimly he looked around a second time. Whoever had been in here had done a damn professional job. If Caine hadn't been a professional himself, he never would have known.

He gathered his belongings quickly and efficiently. Then he mussed the bed and punched in the pillow, making it look as if he'd been lying on it. If anyone glanced into the room, they would think that he'd put his things away and rested, then gone out again.

Luckily the window in his room looked out on the dense green forest behind him. Dropping his two bags onto the ground, he angled himself through the window and climbed down. Looking both ways to make sure no one had seen him leave, he stepped into the jungle and let the green sea swallow him.

Lexie listened to Ana fussing in the other room and smiled wearily at the woman sitting on her small exam table. "Your arm is healing well, Angelita. I'll rebandage it, and you can come back in a week for me to take out the stitches."

"Why don't you get the little one first? My arm can wait that long."

"I'm afraid she can't," Lexie answered wryly, reaching for the gauze and tape. "If I go pick her up and don't feed her right away, they'll hear her screaming two villages away."

"She is a willful one." Angelita, her best friend in the village, smiled at her. "Does she get that from you or her father?"

Lexie's smile faltered. "I don't know. I think both of us are pretty bullheaded." She bent her head and tried to concentrate on Angelita's wound.

"This is the first time you've even admitted that Ana has a father." Angelita's voice was very gentle. "This is eating at your soul, Lexie. You must do something about it. You must tell him that he has a daughter."

Lexie pressed the last strip of tape over her friend's wound and looked up at her, knowing the bleakness in her soul was reflected in her face. "He knows."

Angelita looked at her for a moment, then realization sprang into her eyes. She took Lexie's hand. "The stranger who came to the village this morning, looking for you? He is Ana's father?"

Lexie turned away and nodded. She couldn't bear for the other woman to see her pain. "He came looking for me to take me back to the United States. He claims that I'm in danger here from El Cuchillo." Taking a deep breath, she turned around to face Angelita again. "I told him that I was as safe here as I would be at home."

Angelita didn't answer immediately, and Lexie felt a tiny lick of fear. "Why aren't you agreeing with me, Angelita?"

"Because he may be right," the other woman answered slowly. "El Cuchillo doesn't want anyone from the United States in this country. There is talk of much money being offered for information about Americans."

Fear rippled up Lexie's spine as her friend's words echoed Caine's. She had assumed that Caine was just trying to scare her into listening to him. While she stared at Angelita, another cry came from the other room, more insistent this time.

"You'd better get her," her friend said with a smile. "She's not a very patient baby."

Lexie nodded. "I'll be right back. Don't leave. I want to hear more about this."

She hurried into the other room. Just as she reached for Ana, lying in her basket, she saw a man's shape standing in the corner of the room. He blended into the shadows, but not enough. She could just pick out his large, dark form pressed up against the wall.

As she opened her mouth to scream, he stepped away from the wall and clamped his hand over her mouth. The moment she felt his hands on her she realized it was Caine.

Bending closer to her, he breathed in her ear, "Quiet. Don't let whoever's out there with you know I'm here. Get rid of her so we can talk. All right?"

He kept her mouth covered until she nodded. When he let go of her, he faded into the shadows until she had to strain to see him. It was getting darker outside, and in another few minutes she wouldn't be able to see him at all.

Trying to ignore the way her skin prickled as she felt his gaze on her, she picked up Ana and turned away from him. How had she known it was Caine the moment he'd touched her? The obvious answers all disturbed her, and she decided she must have gotten a glimpse of him as he'd moved toward her. It was a much more comfortable idea than the dangerous notion that she had recognized his touch and his scent, even after almost a year.

She carried Ana to the other room, where Angelita stood smoothing the sleeve of her dress over the bandage on her arm. The other woman watched with anxious eyes as Lexie settled herself in the chair and put Ana to her breast.

"Tell me more," Lexie said.

"There isn't much to tell." Angelita shrugged. "You know how rumors are. There has been talk among some of the people of large amounts of money being offered for information about Americans in the country."

Even in the heat, Lexie felt cold. "Are you saying that someone in the village might turn me in?" she asked carefully.

Angelita's pause was just a hair too long. "We are all very grateful for what you've done, Lexie. Never before has anyone bothered to make sure that our children were vaccinated, or cared when one of us got sick. Even when Dr. Juan was alive, he was more concerned about pleasing his superiors at the coffee plantations than about the health of the people here. You have been good for our village."

Lexie heard a small sound in the other room. Caine was moving closer to hear what they said. She could almost imagine his vitality seeping through the thin wall that separated them, surrounding her and chasing away the chill that had settled in her chest at Angelita's words. Thankful for his presence in the other room, she turned to her friend again.

"Are you saying the answer is yes, that someone would turn me in?"

"I would like to say no, my friend, but I can't. I don't think it would come to that, but who knows what people will do for money? I think you should be careful. If this man wants to take you back home, you should consider it. You have more than yourself to think of, now."

Lexie looked down at her daughter, snuggled drowsily in her arms, her hunger satisfied. Angelita was right. She had to think of Ana first. "All right," she said slowly. "I'll tell Caine I'll leave with him. But I can't go just yet. I have a shipment of vaccine ordered that should come any day now. Once I get it in and use it up, then I'll leave."

A look of sorrow passed over her friend's face as she stood to leave. "We will all miss you, Lexie. You have brought much to this village."

"No more than you've given me." Lexie rocked her daughter and looked up at Angelita. "I'll never forget you, Angelita. Or anyone else in Santa Ysabel. You gave me my life back."

Angelita walked to the door, then paused before she left. "The stranger who came looking for you? He is a man who will take care of you, my friend. Listen to him."

Before Lexie could answer, Angelita was gone. As soon as the door closed behind her, Caine emerged from the shadows of the other room as silently as a ghost.

"How long will it take you to pack?" Caine looked everywhere but at her and Ana. "I want to leave as soon as possible."

"You obviously heard what Angelita and I said. Did you forget that I want to stay until my next shipment of vaccine comes in?" Lexie stood, cradling Ana in her arms, and went over to the stove to stir the pot simmering there.

"I heard."

Caine's voice was grim, and involuntarily she looked over at him. Tension radiated from him, and for a moment she almost didn't recognize him. He was poised for action.

"Dammit, Lexie, use your head. Your friend told you to get out. How much more warning do you need?"

He was a warrior, she suddenly realized. She had never seen this side of him before. He stood in the middle of her house, all his instincts on alert, fully prepared to do battle.

The wooden spoon she was using to stir the stew clattered against the edge of the pot. "Stop it, Caine," she cried. "Stop trying to scare me. Angelita didn't say that there was someone in the village who had turned me in. She just warned me that it was a possibility. I've already told you I'll go with you. I just won't go right now."

He stared at her for a long moment, then finally moved to stand by the window. "The equation has changed in the last couple of hours." As he spoke to her he kept his gaze fixed on the street outside. Watching him, Lexie realized that his eyes never stopped moving. His gaze swept back and forth through the quiet, resting town, cataloging everything he saw.

"Who owns the inn at the other end of the village?" he asked abruptly, still watching out the window.

"Maria Tiotempe," she answered, picking up the wooden spoon and stirring the stew again. "Didn't you meet her?"

"She was there when I checked in, but I didn't see her this afternoon."

His voice was grim, and she put the spoon down again and joined him at the window. Nothing moved in the shimmering heat of early evening. It wouldn't be long before Santa Ysabel rose and stretched from its afternoon siesta, but right now the streets were silent and deserted.

And a little bit spooky, she thought as she stepped away from Caine. Even though she wouldn't admit it to him, his intensity was beginning to scare her. She'd looked out this window at this same early-evening scene a hundred times before. Never before had it bothered her. Now, though, Caine's tension and alert watchfulness were infecting her.

"Maria is a very busy woman. She was probably checking on her garden, or visiting one of her daughters," she answered firmly. "Don't imagine trouble everywhere."

"I wasn't imagining the man standing in her kitchen when I went back there this afternoon." Caine's quiet voice was filled with coldness and danger. "I didn't imagine the way he studied me, either. As if he was memorizing my face for future reference."

Lexie laid Ana gently in her child seat, then positioned it next to the table so she could watch her. Serving two bowls of stew, she sat down and waited for Caine to join her. He kept staring out the window.

Finally she said, "Even in this heat, food does get cold and I'd like to eat. Please, come sit down, Caine."

At that he looked over at her. "I didn't realize I'd been invited."

She ignored her burning cheeks. "I'm sorry I didn't have time to engrave an invitation. I assumed you'd know I wouldn't eat in front of you. Please, join me."

Surprisingly, a fleeting smile passed over his face as he turned away from the window. "A lot of things have changed about you, Lexie, but I see you still have your sharp tongue. Thank you."

He sat down and they ate in silence for a few minutes. Lexie was excruciatingly aware of him sitting just inches away from her, his knees almost brushing hers. The air in the room, already heavy with heat and humidity, became as suffocating as a thick woolen blanket. His nearness swirled around her, more intoxicating than any wine.

"Tell me about the man who lives with the woman at the inn." His abrupt words broke the spell that had entangled her.

"Maria?" She frowned, trying to banish the images that had been flitting through her head. "She lives alone."

"Then who was the man in her house earlier?"

"I have no idea, unless it was one of her sons-in-law."

"This man was in his fifties. Short, thin, salt-and-pepper hair."

Lexie shook her head slowly. "None of Maria's relatives look like that." She looked at Caine, her fear suddenly an almost-palpable thing. "What did you say earlier about the way he was looking at you?"

"I said it was enough to make all the warning bells go off." His voice was blunt. "Believe me, I have enough experience to pay attention to things like that. I made it look as if I'd settled into the room, then I ducked out the window. I've been hiding in your other room all afternoon, half expecting El Cuchillo himself to show up at your door. There's something wrong here, and I want to leave tonight. Right now, if possible."

"Half the people here are waiting for their children to be vaccinated." Her whispered words were as much to convince herself as Caine.

"Well, someone in the other half has another agenda. Trust me on this." He leaned over the table toward her, and she found herself wishing passionately that he would move closer. She had to force herself to back up. She had fought the attraction between them for the short month they'd known each other, almost a year earlier. Now she found, to her dismay, that their separation had only made it grow stronger.

"I can't just disappear in the middle of the night. There are things I need to take with me, and things I need to give to other people."

"My God, Lexie, you give the word *stubborn* a new meaning." He ran his fingers through his long dark blond hair and leaned back in his chair. She wasn't sure if she was relieved or disappointed that he was no longer close enough to reach out and touch.

"All right." The front legs of his chair came crashing down to the floor. "I'm willing to compromise with you, if only so you'll realize I know what I'm talking about. Something is going to happen tonight. I can feel it. So you and I and the kid are going to make ourselves scarce. If nothing has happened when we show up in the morning, you win. But if someone has been here looking for you, we pack up and leave on the spot."

She was trapped and she knew it. She could find no argument to fight his suggestion. In fact, although she would die before telling him, she was glad he was here with her and relieved by the action he proposed.

Glancing out into the darkened streets, she realized that the afternoon siesta was over. People going from one house to another were shadows moving through the town. Yesterday they had all belonged to friends, people she knew and trusted. Today, she wondered who among them might have betrayed her and sold her to El Cuchillo.

"All right. I suppose that's a reasonable suggestion." She glanced down at Ana, wide-awake and staring back at her. "But where will we go?"

"Into the jungle. No one will be able to find us there in the dark, even if they were inclined to look."

"The jungle?" She stared at him. "No one goes into the jungle at night. It's too dangerous."

"I know." He smiled grimly. "That's what I'm counting on to keep you safe."

"There are things in the jungle far more dangerous than El Cuchillo." She stood abruptly, afraid he would see her fear.

"Nothing I can't handle. Trust me, Lexie. This is what I do." His smile was devoid of humor. "You never cared for my job before, but right now, what I do for a living can save your little fanny."

She looked down at Ana, still wide-awake in her basket. She could face anything for her child. And if going into the jungle at night was what it would take, she could do that, too.

"All right." She spoke too quickly, but she didn't care. She needed to say it before she had time to change her mind. "Let me clean up the dishes and get a few things for Ana."

"Leave the house looking like you'd just gone to bed. Take only what's absolutely necessary for you and the kid. I'll take care of everything else."

Lexie moved through the tiny house, washing up the dinner dishes and doing what she normally did as she prepared for bed. Finally she gathered clean diapers and some extra clothes and blankets for Ana and stuffed them into a bag. Switching off all the lights, she picked up her daughter and held her close, then turned to stand in front of Caine in the darkened main room.

"I'm ready."

She barely saw him nod in the shadows. "We'll go the same way I came in. That way, whoever's watching the house won't see us leave."

He took the bag from her hand, then slid his palm against hers and led her into the back room. His hand was hard and warm, swallowing her smaller one, and her skin tingled from the electricity of his touch. She knew she should pull away, but suddenly she couldn't bear to let go of him. She'd dreamed of his touch for eleven long months, woken from sleep with the taste and feel of him imprinted on her body.

She knew he'd taken her hand only to guide her safely through the dark room, but for a moment she let her fantasies have free rein. It was a small enough thing, and it would have to last for a long time.

Lost in her thoughts, she bumped up against him when he stopped abruptly. Letting go of her hand, he pulled her to the side, away from the window. He didn't need to gesture to her to be quiet. Watching him stare out the window, his body tense and coiled, was enough to paralyze her.

Chapter 3

"We'll have to wait." Caine's voice was no more than a breath caressing her neck. "There's someone watching the back of your house, too."

Without thinking she leaned toward the window. "Where?"

He curled his hand around her shoulder and held her away from the window. "Don't. You can't see him, anyway." His heat seeped through the thin cotton of her blouse and made her skin tingle. As he drew back, she thought his hand lingered on her neck for an instant longer than necessary.

It didn't mean a thing, she told herself, cuddling Ana a little closer. Neither of them had ever denied the physical attraction that had flamed between them from the moment they'd met, although she had certainly tried. Lust was a basic human urge, and like all other urges, it could be controlled. For all that Caine had wanted her, she was certain it had never gone deeper than that. And she wasn't about to succumb to her urges again.

Caine stared into the gathering darkness, holding himself perfectly still. His body throbbed with awareness of the woman standing next to him—an awareness only intensified by the still, heavy air surrounding them and the danger swirling outside.

The feel of her skin still burned on his fingertips, and no matter which way he turned, he could smell her faint scent.

Trying to will his body into submission, he deliberately faced away from her and stared into the gloom until he pinpointed where the watcher was concealed. This was no time to be replaying futile fantasies involving Lexie, he told himself harshly. If he wanted to get her out of here in one piece, he'd better concentrate on the matter at hand.

"What's going on?" she whispered behind him.

He didn't turn around. "I know where the guy is. Now all we have to do is wait. Sooner or later he'll get bored and make a mistake. That's when we'll move."

He could almost feel her shiver behind him. "Why are you so sure he'll make a mistake?"

"Because he's already made one. I know where he is."

A tiny, restless grunt came from the darkness behind him— a noise he didn't think came from Lexie. Then he heard the whisper of cloth against wood that told him she'd sat down.

"I have to feed her. I'm sorry." The soft words seemed to wrap their tendrils around him.

There was another rustling, then a satisfied murmur. He knew what he would see if he turned around. In the darkened room, Lexie's breast would be only a darker shadow, and just the back of the baby's head would be visible. Tightening his grip on the windowsill, he tried to ignore what was going on behind him.

"Are you almost done?" he asked finally. The tiny sounds that came from the two of them were getting on his nerves.

"She's almost asleep."

"Good. We're just about ready to go."

He heard her stirring behind him, heard the sound of cloth being pulled together. He wondered what it was, but he didn't dare move away. Whoever was watching them was getting restless. He'd shifted a few times in his hiding place, moving into Caine's line of sight. It wouldn't be long before he and Lexie had their opportunity.

"You ready?" he asked.

"Yes."

Her voice trembled over the word, and he looked back at her sharply. She met his gaze and lifted her chin, one hand resting on the bundle strapped across her shoulder. "What do we do now?" she asked, defying him to mention the fear in her voice.

He turned back to look out the window, unwilling to think about what it had taken her to ask him that. He didn't want to admire anything about Lexie.

Thinking about Lexie, he almost missed the shadow that flitted from its hiding place and disappeared toward the front of her house. Cursing himself for allowing her to distract him, he said, "It's time to move. We need to get through this window, as fast as possible."

She came up beside him and laid her palms on the windowsill. Just before she boosted herself up onto it, he grabbed her hand and stopped her.

"Not quite yet."

Easing himself away from the wall next to the window, he leaned out and looked around. As far as he could tell, there was no one waiting for them. It wouldn't be long, though, before the watcher was back. They had to go now.

"I'll lift you up," he whispered to Lexie. "Once you're out, I'll hand you the bags. Okay?"

She nodded, one hand curling around the lump in front of her. She'd slung some kind of scarf over one shoulder, he realized, and the baby lay inside it. When he put his hands around her waist, he could feel the warmth of the child through the fabric of the scarf.

He swung her onto the windowsill more quickly than necessary, and let his hands drop away almost immediately. Silently she twisted around and slid to the ground on the other side of the window. In another few seconds he'd handed her the bags and dropped lightly down beside her.

Taking her hand, he pulled her toward the darkness between two houses across the street. As they melted into the shadows, he heard someone coming down the street toward them. He didn't have to urge her to hurry. Her hand trembled in his, and beneath his fingers he could feel her pulse leap in her wrist.

As soon as they were behind one of the houses, he stopped. Pressing into the cool mud brick, he waited as the footsteps came closer and closer. When they were even with the house, he risked one quick look.

"What?" she whispered into his ear as he jerked back. "Who was it?"

Slowly he turned to look at her. "It was the man who was at the inn this afternoon."

Even in the darkness he could see her turn pale, but she tried to cover it up. "That doesn't prove anything. Since he's obviously visiting here, too, he's probably on his way to a friend's house."

"I don't hear him anymore."

She licked her lips. "There are a lot of houses he could have stopped at." Although her words were nonchalant, her tone of voice wasn't. He could hear the fear shiver through.

"I don't want to stand here all night and debate about it. Let's get going."

She nodded once, jerkily, and pushed away from the wall. When he took her hand, it was cold and damp. Fury crashed over him like a wave. He wanted to reach out and fasten his hands around the neck of the person who was making her afraid. The Lexie he had known hadn't been afraid of anything.

As he tightened his grip on her hand, he felt an answering pressure so brief he wondered if he'd imagined it. He glanced over at her sharply, but she wasn't looking at him. She examined each street they crossed, each dark alley they passed. She might be afraid, he thought with reluctant admiration, but she wasn't falling apart on him.

They reached the edge of the village quickly. Pulling her into the shadow of a lone building, he stood and waited for what seemed like a long time. When he was sure there were no footsteps behind them, he took her hand again and led her toward the blackness of the forest in front of them.

They hadn't gone more than ten or fifteen feet into the jungle when the darkness seemed to swallow them completely. Even the lights from the village were no longer visible. He slowed down, but continued to move steadily forward. He had picked out this route this afternoon, and had mentally marked all the obstacles in their way. Still, he used his free hand to make sure there were no vines in front of them to snap in their faces.

Lexie held tightly to his other hand. She made no sound, but the desperation of her grip told him all he needed to know.

"It's only a little farther," he murmured, turning back to look at her shadowy outline in the inky darkness. In answer, she tightened her fingers around his.

In another ten minutes he stopped and pulled a flashlight out of his backpack. They had gone far enough into the forest that there was no chance the light could be seen from the village. Turning on the thin beam, he played it over the trees to try to get his bearings.

The vines and flowers that trailed down from the tall trees looked ghostly and surreal in the weak light. Night creatures chirped and clicked in the darkness, adding to the eerie sensation. Inhospitable during the day, the jungle at night was downright forbidding. As he played the light in a circle around them, it glanced off Lexie's face.

Her eyes were huge and black in her pale face. When he gently loosened his hand from hers, she immediately stepped closer to him. Clutching the bundle that was the baby tightly to her chest, she was so near she almost brushed up against him.

"It's okay now," he said in a normal voice. "We're far enough away that no one from the village can see or hear us. We'll be safe until morning."

"That's a matter of opinion," she muttered, her gaze following the beam of light as it outlined the trees surrounding them.

"You're not afraid, are you, Lexie?" he said, forcing a mocking tone into his voice.

It was exactly the right thing to say. Moving away from him, she stood straighter. "Of course not. The jungle at night is just a little spooky, that's all."

Spotting the tree he was looking for, he took her hand again and led her toward it. "Thank God for that," he answered. "It should keep everyone else away from us tonight."

Pushing away the tangle of vines that he'd amassed earlier in the day, he used the flashlight to illuminate a dark hole in the trunk of a towering tree. "Welcome to the Santa Ysabel Ritz."

Lexie took a step backward. "What's that?"

"Our accommodations for the night. Go on in."

She gave him an incredulous look and didn't budge. "How do you know what's in there? There could be animals sleeping in there, or worse. You go first."

"I need to make sure the opening is covered up," he said patiently. "There's nothing in there. I made sure earlier."

She took a step forward, then stopped again. "I'm sorry, Caine, but I can't walk blindly into that black hole. I need to see in there first."

Obligingly, he shone the flashlight into the hole in the base of the tree. All she would see was the blankets he'd put there earlier, plus the wad of mosquito netting he'd stashed by the door. It wasn't much, but the hollowed-out tree trunk would keep them protected and hidden until morning.

He felt her start of surprise when she looked inside. "*You* put the blankets in here?"

"I like to plan ahead." He unslung his backpack and swung it through the hole, then reached out for hers. She jumped when she felt his hands on her shoulders, but quickly shrugged out of her knapsack when she realized what he was doing. Finally, he heard her take a deep, trembling breath before she bent over and twisted through the hole.

Pulling the vines back in front of the opening, he followed her inside. He set the flashlight on the floor and looked at her. She sat in the center, her legs crossed and her back very straight. Apparently the baby was still sleeping, because he didn't hear a sound from the lump in the scarf still strapped across her shoulder.

"When did you bring this stuff here?" she whispered.

"This afternoon." Easing back, he leaned against the dry wood and stretched his legs out in front of him. "As soon as I realized something was up, I gathered what I thought we would need and brought it here."

She was silent for a long time. When she finally spoke, she said, "Don't you get tired of always being suspicious, of always thinking the worst of everyone? It's an awfully depressing way to live.''

Her words surprised him. No one else had ever wondered about that aspect of his job. Trying to hide his uneasiness with her perception, he shrugged and said, "It may be depressing, but it's what's kept me alive.''

"In this case, I still think you're overreacting. The man you saw at Maria's inn was probably just another guest, and the man you thought was watching my house was probably just waiting to meet his lover. In the morning we'll see that this has all been unnecessary.''

"Maybe so, maybe not. I hope you're right, but I don't think so. Either way, we'll find out in the morning.'' Spotting the mosquito netting, he sat up and reached for it. "Let me put this up, then we can go to sleep.'' He glanced over at her, dimly illuminated in the cramped space. "Unless you have other ideas how to spend the night.''

It was hard to tell, but he thought her face turned a dull red. Ignoring his comment, she looked into the darkness for a moment, then turned back to him, licking her lips. "I, ah, need to step outside for a moment.''

It took him a second to understand what she was saying. "Oh. Well, then, take the flashlight, and don't go very far.''

"You don't have to worry about that,'' she muttered. Rising to her knees, she clutched the baby awkwardly and began to crawl toward the opening.

"Wouldn't it be easier if you left the kid here?''

She stopped and looked over at him. "I'm sure it would, but I have no intention of laying her on the ground. God only knows what's down there.''

"Give her to me,'' he heard himself say. "I'll hold her until you get back.''

She went perfectly still and stared at him for a long time. Finally she untied the scarf and eased the sleeping baby away from her. Her hands trembled.

"Here.'' She laid the soft bundle in his arms, stared at them for a moment, then disappeared into the blackness. He couldn't be sure, but he thought he'd seen a glittery wetness in her eyes just before she turned away.

He looked down at the tiny, still figure in his arms. He couldn't see a thing, but a sweet fragrance drifted up to him. It smelled like innocence and love, and he closed his eyes against the pain that filled him. He'd always known he wasn't father material and had sworn he wouldn't do to another kid what had been done to him, but it hadn't made any difference in the end. It had happened anyway, and now this bundle in his arms mocked him, taunting him with the things he would never have.

Maybe Lexie had been right, after all, to keep this baby a secret from him. Maybe somehow she'd known about the empty places inside him—the places that could never be brought back to life. Maybe it would have been better if he'd been able to refuse James's request, if he'd never come down to San Rafael at all.

The child stirred in his rigid clasp, and he stared down at it with a brief rush of panic. Where was Lexie? What if the kid started screaming? What was he supposed to do then?

The beam of light from the flashlight bounced off the trees and Lexie appeared in front of the vines. Crawling into their hiding place, she reached out and took the baby from him.

"Thank you for holding her, Caine."

"You're welcome." His voice was gruff, and he turned his back to her to rearrange the vines in front of the opening. "I think she's getting hungry or something."

"There's no 'or something' about it." He heard her scoot back so she was leaning against the wood. "She's nothing but a little eating machine." Her words were murmured in a low, loving voice, and he glanced over in time to see her bend down and brush a kiss through the baby's hair. When she reached for the buttons on her blouse, he turned away abruptly and switched off the flashlight.

It seemed as if all the creatures of the night were suddenly silent. All he could hear was the faint suckling sounds of the baby nursing. He listened for a minute, then turned blindly toward the opening in the tree.

"I'll be right back." He stumbled into the darkness of the jungle, away from the tree that hid Lexie and the baby. Then he leaned against the smooth, cool bark of another tree and wondered how long it would take her to feed the kid.

Lexie listened to Caine moving outside, and bent her head to nuzzle her daughter's cheek. She had no idea why he wasn't interested in his child, but each time he shoved her away it felt as if her heart would break. "Don't worry," she whispered fiercely into the darkness as Ana nursed contentedly. "He may not want you, but I want you at least twice as much as I ever thought possible. We'll have each other, and we won't need anyone else."

Ana finished eating, and Lexie laid a blanket on the floor of dead leaves and dirt and changed her diaper. Then, wrapping the baby in another blanket, she cradled her in her arms and lay down on the dirt floor.

She wouldn't think about Caine, she told herself firmly, but all she could see was him rushing outside, fleeing from the sight of her feeding his child. The pain went deep and gnawed at her soul, mocking all her futile dreams about their being a family someday. She didn't need him, she told herself again. She and Ana would do just fine by themselves.

They would go back to Santa Ysabel in the morning and find that all this melodrama had been for nothing. Then he would go away and they could live in peace again.

Telling herself that was what she wanted, she brought Ana closer and willed herself to relax. The fear she'd felt as they were slipping out of Santa Ysabel, even the pain that clutched her heart every time she thought about Caine, couldn't keep her awake. Ana would awaken in a few hours, needing to be fed again, so Lexie closed her eyes and forced herself to sleep.

She woke, disoriented, to utter blackness. Her breasts were heavy and throbbing with milk, and Ana was sputtering beside her. When she reached out, her hand encountered dirt, and suddenly she remembered everything.

She and Ana were in the hollowed-out trunk of a tree, somewhere in the jungle, hiding because Caine thought someone would come for her during the night. He was invisible in the darkness, but she heard Caine's deep, even breathing over the sounds coming from the dark forest just outside their hiding place.

Sitting up, she reached for Ana and had just picked her up when suddenly she felt Caine looming over her.

"What's wrong?" he asked in a low voice.

"Nothing. She needs to eat again."

Even though she knew he couldn't see her, she still hesitated before opening her blouse. He was too close. Finally he settled back onto the floor. She thought he'd fallen asleep again when his quiet voice said, "How come she never cries?"

Bringing Ana to her breast, she waited until the baby was nursing before she answered. "She has a scream that could pierce metal at thirty feet. Since I didn't think you wanted to advertise where we were, I've been trying to anticipate her and feed or change her before she can start."

There was a long silence, then she heard Caine shift on the floor. "Lucky kid," she thought she heard him mutter under his breath. After another tense silence, he asked, "Do you need anything?"

Vaguely surprised and touched that he would ask, she licked her dry lips and murmured, "I could use a drink of water."

He switched on the flashlight and she looked away, squinting against the too-bright whiteness. When he knelt next to her and handed her a canteen, she took it without looking at him. She couldn't bear to see the distance that crept into his eyes whenever he was close to Ana.

She handed the canteen back to him with a quiet, "Thank you," then looked down at Ana and realized the baby was asleep again. Laying the child across her lap, she rebuttoned her blouse and lay back down on the floor. Caine switched the flashlight off and settled into his spot on the other side of the makeshift shelter.

Lexie's eyes fluttered closed as her body cried out for sleep. She had almost drifted off again when she heard Caine moving around.

"It's almost dawn," he said, his voice abrupt. "I'm going to take a look around. Go back to sleep."

The vines at the entrance to their hiding place rubbed together with a crackling whisper, then he was gone. Even though it was as black as the depths of the sea inside the tree trunk, Lexie knew as surely as her heart beat that he wasn't with her anymore. Rising up on one elbow, she listened intently, trying to figure out where he was. The only sounds she heard were the mysterious nighttime murmurs of the jungle.

She lay back down slowly and pulled Ana closer. She had dated Caine for a month, had conceived a child with him, but she'd told him the truth earlier: she had never really known him. These skills of his, honed over the years in the covert world in which he lived, were completely alien to her—and more than a little frightening.

They made her wonder exactly what he did, in his so-secret work for her father. And they made her wonder what parts of himself had died while he was learning them.

Curling her body around her daughter's, she closed her eyes and willed herself to sleep. But she woke frequently, startled by a vague and disturbing shadow in her mind. When she finally fell into a dreamless sleep, light was beginning to seep into her hiding place.

Caine hurried back to the hollow tree, grimly examining and discarding options. Creeping through Santa Ysabel in the pre-dawn darkness, he'd gotten his answers. Now he just had to convince Lexie to accept them.

By the time he reached the wall of vines, the faint light of dawn was filtering down to the forest floor. He paused before he entered, afraid of disturbing Lexie in the middle of some intimate task. But no sounds came from behind the vines.

Pushing them aside, he crouched in the opening and looked in at Lexie and the baby, both sound asleep. Something clutched at his gut at the sight of Lexie curled so protectively around her child. He wanted to sit and watch them for a while, and when he realized it, he cleared his throat and let the vines rustle closed.

She sat up abruptly, looking around almost wildly before she spotted him. "Oh, it's you." She exhaled. "You startled me."

"Sorry," he said gruffly. "But it's time to get moving." He nodded at the baby lying next to her. "Can you keep her quiet for another hour or so?"

"Why?" She looked at him suspiciously. "It won't take that long to get back to Santa Ysabel."

"We're not going back there." He reached for one of the packs and slung it over his back. "I just came from the village, and someone was definitely looking for you last night. I hid the Jeep in the brush and we're going to leave right now, before anyone organizes a search."

She stared at him, her eyes huge. Even in the dim light he could see the fear. "What do you mean, someone was looking for me last night? How do you know?" Her voice was barely above a whisper.

He stopped gathering their belongings and looked down at her. "Because whoever searched your house wasn't careful. They left plenty of signs. If we go back there now, we'll be walking into a trap."

"I can't just leave. I need more things."

She was close to panic, and he longed to scoop her up and comfort her. Thrusting that unwanted thought away, he squatted down next to her. "What things, Lexie? What's more important than your life, and hers?" He looked at the baby, still asleep.

"Nothing, I guess," she answered reluctantly. "But I have only one change of clothes for her. I'll need more than that. And I'll need more diapers, too."

Caine rocked back on his heels, calculating quickly. She was probably going to have to feed the baby again before they left. The kid seemed to have an appetite like a lumberjack's. It was early enough that most of the people in the village would still be asleep, so it probably wouldn't be that big a deal to go back and get what she needed. And God knew, he was supposed to be an expert at gliding in and out of places unseen and unsuspected.

"All right. You tell me what you need and I'll go back and get it. Do whatever it is you need to do in the mornings with her, but be ready to leave when I get back."

She looked at him, startled. Was she that surprised that he would give in so easily? "I figure it's easier to go back than spend the next half hour arguing with you." He told himself that it was better if she thought he was a jerk. It would be a lot less complicated.

"Thank you, Caine." Her low voice seemed to resonate inside the hollow tree trunk. Quickly she told him where to find more clothes and blankets for the baby, and more diapers. "And my emergency medical kit. It's on top of the chest in the bedroom." He nodded and turned to go.

"Caine?" The word was hesitant, and he turned around slowly.

"What?"

"There's one more thing."

When she didn't continue, he said impatiently, "Tell me, Lexie."

"An envelope of pictures." She looked down at the baby, lying on the ground. "Pictures of the village when I first got here, of my friends here." She paused, but he knew she wasn't finished. Finally she swallowed and whispered, "Pictures of Ana when she was first born." She looked back up at him, pain in her eyes. "I can't leave them here. They're the only ones I'll ever have."

"Where are they?" He had to be nuts, he told himself. While someone searched for her and her kid, he was going to be looking for a bunch of damned pictures.

"They're at the bottom of the trunk of clothes in the bedroom. In a manila envelope." As she looked up at him and smiled softly, he could see the tension easing out of her. "Thank you, Caine. You're being very understanding, especially since I know you think I'm being a pain in the rear."

"You have no idea what I think of you." As soon as the words were out of his mouth, he wanted to bite them back. The last thing he wanted to do was issue an invitation for a personal conversation. Turning away, he grabbed his backpack and shoved aside the vines that hung in front of the opening. "Stay here until I get back."

Lexie watched the vines rustle back into place in the weak sunlight. He was right, she thought slowly. She had never been able to tell what he was thinking, or read him in any way. Caine O'Roarke had been an enigma to her from the first day she'd met him. That, however, hadn't stopped her from wanting him.

Which only proved that she'd had a lot of growing up to do when she met him a year ago. Thank goodness the past eleven months had forced her to come to her senses. Becoming a mother had a way of doing that, of focusing a woman's thoughts and narrowing her vision until everything but the essentials was stripped away. Coming to Santa Ysabel and having Ana had taught her how useless her life had been.

Not anymore. Stiffly she got to her feet and laid Ana over her shoulder. Maybe it wasn't possible to stay in Santa Ysabel any longer, but she wasn't about to pack up her things and follow Caine home like a docile little mouse. For the first time in her life she'd found something she was good at, something that made her feel good. And she wasn't about to give it up without a fight.

Gathering the things she'd used during the night, she stuffed everything into her backpack, then pushed aside the curtain of vines and stepped into the jungle. Even during the day it wasn't a welcoming place, but it didn't make shivers run up her spine the way it had during the night. And at least it wasn't dark.

Laying Ana once again into the scarf she had tied across her chest, she slung her backpack onto her shoulders and looked for Caine's path through the undergrowth. There was no reason she had to wait in the tree trunk like a frightened child. If they had to leave Santa Ysabel, the sooner they got started, the better. If she could follow his trail through the jungle and meet him near the village, they would have that much more of a head start.

It wasn't difficult to see which way Caine had gone. The tangled vines and low plants grew so profusely on the jungle floor that the only way through them was to cut your own path. When she found the small opening through the vines that were as thick around as a man's wrist, she held Ana closer to her and started walking.

Chapter 4

The jungle was alive with foreign sounds. Monkeys chattered in the tops of the tallest trees, birds shrieked and cooed as they soared through the air above Lexie, and even the dead leaves on the ground seemed to rustle with life. Her arm tightened protectively around Ana. Even though she'd lived surrounded by the tropical forest for the past eight months, she was far from being comfortable with its strangeness.

But she could see Caine's path. It was faint but definitely there, a narrow passage hacked out of the luxuriant foliage. As long as she stayed on the path, she would be safe. Keeping her eyes firmly fixed on the way back to Santa Ysabel, she tried to ignore her surroundings and concentrate on where to put her feet, one after the other.

Ana shifted in the shawl and Lexie stopped to rearrange her, trying to open the shawl so the baby got more air. She was probably too hot, wrapped in the heavy cotton and lying next to her mother's body. Even though it was early in the morning, the heat and humidity dragged on Lexie like a thick cape draped over her shoulders.

Thank goodness Ana was still asleep, she thought fervently as she unbuttoned the baby's shirt. If she had to carry a fussing baby, she would never be able to negotiate her way through the vines. Pushing the edge of the shawl away from Ana's face, she adjusted her once more and began walking again.

She hadn't taken two steps when she heard the sound of someone coming toward her. *Caine.* She began walking faster, more relieved than she cared to admit, when the sound of voices drifted to her in the still air.

Stopping abruptly, she strained to listen. Surely Caine wouldn't have brought anyone with him. The whole idea was to get out of the village before anyone realized they were gone.

The words were indistinguishable, but there were definitely two voices. And judging from the deep sound, it was two men. Uneasily Lexie sidled off the path, moving closer to the huge tree that stood next to her. The two men were getting closer, the rumble of their voices louder. Why didn't either of them sound familiar?

Their low, murmured Spanish seemed to bounce off the vegetation surrounding her, and she realized with a burst of fear that neither of the men was Caine. Her heart bounded in her chest and a shiver crawled up her back. The air that had been so oppressively hot just a moment ago was now bone-chillingly cold.

What should she do? She looked around frantically at the endless, choking tangle of green. She couldn't simply stand here like a deer caught in the headlights of a car. In less than a minute the men would see her. They were already close enough for her to clearly hear their conversation.

A conversation in which her name was mentioned more than once.

There wasn't any time to run, even if there were a place to go. And with Ana on her chest and a pack on her back, she would move about as fast as one of the sloths in the jungle.

She was out of time to think about her options. In another few seconds the men would spot her. Easing behind the huge kapok tree, she sank to her knees and edged backward until the low bushes formed a screen in front of her. She wouldn't be hard to spot, if they were looking. All she could do now was pray that they weren't and thank God that Ana was still asleep.

* * *

As Caine slipped back into Santa Ysabel, the yellow glow of lights was beginning to show in the windows of some of the houses. The day began early here in this farming village. Threading his way between houses and shops, he avoided the few people who were on the street, clinging instead to the already fading shadows.

He reached Lexie's house without being spotted. He was very certain of that. After ten years of working in covert operations for the United States government, he could tell when someone was watching him.

A quick look into the window they'd crawled out of last night told him there was no one in her bedroom, at least. With one fluid movement he was in the room and crouched in the shadows. He listened intently for a long time, but didn't hear anything from the other room. If someone was waiting for them to return—and he was certain someone was—they weren't waiting in the house.

He moved silently across the floor to the chest Lexie had described. It took only a few seconds to find the clothes and diapers she needed and stuff them into his pack. Then he turned and looked for the trunk that held her pictures. Seeing its location, he swore silently to himself. It stood against the opposite wall, in plain view of anyone in the other room—or anyone who happened to look in the window of the other room.

He was tempted to leave and tell her she would have to forget about the pictures. It was the safest thing to do, he told himself. He'd been damned lucky so far, getting into the village unseen two times. Standing in front of a window to retrieve some lousy pictures was really pushing his luck.

He remembered the look in her eyes when she asked him to get the photos and swore again. If she had whined or demanded that he get her pictures, he would have turned around and left right now. But she hadn't. She had simply asked, while trying to disguise the longing in her eyes. There was no way he could leave here without them.

Moving as close to the chest as he could without being seen, he squatted on the floor for a long time, listening intently. He heard several people pass by Lexie's house, but there were no signs that anyone waited outside her window.

Finally he forced himself to move. The longer he waited, the bigger the risk. More and more people would be on the street, and it would be harder to get out of the village without being seen.

After a quick glance at the window to make sure there was no one there, he lifted the lid of the chest and shoved his hand through the layers of clothing. Refusing to let himself think about the soft fabrics and how they would lie against Lexie's skin, he fumbled around until he felt the stiff manila envelope beneath his fingers. Without looking at it, he tossed it onto the floor behind him, out of sight of the window.

As he was lowering the lid of the chest, he grabbed a handful of the clothing and tossed it behind him, too. As long as he was here, he told himself, he might as well get Lexie a change of clothes, too.

Safely out of sight once more, he stuffed the clothing into his backpack and then picked up the envelope. His hand tightened around it as he stared at it for a moment, then with an abrupt movement he shoved it into the backpack as well. He didn't want to see the pictures of his newborn daughter, he told himself. And even if he did, this wasn't the time or place. Right now he had to concentrate on getting her and her mother out of this hellhole of a town.

It took longer to get out the window this time. It was fully light now, and more and more people were on the streets. Finally he saw his chance, and in the time it took to draw three breaths he shimmied out of Lexie's house and hid between two buildings across the street. He slipped around behind one of the houses and was about to head for the next block when he heard voices coming from the direction he'd just left.

One belonged to a woman, and she sounded furiously angry. The men's voices were abrupt and cold, and a curt order cut the woman's words off in midstream. The voices stopped at the back of Lexie's house.

Caine's muscles tightened and he reached for the knife concealed in his boot. He waited, tensed, while the two men debated the best way to apprehend Lexie. The woman's voice interrupted frequently with scorching remarks about the men's ancestry, breeding and virility, but the men didn't seem to be paying much attention. As far as he could tell, they simply ignored her.

Caine listened long enough to make sure they hadn't found his Jeep, then he replaced his knife in its sheath and began to move. He had to find Lexie and get out of here before anyone thought to organize a search.

It took him longer than he liked to get to the jungle, but no one saw him. Once he was hidden by the foliage, he began to lope down the path he'd cut the day before. If Lexie had listened to him, the kid would be fed and they would both be ready to go. It would take about six hours by car to get to Limores, the capital city of San Rafael, and with any luck they could get a plane out that evening.

As he jogged down the path he'd cut through the jungle, something shiny on the ground caught his eye. Stopping abruptly, he stooped to look at it and felt a cold hand clench his gut.

It was a brightly colored candy wrapper, and it hadn't been there when he'd left earlier—he was sure of it. Someone had found his path and decided to follow it. And he was damned sure they hadn't been on a pleasure expedition.

He began to move again, but this time he was silent as well as swift. The hole in the base of the tree had been fairly well hidden by the vines, but had the kid been crying? Had Lexie been talking to her just as the unknown person walked by the tree? And what would that person do when he or she realized that the path ended right there? Anyone skillful enough to follow them into the jungle would recognize the significance of that immediately.

Caine moved a little faster, straining to be quiet enough to hear anyone ahead of him on the path. If he was very lucky, he would hear them coming before they heard him.

He saw a flash at the base of the kapok tree out of the corner of his eye and dived into the bushes on the opposite side. Unsheathing his knife in one smooth motion, he eased the pack off his back and squatted in the dead leaves, waiting for the other person to make the first move.

"Caine?" He heard the shaky whisper and shoved the knife back in place. Listening one more time to be sure no one else was coming, he slid out of the bushes and stood.

"Lexie. Where are you? Are you all right?"

The bushes rustled in front of him, then she stepped out onto the path. The urge to hold her was so overwhelming that without thinking, he stepped forward and wrapped his arms around her.

The baby squirmed between them, but for just a moment he didn't care. Lexie was in his arms again, and nothing else mattered. It felt like a lifetime had passed since the last time she'd been there. His arms tightened around her, and for the space of one heartbeat she held him just as fiercely. Then she let him go and stepped back.

"Are you all right?" she whispered, the fear still sharp in her eyes. "You were gone so long that I thought..."

"I'm fine." His voice sounded gruff. "It just took longer than I thought to get out of the village." Now that he knew she was safe, the fear was fading, replaced by anger fueled by the helplessness he'd felt. "What are you doing here? I told you to wait in the tree."

"I know," she said calmly. "But I decided there was no reason to do that when I could meet you at the edge of the jungle and we could leave that much more quickly. It was easy enough to follow your trail."

Fear about what might have happened to her made his words sharper than he intended. "I told you to stay in the tree. You could have gotten yourself killed."

"If I'd listened to you and stayed in the tree, those two men would have found me there," she retorted.

"You could have walked right into them!" he exploded. "At least in the tree you were hidden." One part of him knew he was being irrational, but anger at the two men hunting her and his overwhelming relief at finding her unharmed had swamped his reason. "I give the orders on this little expedition, Lexie. If you want to make it out of here in one piece, you're going to have to do what I tell you."

She tightened her lips and glared at him. "First of all, I never said I wanted to leave Santa Ysabel. That was your idea. Even now, I'm only taking your word for it that someone is looking for me. And second, I don't recall crowning you king. I had twenty-six years of being ordered around by a man, and I don't intend to put up with it again. If you want me to do something, you can ask me like a reasonable human being."

"You haven't fit the definition of reasonable since the day you were born." He wanted to grab her and shake some sense into her. He watched her staring up at him, her face tight and determined, and with a silent groan he stopped himself from stepping closer to her.

Hell, who was he trying to fool? He just wanted to grab her. He needed to feel her under his hands, her mouth opening under his, her body softening and responding to him. He needed to reassure himself that she was alive and unharmed. Curling his hands around the straps of his backpack to stop himself from reaching out to her, he backed up another step.

"I'm in charge, Lexie. As long as I'm responsible for getting you and the kid out of here safely, you'll do as I say." With an effort, he managed to keep his voice level and controlled.

She smiled at him sweetly. "Since I would like to get out of this jungle safely, don't you think we should be leaving now? Who is or isn't in charge here is a fascinating subject, but right now I'd prefer not to meet up with the two men who are undoubtedly on the trail behind us."

He stared at her as she picked up her pack that was lying on the ground, then swore viciously as he looked down the path behind them. There was no sign of the two men, but she was right; it wouldn't be long before they were back. When the trail ended and their prey was nowhere in sight, they would retrace their steps. If he stood here arguing with Lexie much longer, the two men would walk right into them.

"Let's go." Swinging his own pack onto his back, he motioned for her to precede him, then took one more look back at the path behind them. There was still no sign of the two men. Furious with himself for allowing his fear for Lexie to override his common sense, he strode after her in grim silence.

Lexie walked along steadily, one arm shielding Ana from the vines that hung over the path and the other helping to support her weight. Caine was close behind, but he didn't say a word. Her body was quiveringly aware of him, and when she realized she was slowing down so he would get closer to her, she deliberately speeded up. The last thing she needed or wanted was any more closeness to Caine O'Roarke.

It seemed as if they'd been trudging through the endless green forever when Caine muttered behind her, "Slow down."

She stopped immediately and turned around. "What's wrong?"

"Nothing."

He cocked his head as if listening, and she instinctively moved a step nearer to him. "What do you hear?" She was disgusted with herself at the breathless, fearful quality of her voice.

"Nothing."

She opened her mouth to ask again what was wrong, but he shushed her with one hand. After what seemed like a long time, his mouth thinned into a grim line and he stepped in front of her.

"We're changing the plan a little. I hid the Jeep in the jungle near the road away from the village, but we need to cut a new path to get to it. I want to approach it from a different direction."

"What's wrong, Caine? And don't say nothing again," she warned. "I saw the way you looked."

He gazed at her for a moment, then his eyes softened momentarily. "I won't lie to you, Lexie. Whatever happens on this trip, I'll be straight with you. If there's something wrong, you'll be the first to know. And I promise you, nothing's wrong right now."

"Then why are you changing the plan?" she challenged. She would never admit it to him, but she was fervently glad he was on her side right now.

"Because I decided the old one was too predictable," he answered easily.

When she continued to stare at him, unconvinced, he sighed. "I swear to you, Lexie, I didn't hear a thing. Something just doesn't feel right. I can't explain it, but there's something about the quality of the silence that— Oh, hell, I don't know. I just know I'm not going to go the way I'd originally planned. All right?''

She nodded, fear reaching out to grip her again. ''Tell me what I need to do.''

His eyes softened again, then he turned away and gazed at the wall of green in front of them. When he looked back at her, he was the impersonal commando again. ''I'm going to try to find a way to get through this stuff without cutting anything, at least until we're out of sight of this path. Stay here for a moment. I'll be right back.''

Without another look, he crouched down and crawled into the greenery. She stood alone on the tiny path, cradling Ana with one hand and listening anxiously with all her concentration. All she heard was the sounds of the jungle echoing around her.

Surely they were getting close to the village, she thought with another stab of fear. There should have been some noises that she could identify, even if they were only a vague whisper above the forest cacophony. But it was as if the cries of birds and other animals and the ever-present rustling in the dead leaves underfoot were the only sounds in the universe.

The lack of human noises made her heart pound with terror and her head throb with the effort of listening. When the leaves swished next to her, she spun around so fast she almost lost her balance.

Caine reached out to steady her, gripping her upper arms. ''It's only me, Lexie,'' he said. ''I've found a way. Let's go.''

She managed to nod. ''I'm ready.''

''Give me your pack first,'' he said, and she turned and looked at him in surprise. ''You're going to have a hard enough time getting through with a baby on your chest. You don't need to worry about that pack, too.'' He waited impatiently as she shrugged out of the cumbersome backpack, then slung it onto his shoulders as if it weighed no more than an armful of the flowers that hung from the trees.

"Turn around," he ordered, and she slowly pivoted. She felt his hands hesitantly moving on the knot she'd tied in the shawl, careful not to touch her back.

"What are you doing?" she whispered.

"Making this thing tighter. It might be uncomfortable for you or the kid for a few minutes, but it'll be easier for you to get through the brush. If it's a little tighter, you won't catch on so many branches."

The shawl pulled taut around Ana, lifting her higher and tighter against Lexie's breasts. The baby moved sluggishly, and Lexie put a hand on her to quiet her. The last thing they needed right now was a baby crying.

"There. That should do it." She could feel the knot on the shawl being pulled snug, and then Caine's hands rested on her shoulders for a second. He removed them almost immediately, but not before her skin came alive. Each place his fingers had lingered throbbed with awareness. Turning away so he wouldn't see her reaction to his casual touch, she made a production of covering Ana's face.

When she looked back up at him, he was watching her with an inscrutable look on his face. The silence stretched between them as the chatter from the jungle seemed to fade away. Then he said abruptly, "Follow me. You'll only have to crawl for a short distance, but watch where you put your hands."

He knelt on the ground and wriggled between two bushes, and after a moment she dropped down and followed him. The rich, moist scent of the earth surrounded her. Branches and vines clawed at her face, and she tried to use one hand to protect herself and Ana. When she paused to push a particularly thick vine out of the way, she heard a noise from the direction of the path behind her that made her freeze.

Apparently Caine had heard it too. He halted in front of her and swung around, motioning for her to stop. Looking around fearfully, she wondered if they had gone far enough to be invisible from the narrow path they had just left. Caine must have seen the fear in her eyes, because he took her hand and gripped it tightly.

Under any other circumstances she would have been ashamed of how she clung to him. Now she just held on, finding more comfort than she would have ever thought possible in the warm fingers engulfing hers. Comfort wasn't a quality she had ever associated with Caine, and the thought crept into her mind that she could have sat here with him, like this, for a long time.

They sat, silent and unmoving, for what seemed like ages. "Let's move," he finally whispered, drawing his hand away from hers. "They're gone."

She thrust the bereft feeling aside and followed him through the tangled greenery again. It seemed to stretch on forever. By the time he stopped in front of her, she felt bruised and disheveled from forcing her way past the endless branches.

"This should do it." Caine stood in front of her in a tiny clearing and reached down to pull her to her feet. "We've come far enough that no one should be able to find our path unless they crawl through the jungle the same way we did."

"Won't they be able to see where we left the path?" Lexie looked around her at the unending greenery, and shivered at the thought that someone would want her so badly that he would pursue her even through this.

"Only if they have people trained in tracking," Caine answered grimly. "And right now, I don't think they do. If they did, they would have found you in the jungle."

"You're so reassuring," she muttered.

One of his rare smiles flashed across his face. "Cheer up, Lexie. The worst is behind us. Now all we have to do is get to the Jeep and leave this village in the dust behind us."

An unexpected sheen of tears filled her eyes at the thought of what she'd be leaving behind. Besides the people of Santa Ysabel, who she'd thought were her friends, it was the place where she'd learned she was pregnant with Ana, the place where her child had been born. Now she was sneaking out of the village, unable to say goodbye to any of her friends, not sure if she would ever be back.

"Tell me what you found that made you so sure there were people looking for me," she said suddenly to Caine. "You never told me."

Caine unsheathed a machete from his belt and began methodically hacking away at the vines. "Yes, I did. I told you someone had been searching your house."

"It might have just been someone looking for me, someone who needed medical help," she protested. The longing to go back to the village was so intense she had to stop herself from turning around and fighting her way through the undergrowth.

Caine lowered the machete and faced her. "Lexie, someone had gone through all your belongings. And it wasn't a friendly search, believe me. I know the difference." He stared at her for a moment, impatience in his gaze now. "Have you forgotten the guy watching your house last night, or the two men in the jungle just now?"

"No," she whispered, holding Ana more tightly. "I guess I just don't want to believe it."

He dropped the machete and stepped over to her. He slowly reached out and tilted her chin upward until she was looking at him. "I know." His voice was quiet. "You feel betrayed and hurt, and you're trying as hard as you can to convince yourself that what I'm saying isn't true. I understand, Lexie, and I wish I could fix it for you, but it can't be fixed. Someone *did* betray you, and there *is* someone waiting in the village for you."

She was horrified to feel her eyes filling with tears. Turning away, she made a production of adjusting the scarf that held Ana in order to avoid looking at him. She desperately wanted to hold her child, but knew if she woke her now, they would have to wait while she was fed. Instead, she ran her hand gently down Ana's back and gulped twice, swallowing the sobs that threatened to erupt.

Caine's hands gripped her shoulders from behind and gently turned her around. "It's all right, Lexie." His voice was softer than she'd ever imagined it could be. "I know how you feel. Betrayal hurts more than almost anything in the world. But you can't give in to the hurt, because if you do, they've won. You have to get angry and use that anger to save yourself and the baby."

She was close enough to smell his crisp, male scent and to see the dark shadow of hair on his chest through his T-shirt. Memories came flooding back—of lying against his chest, hearing his heart racing beneath her ear. She remembered in vivid detail the strength of his arms wrapped around her, the taste of his mouth on hers.

There were a lot of things about Caine that she hadn't forgotten.

Their eyes met and she realized he hadn't, either. There was more than comfort in his eyes now. They glittered with something hot and primitive, something that would burn her if she gave it half a chance.

This was the time to back up, to thank him for comforting her and step away from him. She found she couldn't move. His hot gaze had mesmerized her, holding her in place.

He brought one of his hands up and tangled his fingers in her hair. Even in the jungle heat she shivered.

"Lexie," he whispered. His hand caressed her scalp and he bent his head and brushed his lips over hers.

It was the softest of kisses, a mere sweep of his lips over hers. It shouldn't have made her tremble. Caine shouldn't still have the power to make her ache inside, with just one touch of his mouth. She'd worked too hard to forget about him.

He raised his head, and she saw the triumph and fierce desire in his eyes. "Lexie," he said again, thickly, as he lowered his mouth to hers again.

This time the kiss wasn't gentle or comforting. His mouth was hard and bruising, demanding her surrender. She knew she had to stop, to move away, but she was caught in the sensual web he knew how to weave around her. Her senses spinning, desire coiling tightly inside her, she gripped his forearms and held on to him.

He steadied her with one arm around her back and one behind her neck as his mouth moved on hers. Lexie forgot about Ana, still lying between them. She forgot about the jungle, about Santa Ysabel, about everything except Caine kissing her.

When he took her lower lip between his teeth and ran his tongue over it, sensations speared through her and she tightened her hold on his arms. She heard a moaning sound, and realized with a shock that it was her. He slipped his tongue into her open mouth, and one of his hands slipped down to caress the curve of her hip.

Desire pounded through her blood, pooling in her lower abdomen, and she tentatively touched her tongue to his. He groaned into her mouth and tried to pull her closer. For a moment she didn't recognize the whimper, then she realized it was Ana, jostled by their two bodies straining toward each other.

Her desire vanished as quickly as if someone had dashed a bucket of ice water over her head. Letting go of Caine, she stumbled backward, staring at him with shock.

His eyes glittered with passion and the sharp planes of his face were taut with arousal. He reached out to touch her, but when she backed up a step he let his hand fall to his side. He stood staring at her as the moment stretched on, the tension between them pulling tighter and tighter.

"Thank you for trying to comfort me." She knew her words tumbled out too quickly, but she was desperate to break the tense, throbbing silence. "I'm sorry I acted like such an idiot about leaving Santa Ysabel."

Something shifted in his eyes, and it was as if his face had been suddenly shuttered. His eyes, alive with desire just a moment ago, were now flat and opaque, unreadable. She had no idea what he was thinking.

"You're welcome." His words were flat, too, without inflection. "Are you ready to go?"

She nodded, unable to hold his gaze.

"Follow me. Stay far enough behind that I can swing the machete."

He turned and picked up the huge knife and began hacking at the vines. Every blow looked vicious, and she could see his muscles bunching for each massive swipe. He moved ahead at an almost-inhuman pace, hardly seeming to take a breath between swings of the razor-sharp machete.

Waiting for him to move a few feet ahead of her, she picked up her pack and swung it over her shoulder, then began to follow him. She looked down at Ana worriedly. She should be waking up soon, hungry and ready to eat. She was sure Caine wouldn't want to stop now so she could feed her.

"How much farther until we get to your Jeep?" she called to Caine.

He didn't even pause in his rhythmic swings of the machete. "Another ten minutes or so."

As long as they kept moving, Ana could probably wait that long. The motion would soothe her enough to make her forget her empty stomach, at least for a few minutes.

She looked up at Caine again, wondering at the fury that propelled him. Was it directed at her, or at himself? It didn't matter, she decided. What had happened just now was a mistake, brought on by her momentary vulnerability. From now on, she vowed, she would control herself. She wouldn't let down her guard for an instant.

If Caine thought he could control her by exploiting her body's traitorous reactions to him, he was going to find out how wrong he was. Less than a year ago she'd surrendered to him, and then he'd abandoned her without a word of explanation. He might be Ana's father, but that didn't mean she was going to be putty in his hands a second time.

No, she didn't care if he was angry at her. He might as well learn now as later that she had grown up, and she wasn't the infatuated little fool she'd been a year ago.

Chapter 5

Caine cursed himself with each swing of the machete. Every vine in front of him, each bush in his path mocked him for his desire for a woman who represented everything he couldn't have in his life and didn't want anyway. He slashed desperately at them, trying to rid his mind of the demons that haunted him.

He could hear Lexie behind him, staying well back from the machete. It had been the hurt in her eyes that had managed to get past his barriers and make him touch her. And once he'd touched her, he'd been lost.

It wouldn't happen again, he told himself with a particularly brutal sweep of the blade. It had been far too appropriate that the baby had physically separated them a few minutes earlier. She represented everything that he'd always known was out of his reach, and now everything that stood between him and Lexie. The taste of the past was bitter in his mouth, taunting him with the fact that he was a lousy choice as a father for any kid.

"Caine?" Lexie's voice came from behind him. She sounded worried. "I'm going to have to feed Ana soon. Do you think we should stop?"

"No." He drew a deep, shuddering breath and wiped the sweat out of his eyes. His muscles were protesting their unrelenting workout, but he ignored his body's warning. "We can't stop now. She's going to have to wait."

"I'm not sure if I can keep her from crying."

"Dammit, Lexie, if we stop now we'll be sitting ducks!" he exploded. "You're her mother. Do something to keep her quiet."

"I'm not a miracle worker," she snapped. "She doesn't know that it's inconvenient for her to eat right now."

"Then give her some water."

"In what?" she asked sarcastically. "The bottles are in my backpack, and I'd have to stop to get them. Or should I just pour it down her throat?"

"How the hell would I know?" he snarled. "What do you normally use?"

"My breast," she shouted.

She seemed to realize what she'd said the moment the words were out of her mouth. There was dead silence from behind him as he froze momentarily. He could almost feel the embarrassed heat radiating from her body.

Now was not the time to think about her breasts, he reminded himself savagely as he resumed swinging the machete. Another vine fell from a particularly vicious blow. His body stirred as he remembered the smooth, creamy skin that she'd exposed when she fed the baby. Cursing, he called himself ten different kinds of pervert. He tried to think about their escape route and calculate what obstacles they might meet.

Instead, visions filled his mind of another time, another lifetime. She was lying next to him, naked. Her small, round breasts with their pink tips had fit perfectly into his hands and his mouth.

There was a whimpering noise behind him, and the sound fueled his temper. They were too close to the Jeep and freedom to let a crying baby stop them. "Keep that kid quiet," he warned in a low, deadly voice. He didn't even bother looking back.

Lexie didn't answer, but after a few moments there was silence again. He was free to concentrate on getting them back to the Jeep and away from this town before all hell broke loose. As he swung the machete in rhythmic strokes, the tension in his body eased and he was able to channel his thoughts away from Lexie and concentrate on what to do next.

In another ten minutes he saw the dull gleam of metal in the distance ahead of him and he allowed himself a small smile of satisfaction. The Jeep was still where he'd left it. Stopping immediately, he turned around to find that Lexie was nowhere in sight.

Pushing down the wave of panic that threatened to wash over him, he began walking back along the path he'd cut. As he rounded a small bend, he saw her walking along with her head bent over the kid. Anger immediately replaced the panic, and he strode forward to meet her.

"You were supposed to keep up with me," he said in a harsh whisper. "What's the problem?"

She looked up, and he saw the weariness etched on her face. She straightened and looked directly at him. "I was doing the best I could. I assumed you'd rather I walk more slowly than allow Ana to scream."

He glanced down and realized that she had been feeding the baby as she walked. The arm that cradled the child to her breast shook slightly with fatigue, but she continued to hold the baby steadily in place. When he looked up at her face, she held his gaze defiantly.

Guilt flooded him. It couldn't have been easy for Lexie to hold the kid in that position while she walked, and one look at her trembling arm told him what a strain it was for her arm muscles.

"Sit down," he said, more gently. "The Jeep is just ahead, and I have to make sure no one's found it. Stay here until I get back."

She sank to the ground immediately and leaned against a tree that stood next to the path he'd cut. Tilting her head back, she closed her eyes and brought her knee up to support the baby. Her trembling arm dropped to her side. The weariness in her face released another flood of guilt in him.

"I'll be right back," he muttered as he turned to go.

After he'd gone a few steps he looked back at her, but she hadn't moved. He paused for a moment, wondering if he should go back to her, then forced himself to move forward. If they didn't get out of here, it wouldn't matter how tired Lexie was.

Ten minutes later he stepped away from the Jeep and allowed the vegetation to spring back into place around it. After thoroughly inspecting the area, he'd decided that no one had found its hiding place—at least, not yet. It was time to get Lexie and the kid and get going.

When he arrived back at the tree where he'd left them, he found Lexie wrapping something in one of the huge leaves that hung down from the tree behind her. The baby lay on the ground next to her, kicking her legs and waving her arms.

He hadn't looked closely at the kid before this, and he found himself watching her agitated-looking movements. "What's wrong with her?" he finally asked.

Lexie looked over at him, puzzled. "What do you mean, what's wrong with her? There's nothing wrong with her."

"Why is she jerking around like that?"

She looked over at the baby, and a soft smile lit her face. "She's just happy to be out of that shawl for a while. Even babies have to get some exercise, you know."

"Oh." He tried to ignore the baby and concentrate on what they had to do, but he couldn't seem to tear his gaze away from the kicking legs and gently swaying arms of the child on the ground. *His child,* a small voice reminded him. Whether he liked it or not, this child was his flesh and blood. Would she look like him? he wondered, staring at her. Would he see himself in her smile, her eyes?

If they didn't get out of here right now, no one would ever know, he reminded himself harshly. Pushing away from the tree, he said, "Let's go. No one's found the Jeep, but if they're looking for you it's only a matter of time."

She nodded and scooped the baby up, replacing her in the shawl. For one insane moment he opened his mouth to offer to carry the kid. Lexie's arms probably still ached from their last trek. Then he regained his senses. The last thing he needed was to have his hands full of baby. If there was trouble, he needed to have his hands free.

"How far away from the village are we?" Lexie asked in a whisper.

Disturbed by his sudden, inexplicable need to touch the baby, he was glad to have the distraction. "Far enough. This morning I pushed the car down to the road, then drove it five minutes away and hid it. You're going to steer and I'll push until we're on the main road and heading away from the village. As long as no one hears us leaving, I think we'll be safe."

"If they realize your car is gone and think we've left, won't they be looking for us on the road?"

He could hear the worry in her voice and wanted to reassure her. "No one saw us leave, so I'm hoping that they'll assume I've done just what I did—hidden the car somewhere near the village. I'm counting on them continuing to look for us and the car for a while yet. By the time they realize that we've gotten away, we should be close to Limores."

She was silent for a while. Then she said quietly, "I've heard a lot of things about El Cuchillo, but never that he was stupid. Are you sure this isn't a trap?"

"If it is, there's nothing we can do about it now." His voice was too harsh, but he didn't like the fact that she'd glossed over his reassurances and zeroed in on his main worry. "We'll just have to deal with it if it happens."

The metal of the Jeep flashed at him through an opening in the brush, and he stopped her with an outthrust hand. "Wait here."

A quick inspection showed him that everything was just as he'd left it. Holding back the shrubbery, he motioned for her to join him. "I'll clear out these branches and make sure there's a path to the road. I'll be right back."

Quickly he removed the camouflage he'd placed around the Jeep in the early morning. When there was a narrow path through the jungle to the road, which was just out of sight, he returned to the Jeep.

Lexie was in the back seat, hunched over. "What are you doing?" he asked her.

"I'm trying to get Ana strapped into the car with some semblance of safety. It'll just take me a minute."

As he waited, sweat trickling down his back, he could feel his temper rising. "Maybe we ought to go back to the village and get a car seat for her," he growled, anger tingeing his voice.

She looked up then, a mutinous expression on her face. "Sarcasm isn't necessary," she snapped. "Do you want her to bounce out of the car, or get thrown into the windshield if we have to stop suddenly?"

The visions she conjured up made him feel slightly sick and he was ashamed of himself for losing his temper. "Just hurry up," he muttered. "The longer we sit here, the closer they're getting."

"I'm finished," she said after a few more minutes, and she slid into the front seat. "What do you want me to do?"

"The road is straight ahead. There. Can you see it?"

She peered through the greenery. "I can see a lighter area ahead of us."

"That's it. Just aim toward that. When we get to the road, turn right. The road is heading downhill, so we should be able to coast for a while before we have to turn on the engine."

"Should I stop for you to get in?" She turned to look at him, and all he saw in her eyes was a slight tension. He knew she had to be terrified, both for herself and her kid, and he admitted to himself with grudging respect that she was doing a lot better than he'd expected.

"Just let it go. Don't brake, whatever you do. We need to get as far away as possible before starting the engine. I can jump in while the car's moving."

Her gaze held his for a moment. "Be careful," she said finally as she turned away to look out toward the road. He saw her hands tighten on the steering wheel as she shifted slightly in the seat.

Putting his shoulder to the back of the Jeep, he strained until he felt it begin to move. From now on, the weight of the vehicle would keep it moving, and all he had to do was urge it along. It began gliding silently through the jungle, but as they neared the road he tensed. He heard the sound of another car on the road, approaching them quickly.

Lexie heard it, too, because she turned around to look at him, a question in her eyes. Gauging the sound of the engine, he realized that the car would probably reach them just as they were emerging from the jungle. Cursing the luck that had brought a vehicle down the seldom-used road just as they were trying to make their escape, he made his decision quickly.

"Brake!"

She stomped on the brake pedal and the Jeep shuddered to a halt, barely concealed by the few bushes between them and the road. The next instant a car roared past them, heading in the direction of Santa Ysabel.

Lexie turned to face him, and this time the fear in her eyes was easy to read. "That was another jeep, and it was painted in camouflage. Do you think it was someone looking for...?"

"We don't have time to think about it," he answered grimly. "Let's get this car on the road and get going." He put his shoulder to the Jeep again and began pushing. He didn't want to think about whether or not the other car had seen them as it flashed past. The camouflaged jeep had been going awfully fast. On the other hand, if it belonged to El Cuchillo's men, they would have been trained to be observant.

The Jeep burst through the last of the bushes and Lexie turned it sharply to the right. Caine gave it one last push and felt it gain momentum as it rolled down the gentle incline. Swinging himself into the passenger seat, he handed Lexie the keys and watched her put them into the ignition with a hand that trembled slightly.

He let the car roll for as long as he dared. When he felt it slowing down, he looked over at Lexie grimly. She clung to the steering wheel, staring at the road ahead of them. They weren't as far away as he would have liked, but they didn't have any choice. "Go ahead and start the engine."

Lexie sat in the passenger seat of the Jeep, feeling the hot, damp air flow past her face, and looked over again at Caine. Not long after she'd started the engine he'd told her to stop so he could drive, and she'd been happy to oblige him. Even now, three hours away from Santa Ysabel, she still couldn't stop herself from turning around every few minutes to see if they were being followed.

There had been no signs of pursuit, but she knew she wouldn't feel safe until they were in Limores and she could lose herself in the urban bustle. She'd thought that as they got farther away from the village her feelings of betrayal and desolation would fade, but they came flooding back, stronger than ever, each time she thought about what she'd left behind.

She twisted around in her seat again, this time to check on Ana. The baby had never ridden in a car before, and it was having a magical effect on her. She hadn't woken once in the last three hours.

"Is she okay?"

Caine's voice was gruff, and he didn't look at her. Blinking in surprise at his sign of interest, she glanced over at him. "She's fine. Still sleeping."

"Good. I don't want to have to stop yet."

She should have known why he'd asked about Ana, she told herself, trying to ignore the tiny stab of pain in her heart. His actions the previous day had made it clear he wasn't interested in the baby.

She would never let him see how much his words hurt. Giving her daughter an assessing look, she said, "It doesn't matter whether you want to stop or not. She's going to need to eat soon."

"Can't you feed her while I drive?"

"It's too dangerous," she said instinctively. "What if you hit a hole in the road while I was holding her? She could get hurt."

He glanced over at her, a hard expression in his eyes. "You'd rather take the chance on the men behind us catching up? I can guarantee you she'll get hurt if that happens."

"There haven't been any signs that we're being followed," she protested. "Maybe they gave up when we got away." From what she'd heard of El Cuchillo, that wasn't very likely, but surely the rebel leader had bigger fish to fry than searching for one American woman.

He glanced over at her again. "You want to pull over and wait awhile to see?"

Swiveling around in the vinyl seat, she stared back the way they'd come. There was nothing to see but an endless ocean of green undulating into the distance on both sides of the highway. The asphalt was merely a tiny ribbon of dull black that only emphasized the vastness of the tropical forest behind them and the isolation surrounding them.

"No," she muttered. "I'll feed her while you drive."

The only sign that he'd heard her was the slight relaxation of his hands on the steering wheel. It didn't make her feel any better to realize how tense he was, even though there were no signs of pursuit.

Braking suddenly, he pulled the car over to the side of the road. "Do it now," he ordered, peering down the road ahead of them.

Her heart turned over in her chest and began a slow, heavy thumping. "What's wrong?" she whispered, staring at him.

He didn't answer for a moment as he continued to look down the road. Finally he said slowly, "I don't know. I thought I saw a flash of light ahead of us, but I don't see anything now."

"Maybe it's another car coming toward us." She didn't like the sick dread she heard in her voice.

"Maybe." He didn't sound convinced. "Go ahead and feed her while we wait here for a few minutes and see."

She climbed into the back seat, her fear making her feel clumsy and awkward. Ana was just beginning to stir now that the hypnotizing motion of the car had stopped. Quickly Lexie roused her and put the baby to her breast. They didn't have time for a leisurely feeding session right now.

Caine continued to stare into the distance, and his utter stillness only increased her fear. Finally she burst out, "What do you see? Is there a car coming?"

"No." He didn't turn around to look at her. "I saw another flash of light, but there are no cars on the road ahead of us."

The contrast between the utter normalcy of Ana nursing at her breast and the fear that was beginning to pound through her veins was disorienting. She looked at Caine again, at his almost-frightening quiet. "What are we going to do?"

He didn't move or answer her for a long moment, then he turned around. She noticed that he was careful not to let his gaze drop below her face. "I'm going to hide the Jeep in the trees and go take a look. You do whatever you have to do to keep her quiet."

"She'll be fine since she's just eaten." Gulping once, she asked, "How long do you think you'll be?"

Slowly he let his gaze drift below her neck. "Eager for my company, Lexie? That's a change."

Flushing, she turned away and began to rebutton her blouse. "I just want to know how long to wait before I get worried." Her hand shook as she fumbled with the buttons on her blouse, and she laid Ana on the seat so she could use both hands.

"I'm sorry, Lexie." Caine's voice behind her sounded regretful, but she refused to turn around. "I shouldn't have said that."

She lowered her head to force the last button through the impossibly tiny hole. "Forget it. It's not important."

His hands settled on her shoulders, the warmth of his fingers burning through her thin T-shirt and starting the heat coiling deep inside her. Cursing her traitorous body, she tried to shrug away from him. His hands merely tightened on her.

He turned her around in the seat with what seemed like very little effort. "It is important, and I'm sorry. I didn't mean to hurt you."

She couldn't interpret the expression flickering in his eyes. Shrugging again, she managed to pull away from his hands. "Don't worry about it. I'm a big girl, Caine. It takes more than a few nasty words to hurt me now." As she watched him she forced herself to remember how he'd left her eleven months earlier, and how, when he'd found her again, he'd ignored the child they'd created together. Pain throbbed dully through her chest, a pain she suspected would be there for a long time. "It takes a lot more than that," she said softly. Turning away from him, she bent over Ana and fumbled in her pack for a clean diaper.

She could feel his eyes on her for a long time. Finally he shifted in the seat and turned to face the road again. "There's a spot over there where I can pull into the trees," he said, his voice hard and abrupt. "Hold on."

The Jeep bumped off the road and over the uneven ground to the small gap in the trees. Clutching Ana with one hand and the back of the seat with the other, she felt a start of fear again when the green canopy closed over her and she was once again in the dim, shadowed light of the jungle. She hadn't realized that in spite of her nervousness she'd begun to assume that everything was going to be all right.

Caine didn't give her a chance to let her fear grow. "Help me cover the car up," he said as he jumped out and began to tug an armful of dead vines over the front of the Jeep. "I won't be gone long, but I don't want to take any chances."

Laying Ana back down on the seat, she eased out of the Jeep and felt the familiar squishy sensation as she stepped on the floor of the jungle. Even though they had only driven a few yards off the road, it was much hotter under the leaves than it was in the open. They were approaching the hottest part of the day, and she felt the sweat begin to trickle down between her breasts almost immediately.

A few minutes later Caine stepped back and surveyed the Jeep. It was almost completely hidden under a layer of vines and dead branches they'd found on the ground. He nodded once, then turned to her.

"Nobody will be able to see you from the road. I'm going to get close enough to find out what those flashes of light were." His gaze softened. "It may take me a while, so don't start to worry if I'm not back right away." He examined her face, then reached out to skim her cheek below her right eye. "You look tired. Why don't you take a nap?"

Before she could answer, he turned and disappeared into the jungle. "Caine?" she called.

He reappeared next to the Jeep. "What?"

"Be careful."

He stared at her for a long moment, then raised his hand to cup her face. Brushing his fingers along her cheek, he murmured, "I'm always careful, Lexie. I'll be back."

Her skin tingled where he had touched her, and she raised her hand to the place his fingers had been. Staring at the spot where he'd disappeared, she strained to hear him moving away from her but didn't hear a sound other than the normal jungle noises.

After a long time she turned back to Ana. The baby was wide-awake and staring at her, and Lexie smiled wearily down at her. To her surprised delight, Ana grinned back.

She watched in awe for a moment, then snatched her daughter into her arms and held her tight. "You smiled at me. You really did this time!" she whispered. She knew she was grinning like an idiot, but she didn't care. All the fear that had been building inside her seemed to fall away as if by magic, and she nuzzled the side of Ana's neck.

"If only your daddy had been here to see it, too," she murmured without thinking. Ana gurgled as if to agree with her, and the sound nearly broke her heart when she realized what she'd said. Ana's father had made it abundantly clear that he wouldn't care if she ever smiled.

"You can smile for me all you want, little girl." Her voice was fierce as she laid Ana across her lap again. "Each time will be as precious to me as this first one was."

This was the first time in the past day and a half that she'd been able to relax and enjoy Ana. Pushing thoughts of Caine and the danger they still faced away from her, she smiled down at her daughter and vowed to forget about the whole mess, at least for the next few minutes. Ana was going to get her full attention.

She awoke with a start, her heart pounding. She didn't know when she had fallen asleep, and she looked around frantically for Ana. Finding the baby tucked against her abdomen, she relaxed enough to raise her head and look around. Something had awakened her, and it hadn't been Ana.

There was a crunching of leaves underfoot, the barest whisper of a sound that she caught with straining ears. Someone or something was approaching the Jeep.

Even if she'd had time to run, there was nowhere to go. The tangle of vines and low bushes surrounded the Jeep, and without Caine's machete she was trapped in the middle of the greenery. The leaves crackled again, closer this time. It wasn't Caine. She was certain of that. When he'd left, he'd moved away without a sound.

Easing off the bench seat, she crouched on the floor, out of sight. Picking Ana up carefully, she laid her on the floor, protecting her with her body. If they were very lucky, whoever or whatever was out there wouldn't get close enough to the Jeep to see them.

The intruder wasn't making any effort to conceal himself now. Lexie could hear every leaf as it crumbled beneath the approaching footsteps. Bracing herself, she laid one hand on Ana as she gathered herself to flee.

The sound was right next to them now, and Lexie jerked her head up to face whatever was there. To her surprise, she didn't see anything. The leaves continued to rustle, though, and now it sounded as if it was coming from underneath the Jeep. Swiveling around, she peered over the door just as an agouti appeared, strolling slowly and casually through the dead leaves.

Lexie wasn't sure who was more startled, her or the small, rabbit-like rodent. They stared at each other for a long moment, then the agouti scampered away into the underbrush.

Closing her eyes, Lexie let out a long, shuddering breath. How had she managed to hear that one, small sound over the cacophony of the jungle during the day? Her heart pounding in her chest, Lexie bent over to pick up Ana and cradle her to her chest. She was afraid she knew the answer to that question.

She had thought it was Caine. Even sleeping soundly, she'd awakened because she'd thought Caine was returning.

It didn't mean a thing, she told herself. Of course she would be attuned to Caine—right now her safety and Ana's depended on him. She would be a fool if she didn't pay attention.

Her heart told her she was another kind of fool, but she refused to listen. Caine was just like her father, and she'd spent the last twenty-six years trying to escape from him. To run into the arms of a man who could be his twin would be nothing more than stupidity. Worse, it would be begging for heartbreak. She could no longer deny that the physical attraction between her and Caine was still there, stronger than ever, but that could be controlled and ignored. She refused to acknowledge the possibility that there could ever be anything more.

As if conjured up by her thoughts, Caine suddenly appeared next to the Jeep. There had been no sounds warning of his approach, and she blinked once when she saw him, unsure if he was real or just a figment of her imagination.

He had to be real. If she was imagining Caine, she wouldn't have put such a forbidding look on his face. "What's wrong?" she whispered, reaching out for the still-sleeping Ana.

His eyes flickered to where she touched the baby, then back to her face. "We can't take the road."

His voice was grim and hard. "What do you mean? Do we have to go back and try another route?"

"There is no other route." Reaching behind him, he pulled a map out of the rear pocket of his fatigues. "This is where we are," he said, pointing to a thin red line that represented the road. "Limores is here." He pointed to a spot that was directly below them. "It's not too far, and we're only a half mile or so from where this road joins another and becomes a four-lane highway."

She licked her lips. "So what's the problem?"

He stared at the map for a moment, then looked up at her, his face grim. "The problem is that there's a roadblock where this road joins the other one. They've picked the perfect spot to intercept us, and they know it. We can't continue on this road, and we can't double back and try to pick up the other one. We're trapped between them and Limores."

The jungle heat and the swarming fear were suddenly making her feel faint. "Then what do we do?" Her voice was high-pitched and reedy, sounding completely foreign to her.

Caine looked at her for a moment, as if assessing her and testing what he wanted to say. "We have two choices," he began slowly. "We can let ourselves be caught at the roadblock and hope they listen when we demand to be taken to the American Embassy."

She didn't like the cold, hard look in his eyes. "You don't think that's going to happen, do you?"

"What do you think?" His voice was blunt. "From what I've heard, El Cuchillo doesn't think much of diplomacy or going through the channels."

"No." She shivered. "I don't think that's what would happen if we allowed ourselves to get caught. But what about just waiting until it's dark and driving through the roadblock? If we surprised them, maybe we could catch them off guard."

He shook his head. "Wouldn't work. We're not talking about a couple of sawhorses and a few bored men standing around. Whoever set up this roadblock was serious. There are too many trucks blocking the way to ever hope we'd make it through. And too many sophisticated weapons."

He looked at her, and she didn't like the faint trace of pity she saw in his eyes. "It looks like they don't care if they catch you alive or dead, Lexie. In fact, dead would probably be preferable to them. Less messy, more final." He searched her face. "This is beginning to look like more than an anti-American bias. This is starting to smell awfully personal. Is there something you're not telling me?"

"What could I be hiding from you, Caine? All I know about El Cuchillo is his name. You probably know more about him than I do."

"Are you sure? You've been living in this country for a while now. Maybe there's something you've seen or heard that you don't remember."

She shook her head. "Not that I know of. Santa Ysabel is too isolated. We wouldn't see anyone from one week to the next."

After a moment he nodded. If he was disappointed, he didn't show it. "All right, let's get going."

"What do you mean? You never told me what the other option was."

He turned to face her, pulling on his backpack. "Didn't I? I'm sorry, Lexie, but we don't have any other choice. We're going to have to walk through the jungle to Limores."

Chapter 6

"What?" She couldn't believe she'd heard him correctly. "How can we walk through the jungle? We don't have any food, we don't have any way to cook the food we don't have, and we can't have nearly enough water. It would take days to reach Limores."

"Three, maybe four at the most." His voice was cool and determined. "And we do have food and water. I made sure I was prepared for anything."

She stared at the wall of green in front of her. "How can we get through this?" she whispered.

"We'll cut our way through. Lexie, we don't have any choice." He was starting to sound impatient. "Believe me, I've given it a lot of thought. Limores is on the other side of this mountain. The only way to avoid being caught is to go over it and straight down into the city."

"But..." She gestured hopelessly at Ana. Besides the difficulty of carrying the baby over miles of rough terrain, she didn't have enough clothes or diapers for a trek of several days. "What about her?"

His eyes skimmed over the baby and back to her face. "I'll help you, Lexie. We'll make it because we don't have any choice. It's either this or be caught by El Cuchillo's men, and after seeing what he's got waiting for us down the road, we can't take that chance. He wouldn't go to all this trouble just to escort you out of the country.''

She teetered on the edge of panic as she looked at the jungle ahead of her. Deep inside she knew Caine was right, but she scrambled for another idea. The thought of spending the next few days walking through the hot, airless jungle was too overwhelming to consider. She refused to even think about the nights.

After strapping his small pack to his chest, Caine moved around to the back of the Jeep and pulled out a much larger backpack. Hoisting it onto his back, he reached into the Jeep and pulled out her pack and handed it to her. It held pitifully few items that would help them make it through the jungle. Besides the few items of clothing that Caine had brought for her, it held Ana's diapers and clothes, her medical kit and a few toiletries. And the manila envelope that Caine had retrieved for her.

Whatever happened, she thought fiercely, she wasn't going to leave her pictures behind. Lifting her backpack into place, she turned to Caine and waited for him to move.

He stood back, looking at the Jeep. "I'm going to get more branches and try to cover it better," he said abruptly. "With any luck, they won't find it until we're out of the country."

"All right." She moved to help him, and he laid a hand on her arm with a curious expression in his eyes.

"Don't, Lexie. Let me do this. You need to conserve your energy. We have to get far away from this car today, and we don't have many hours of daylight left."

She slipped the pack off again and sank down onto the ground as she watched him hack at the vines with mechanical efficiency. In a very few minutes she could barely see the Jeep through the matting of green that Caine had arranged over it.

He stepped back and looked at it critically. "It won't be too many days before everything begins to wither, but with any luck it'll stay green for long enough." Sliding the machete back into its scabbard with a fluid motion, he turned to her and held out a hand. "It's time to go."

She slid her hand into his, and he pulled her to her feet in one smooth movement. His fingers seemed to linger longer than necessary, then he dropped her hand and reached for her pack. "Turn around."

His gruff voice was so close to her ear that she could feel his warm breath whisper across the side of her neck. Shivering slightly, she waited with tense anticipation for his hands to touch her shoulders.

She was disappointed when the pack settled onto her back seemingly without any assistance. She turned around to look at him, but he had moved away to settle his own pack.

Lexie was surprised to learn that they didn't need to use the machete to cut a path. The undergrowth was sparse here, perhaps because the canopy of trees above them was so dense that little direct light penetrated to the floor of the forest. For the first time since he'd said they were going to walk through the jungle, her anxiety lifted slightly. If they didn't have to fight for every inch they traveled, maybe it wouldn't be as bad as she'd feared.

Just as she was beginning to relax a little, Caine called back to her, "Watch your step. Without a lot of ground cover, there aren't too many places for snakes to hide. You don't want to step on one."

She froze in mid-step and looked down at the uneven ground. There was nothing to see except leaves and dead branches in various stages of decay. "Ah, Caine?"

Slowing down, he looked back over his shoulder at her. "What?"

"Did you just see a snake?"

"There aren't any right here, Lexie." He stopped and turned around. "They hide under fallen trees and bigger branches. I just wanted to remind you to pay attention."

"You don't have to worry," she muttered, picking her way gingerly past a small branch. "You got my attention, all right."

She looked up in time to see his face soften. "Don't you know snakes are more afraid of you than you are of them?"

"I think that's highly unlikely." Stopping in front of him, she shifted the sleeping Ana and looked around. "How do you know so much about the jungle, anyway?"

The momentary softness in his eyes disappeared. "It comes with the territory. I've spent a little time in jungles like this."

"Working for my father?"

He gave her a curt nod. "That's what I do, remember? I go where James Hollister sends me."

Spinning around, he began walking again. She wasn't sure why she goaded him, but she needed to know for sure. "Is that why you're here, Caine? Because my father sent you?"

He stopped so abruptly that she almost ran into him. When he turned around, she could see the gleam in his bright blue eyes even in the dim light. "I already told you I didn't come to get you because your father asked me to. Do you want to know why I'm here in San Rafael?"

Her heart pounding, she slowly nodded.

He took a step closer, and the clean scent of his sweat filled her senses. Heat seemed to ripple off his body and surround hers. "I'm here because you were a fever in my blood," he said, staring down at her, holding her gaze with his. "I had eleven long months when I could think of nothing but you. You haunted me, day and night. I was obsessed with you, Lexie. Obsessed with wanting you."

He took a step closer. "And I didn't want to be. I wanted to forget all about you, to erase your memory from my mind. I figured if I came down here to save your hide, seeing you again would cure me." He straightened, and the fire went out of his eyes. "That's why I'm here."

Standing taller, she held Ana close and forced herself to hold his eyes. "Maybe if we're both lucky you'll be successful," she whispered, trying not to let him see her pain. Her hand tightened on her daughter. "Thank you for being honest with me."

He stared at her for a moment, as if taken by surprise at her response, then muttered, "You're welcome." Without another word he began walking again, and she squared her already aching shoulders and followed him.

Why the hell had he said that to her? Caine fumed as he walked along, kicking at the branches in front of him. He hadn't missed the pain she'd tried so desperately to hide. And he'd noticed the effort it had cost her to answer him in the same way.

Because he wanted to hurt her, he acknowledged reluctantly. Every time he looked at the baby, he felt the same visceral kick of betrayal. She hadn't told him, and it was apparent that she'd had no intention of telling him anytime in the near future.

It brought back the painful memories he'd tried so hard to bury, and he didn't like the feeling one damn bit. Even though he told himself that what his ex-wife had done was infinitely worse than Lexie's crime, he hadn't been able to stop himself. He'd lashed out, and now the sight of Lexie's face, tight and full of pain, was going to haunt him for a long time.

They walked for a while without speaking, surrounded only by the noises of the jungle. Already the screeching of the colorful macaws high in the treetops was becoming reassuringly familiar. Lexie trudged along in his wake, not saying anything. So far, she was doing a damn good job keeping up with him.

He turned around to tell her so, and was shocked at the bleak expression on her face. She was looking down at the baby, and he could tell the kid was beginning to stir in the sling. She must have felt his eyes on her, because she glanced up at him, making her face carefully blank.

"She's waking up," she said unnecessarily. He could see the squirming inside the shawl.

"We'll stop so you can feed her." Taking his compass out again, he studied it and adjusted their course slightly. Then, scanning the area ahead of them, he nodded toward a spot in the distance. "There's a place up ahead."

She didn't say a thing. Cradling the baby with one hand, she followed him silently. By the time they reached the fallen tree he'd spotted, the baby was beginning to make impatient sounds.

Lexie sank down onto the log and shrugged off her pack. Without even bothering to look at him, she opened her blouse and put the baby to her breast. He couldn't stop himself from watching, and she gave no sign that she noticed.

The inner curve of her breast was pearly white in the muted light. It looked fuller and heavier than he remembered, and a fierce longing shuddered through him. He wanted to hold it in his hand, to feel the weight of it resting against his palm.

Feeling his lower body stir and tighten, he looked at her face to see if she'd noticed his reaction. She hadn't. As she leaned back against a tree trunk, her eyes closed and lines of weariness tugged at her face.

Disgusted with himself, he stood and turned around to pull a canteen out of his pack. Thank God she'd been too tired to see him make a fool of himself. Especially after he'd told her he'd come down here so he could forget about her.

Taking a long drink from the canteen, he waited until she'd finished nursing the baby and had laid her on a blanket spread on the ground. "Do you want a drink?" he asked her.

Startled, she looked up from her backpack, clutching a clean diaper in her hand. She licked her lips, and he felt himself tightening again.

"Yes, I would."

Silently he handed her the canteen, and he watched as she drank deeply. Her mouth covered the place his had been just a moment ago, and he closed his eyes as heat pooled in his loins. Thank goodness he was wearing loose cotton pants. If he was lucky, she wouldn't notice his condition.

Tilting the canteen away from her mouth almost reluctantly, she handed it back to him. There was just a swallow of water left in the bottom. He was shocked at how much she'd drunk.

"Why didn't you tell me you were so thirsty?" he demanded.

She shrugged, looking away. "I knew you wanted to get as far from the road as possible before we stopped, and I knew we'd be stopping eventually so I could feed Ana. I figured I could wait."

The guilt that flooded him didn't do anything to soothe his temper. "Dammit, Lexie, that was just plain stupid!" he exploded. "I can't afford for you to get dehydrated. When you get thirsty, you need to drink."

She stood and shouldered her pack. "I'm sorry, I wasn't thinking. Next time I'll try to have more consideration," she said coolly.

The baby was still lying on the ground, waving her arms and legs again. Lexie didn't look at him as she adjusted the shawl, then bent over to reach for her.

He stopped her with one hand on her arm. "Just a minute."

Watching him warily, she slowly straightened. "What?"

"I'm sorry," he said, his voice stiff. "I didn't mean it that way. I was worried about you, and it came out wrong."

"Don't worry, you made your point. Next time I'll ask when I get thirsty."

"There won't be a next time. You're going to carry the canteen. And you're going to drink whenever you need to." He wanted to do something, anything, to erase that remote look from her eyes. "Will you do that?"

She watched him for a moment, then nodded as she turned away. "Yes, I will. I promise."

He watched in frustrated silence as she picked up the baby and laid her carefully in the shawl. Then, tightening the knot over her shoulder, she looked at him. "We're ready to go."

Nodding once, he spun around and began to walk again. This was a new side of Lexie, he thought uneasily. He'd always known just what she was thinking, had always been able to predict her next words from the expression on her face. Right now, though, he had no idea what was going through her mind, and he didn't like it. She'd never been able to shut him out like this before.

But he'd never told her before that he didn't want any part of her, either, he reminded himself. Calling himself an ugly name, he took out his compass again to make sure they were headed in the right direction.

He couldn't have it both ways, he realized. He looked back at Lexie, walking along behind him with her head down, watching where she put her feet. After he'd made it clear that he didn't want any part of her, he couldn't very well expect her to be open to him.

It was exactly what he wanted. They would be excruciatingly polite to each other for the remainder of the trip, and once they were back in Washington, they would go their separate ways. He would make sure that she and the kid were financially taken care of, and that would be the end of it.

He thought again of the baby, lying on the bright blanket on the jungle floor, waving her arms and legs and looking around, almost as if she was wondering where she was. A tiny arrow pierced his heart, flooding him with pain. He refused to think about what she would look like when she was two years old, or five, or ten. He wasn't cut out to be a father, and she would sure as hell be better off without him.

He heard Lexie stumble behind him, and he stopped and spun around. She'd snatched at a vine to steady herself, and before he could think, he grabbed her shoulders and pulled her upright.

"Are you all right?" he demanded.

She backed away, slipping out of his hands. "I'm fine. You'd gotten a little ahead of me and I was just trying to catch up. I didn't see that dead vine in front of me and I tripped on it. That's all there was to it."

"I'm sorry. I'll try to go a little slower." He'd been trying to run away from his thoughts, and guilt swamped him again. He hadn't even thought about how he would be pushing her.

She brushed her hair away from her face and wiped the sweat off her forehead. "Go as fast as you like. I don't want to be caught any more than you do. I have just as much to lose." She glanced down at the baby, then back up at him again with a fierce look. "More."

Anger welled up in him as he realized that she thought he wouldn't care if the baby was caught by El Cuchillo, but he stopped himself before he corrected her. He hadn't given her any reason to think otherwise. In fact, he'd done his best to ignore the baby's very existence.

It was for her own good, he told himself. But that didn't mean he wanted to see her caught by El Cuchillo. "I'll try to be more careful," he said. "But you're right. I know it's hard on you, but we need to move as fast as we can. If they start looking for us in the jungle, I want to have as much of a head start as possible."

"I didn't ask you to stop," she reminded him in the same cool, detached voice. "You're the one who turned around."

"I may be a bastard, Lexie, but I'm not going to keep walking when you fall down, hoping you'll catch up to me."

She had the grace to flush at that. "I never said you would." She pointedly looked past him at the endless miles of jungle in front of them. "Maybe we should continue this discussion later."

He looked up at the sky and frowned. "We're going to have to stop soon, anyway. We need to find a place and settle in before it gets dark."

He saw the fear sweep over her face and how she struggled to subdue it. Not for the first time that day, he felt a jolt of admiration for her. She'd kept up a brutal pace for the past several hours and hadn't complained once. Now she faced spending another night in the jungle, but she refused to give in to her fears.

"Are there any streams or rivers around?" she asked. "I need to wash out Ana's diapers so they can dry overnight."

He hadn't thought of that problem, but he pulled out the map he'd stuck in his back pocket. "If we've covered as much ground as I think we have, there should be a stream not too far away. We'll stop there for the night."

She licked her lips again. He knew she did it when she was nervous, but he wished she would stop. It was driving him crazy. "Are we going to sleep in the open?"

Forcing his thoughts away from her mouth, he shook his head. "The worst scenario is we sleep in my tent. I'm going to try to find another hollow tree like the one we slept in last night."

She shot him a curious look as he began to walk and she stepped in behind him. "How did you know how to find that tree?"

He looked over his shoulder and smiled slightly. She sounded more normal than she had for a while. "I just looked for fig vines."

"What does that have to do with it?"

"Fig vines strangle a tree and eventually kill it. When that happens, the inside of the tree rots away and it eventually falls down. We just need to find one that's already dead but hasn't fallen yet."

"And that no animals have found," she muttered behind him.

"We can deal with any animals we find." He was feeling more cheerful, and he started looking for signs of water. Lexie was sounding more like herself and less like the remote, chilly woman he didn't know.

Ahead of him the bushes and undergrowth became abruptly more dense, and he walked a little faster. "I think that stream is up ahead," he said over his shoulder, and she began to move faster, too. Before Lexie cleaned the diapers, they could replenish their water supply and get enough to cook the freeze-dried meals he'd packed.

A few minutes later they stood on the edge of what had obviously been a stream at one time. Now it was just a wide strip of mud. He saw her shoulders slump, and he longed to pull her to him and comfort her.

"It's all right, Lexie," he said gently. "There'll be water somewhere close. The ground is still wet here."

She straightened and turned to look at him. "Don't try to make me feel better, Caine. I know as well as you do that there isn't going to be any water in that stream until the rainy season starts. And that's not for a few weeks yet."

"There'll be water." He handed her another full canteen from his pack and took her empty one. "You stay here. I'm going to follow this for a while and see what I can find."

Lexie nodded as her hand closed around the heavy metal container. Caine stood over her long enough to watch her sink down against the base of a tree, then he strode off along the muddy edges of the streambed.

Untying the knot that held the shawl with Ana in place, she lowered the sleeping baby to the ground and slipped out of her pack. The muscles in her shoulders burned with an ache so deep she was sure she wouldn't ever be able to lift another thing. Unscrewing the cap to the canteen with fingers that shook, she gulped the water down. She'd been trying to drink as they walked, but she still found herself with a raging thirst.

The water was tepid, but it tasted wonderful as it slipped down her throat. By the time she'd drained the last drop from the canteen, she was beginning to feel better. Her muscles still ached and she was aware that she needed food badly, but the horrible thirst was gone.

Ana slept on, and Lexie felt her own eyelids drooping. The last conscious thing she did was scoop Ana close as she felt herself dropping off to sleep.

She awoke with a start as she felt a hand on her shoulder. "Lexie, wake up."

It was Caine, and for a moment before she opened her eyes she luxuriated in the intimate words. The bed seemed hard, but she didn't mind as long as Caine was there to whisper to her.

"Come on, Lexie, dinner's ready." His voice was impatient, and she reluctantly opened her eyes. Twilight surrounded them, and she bolted upright in fright. Where were they?

It only took a moment for her to remember. They were in the jungle, and Caine wasn't her lover imploring her to wake up for him. She looked around, disoriented by the darkness, and realized that Ana wasn't lying next to her.

"Where's Ana?" she demanded, twisting to look behind her. "Where did she go?"

"Relax, Lexie. I moved her over by the fire. It looked like you were going to crush her."

She scrambled to her feet and stumbled over to where the fire glowed brightly in the darkness. Ana was lying on her shawl, wide-awake and staring at the dancing fire. She seemed perfectly content, and Lexie felt a gnawing dissatisfaction. She was the only one who was supposed to be able to take care of her daughter.

"Thank you," she said stiffly to Caine. "I appreciate your watching her."

He shrugged. "I didn't want you rolling over her. She might have started squawking, and I couldn't take that chance."

"Thank you for your concern." She couldn't disguise the pain in her voice. "I appreciate it."

"Lexie..."

She spun around and glared at him. "I thought you said dinner was ready. I'm starving."

He hesitated as if he wanted to say something else, but then he shrugged again and moved to the other side of the fire. The flames illuminated the planes of his face, hardening the lines in the uncompromising light.

He indicated an aluminum bowl that had steam rising gently from it. "Here's dinner. I hope you like beef stew."

Her stomach growled in response, and she moved over to pick up the bowl. They were both silent as they ate. Ana slept on, and outside the circle of flickering firelight Lexie could hear the sounds of the jungle settling in for the night.

Scraping the last bit from her bowl, she set it down and looked over at Caine. Still eating, he gave her a slightly surprised look. "Did you get enough to eat?"

His pack was open, and while she'd eaten her dinner she'd noticed the pile of dehydrated meals in their foil packages. There were enough for both of them for three more days. "Yes, thank you, I'm fine," she said politely. Her stomach protested, but she ignored it.

"There's a bag of nuts in there, if you want them."

She had to force herself to pretend to consider it. Finally she said, "I would like a few, I think."

Reaching over to his pack, he drew out a bag and handed it to her. It felt pitifully light. Obviously, when Caine had planned his meals, he hadn't taken into account the appetite of a nursing mother. Even back in the village, she'd been hungry all the time. She didn't want to think of how hungry she might get before they got to Limores.

Taking a small handful of the nuts, she handed the bag back to him. As she savored each one, he finished his bowl of stew and stood.

"I found water a little farther downstream. Give me your bowl and I'll clean up."

"You made dinner," she protested. "I'll clean up."

"Save the polite gestures for when we get back to civilization," he said, but the tone of his voice was gentle. "I don't want you near the water at night. It's too dangerous. And give me the dirty diapers, too."

"I can do that in the morning."

"If you do it in the morning, they won't have time to dry before we have to leave," he explained patiently.

She wasn't sure why she was so reluctant to have him clean Ana's diapers. Before she could think of an excuse, he stepped over to her backpack.

"Did I see you wrapping them in liana leaves?"

Squatting in front of her pack, he reached in just as she scrambled over to it. "I'll get them," she muttered. Pulling out several cool lumps wrapped in rubbery leaves, she piled them on the ground. "But if I fall asleep before tomorrow, wake me up so I can wash them myself."

Gathering the dirty diapers in their green wrappings, he shot her an amused look. "I have washed clothes before, you know. What's the matter, Lexie? Afraid I'll mix up the rinse cycle and the spin cycle?"

Ana began to stir, and Lexie knew he was right. The last thing she wanted to do was try to find her way to the water in the rapidly darkening jungle. In a few more minutes everything would be black. The only place she felt safe was by the fire. Or close to Caine.

"You'd better hurry," she said, turning away to edge closer to the fire. "It's getting awfully dark."

"I have excellent night vision." To her surprise, he leaned over and brushed his lips against her hair. "I'll be right back. Don't get too scared. The fire will keep animals away."

By the time she spun around, he'd disappeared into the darkness. She sat and stared into the night for a long time, wondering why he'd kissed her. Especially after he'd gone out of his way earlier to make sure she understood just how he felt about her.

Ana's whimpering finally registered, and she turned to pick the baby up. Looking around, she spotted a small tree not too far from the fire. As she unbuttoned her blouse, she leaned up against it and closed her eyes. The nap she'd taken that afternoon hadn't begun to help her bone-deep weariness. She felt as if she could sleep for two days straight.

She roused herself when Ana finished eating and changed her diaper, then leaned back against the tree as she held the baby loosely in one arm. Her arms and legs ached with the strain of walking over uneven terrain all day, the muscles in her back burned and throbbed, and her stomach already felt empty again. She should grab another handful of nuts, she told herself, but she was too tired to do even that. Her eyelids had begun to droop when she heard a rustling in the bushes in front of her.

Caine was back, she thought, rousing herself. Surely he would have found a place where they could sleep. Sliding upright, she started to stand when she saw the firelight reflected in a pair of yellow eyes.

She froze, her arm tightening around Ana. As she stared, mesmerized, at the unblinking gaze of the animal in the bushes, she heard a low rumble that seemed to make the ground vibrate beneath her. It swelled and got louder until the growl filled the air of the suddenly silent jungle.

Chapter 7

Caine made his way through the darkness, the distant glow of the fire his guide to where Lexie waited. It had taken longer than he'd expected to collect and purify the drinking water and wash the diapers and the bowls, and he cursed himself for neglecting to bring the flashlight. Lexie had put on a brave front when he left, but he remembered how reluctant she'd been to enter the jungle the previous night. He hoped she hadn't gotten too scared.

When he heard the growl he was fifty feet away from the fire. He began running, searching frantically for Lexie. Hoping she would have enough sense to stay motionless, he drew the long hunting knife smoothly from his boot as he moved through the brush. As he got closer and the growl became a roar, he reached down and grabbed a thick branch outlined by the firelight.

He could see her crouching against the trunk of a small tree, frozen in place. Her wide eyes stared, unblinking, at the tangle of vegetation in front of her.

Don't move! he wanted to shout. Whispering prayers to a God he wasn't sure he believed in, he reached the bush where the animal crouched just as the roar reached a crescendo.

Knowing that the animal was about to leap, he brought the stick down onto its hiding place with all his strength.

The animal roared again, but this time with pain. When Caine slashed at the bushes with the branch he held, the animal turned and charged toward him. Tightening his grip on the knife, Caine slashed at the approaching jaguar with the branch. The animal stopped so close to Caine that its sickly sweet breath fanned his face, then the huge cat abruptly whirled and ran off. The black spots on his yellow coat gleamed for an instant in the firelight, then he was gone.

Caine stood and stared in the direction the jaguar had disappeared for a long time, listening. Then, dropping the stick, he turned around to where Lexie still crouched against the slender tree, Ana clutched tightly to her chest.

"It's all right, he's gone," he said.

She stared back at him with wide, shocked eyes. "What was it?" she whispered.

He slid his knife back into its sheath and squatted in front of her. "It was a jaguar. It's okay, Lexie. He's gone."

"How can you be sure?" The frantic fear she must still be feeling resonated in her voice. "You can't see past the end of your nose in this darkness. Maybe he's sitting a few feet away, waiting for another chance."

"He's not, Lexie." Pulling her to her feet, he wrapped his arms around her and the baby both. He couldn't help himself. "Do you hear all the noise from the jungle? If the jaguar was still around, everything would be quiet. That's how I know he's gone."

One of Lexie's arms crept around his neck. "I saw his eyes, Caine. He was staring at me." Her voice trembled next to his ear, and he tightened his arms around her. "He was staring at me and Ana."

"Shh," he murmured. "He's gone, and he won't be back. And from now on I won't leave you alone at night. All right?"

Her arm tightened around his neck. If she held him any closer he would have trouble breathing, but he didn't care. Even though he knew she did it only because she was scared, his body stirred and responded as she pressed against him.

He smoothed his hand down her back, trying to ease the trembling that racked her. "It's okay, Lexie." Bending his head, he whispered his lips over her hair and drew her as close as he could without crushing the baby.

At the touch of his lips on her hair she raised her head, staring at him with wild eyes. In the flickering light of the fire he watched the fear gradually fade, to be replaced by another emotion. It was only reaction to the fright, he told himself. She just wanted to reassure herself that she was still alive. But he couldn't stop himself from lowering his mouth until his lips brushed against hers.

For one shocked moment she froze. He could see her eyes, wide open and staring at him, could feel her muscles tense to spring backward. Then she melted into him.

Her mouth softened under his, drinking in his taste. The arm she'd clamped around his neck loosened, and he groaned when he felt her fingers slide tentatively into his hair. When he pulled her into the vee of his legs, against the hard bulge of flesh already straining the zipper of his pants, she didn't move away. Instead, she tried to press even closer to him.

When she rose up on her toes, sliding against him as she reached to mold herself around him, he was lost. All his dreams, all the fantasies he'd had over the past eleven months didn't even come close to the reality. Lexie was in his arms again, and the passion that radiated from her set a fire in his soul.

He staggered backward, his knees suddenly rubbery, and sank to the ground. She went with him willingly, still holding on to him with one hand and the baby with the other. Easing her onto her back, he slid one leg between her thighs and braced himself above her.

Slowly she untangled her hand from the baby, leaving the shawl and its occupant lying next to her on the ground. Holding on to his shoulder with one hand, she traced the contours of his face with the other. Her hand moved gently, almost reverently across his forehead and cheek, finally stopping when she traced the outline of his lips.

Blood pounded through his veins, throbbing in his loins and hardening him to the point of pain. He opened his mouth and drew her finger inside, alternately sucking on it and stroking it with his tongue. Her eyes became heavy-lidded as she watched him, and he could feel her pressing closer to his thigh as it rested between her legs.

He wanted her more than he'd ever wanted anything or anyone in his life. His body cried out for her, begging for the release he would find inside her. He ached to watch her respond to him, to see her come apart under his hands and his mouth.

The need to touch her consumed him. He imagined the feel of her skin under his fingers, the way she would react when he caressed her. Before he realized it, he was pulling her blouse out of the waistband of her shorts. When he laid his palm against her belly, he felt her twitch and her muscles tighten. He could feel her skin getting warmer and softening for him.

He barely managed to push the buttons of her blouse through the tiny holes. His hands shook so badly that it took three tries to get the last one. When he brushed her shirt apart, her white bra gleamed in the firelight and he reached out and unfastened it.

Her breasts spilled over into his hands, fuller and heavier than he remembered. As he held them in his palms, he looked up at her face. She was watching him, her features shadowed by the flicker of the firelight. Never taking his eyes off her face, he brushed his thumbs slowly across her already hard nipples.

She drew in a sharp breath, and her hands tightened their grip on his arms. When he did it again, she closed her eyes and arched so that she pressed harder into his leg. He lowered his mouth to hers, and the tiny moan that vibrated into his mouth sent the tension in his body coiling even tighter.

Sliding down her body, he buried his face in the valley between her breasts, drinking in her scent. Her skin warmed by passion, she smelled of darkness and desire. It was the scent he'd dreamed about for so long—a scent that was uniquely Lexie.

He moved over to take her nipple into his mouth, and she moaned again and arched into him. One of her hands slid slowly down his back and traced the curve of his buttocks, finally pressing him against her. The tentative gesture pushed him over the edge, and with one hand he reached down to unfasten her shorts.

His other hand cupped her breast, unwilling to let go of her. As his thumb traced the outline of her nipple, he felt something warm and wet trickle over his hand.

Lexie stiffened and brought her hand up to shield her breasts. Squirming away from him, she sat up and stared at him, her eyes huge and her hand still covering her breasts. Her shirt gaped open and the zipper on her shorts was pulled halfway down.

Desire pounded through him, along with an almost-uncontrollable demand for release. He reached for her, and she scooted backward again.

"What's wrong?" he demanded. He hardly recognized the guttural voice as his own.

Even in the dim light from the fire he could see her face redden. "I'm sorry, Caine. I don't know what I was thinking about."

"Come here and I'll show you."

Shaking her head, she suddenly looked down at her breasts again. He thought she got even redder. Her hands fumbled as she fastened her bra, then buttoned her blouse. Smoothing her hands down her shorts, she realized the zipper was undone and fastened that, too.

He sat and watched her, battling with his body for control. When he thought he could speak without begging her to finish what they'd started, he asked in a low voice, "What happened, Lexie?"

"What do you mean, what happened?" She turned away and picked up a stick to stir the fire. "You were there, too."

"I know what we were doing." He struggled to keep his voice even. "I want to know why we stopped."

He could see her hand clench the stick more tightly. "Let's just say I came to my senses."

He said roughly, "When we stopped, the only thing you were capable of coming to was a—"

"Stop it, Caine," she interrupted, tossing the stick away and turning around to face him. Taking a deep breath, she said more softly, "That's what stress does to people, isn't it? Makes them forget their inhibitions, do things they normally wouldn't do. I guess I just got over my stress.''

"Lexie—'' he began, but she interrupted again.

''I need to go to sleep, Caine, if we have to keep walking to-morrow. Are you going to set up the tent, or is there some-where else I should sleep?''

She stared at him, defiant, but he could see the traces of em-barrassment in her face. Curious, he watched her for a mo-ment until she looked away. Picking up Ana from the ground, she turned aside from him and began to feed the baby. He wouldn't find out now what had happened to make her stop. She had shut him out as completely as if she'd slammed a door in his face, and he knew it.

His lower body still throbbed, reminding him of what he and Lexie had been doing just moments ago. In spite of her words, he was willing to bet that her body hadn't forgotten, either.

Picking up their packs, he slung them into the hollow tree he'd found earlier and waited for her to finish nursing the kid. She didn't know it, but this discussion wasn't over. It had only been postponed.

Lexie started awake and opened her eyes to total darkness, confused and disoriented. Ana snuffled in the blackness next to her, and suddenly her memory came flooding back.

They were sleeping in another hollow tree, the mosquito netting that Caine had strung across the opening a pitifully flimsy barrier against the jungle outside. Spending the day walking through the forest, followed by the encounter with the jaguar, had used up all her energy. Exhausted, she lay per-fectly still for a while, hoping that Ana would fall back to sleep, but her grunts grew progressively louder.

Finally giving in to the inevitable, Lexie rolled over to sit up and bumped into Caine, lying close beside her. She froze, knowing from the tense stillness of his body that he, too, was awake.

After a long moment she moved carefully away from him, ignoring the heat that swept through her when she accidentally brushed against his hand. "I have to feed Ana,'' she whis-pered.

"I figured." Spoken in a normal voice, his words echoed off the walls of their makeshift room, and she glanced fearfully toward the trembling mosquito netting.

"Shh," she whispered fiercely.

She could hear him rising next to her, and wanted to call him back when he moved away. "Don't worry, Lexie. The only ones out there to hear us are the bats and the other night creatures, and they don't care what we're talking about." She heard the almost-silent rustle of cloth as he lifted the mosquito netting and looked outside, then let it drop again. "There's nothing out there except the jungle."

Picking Ana up, she scooted over to lean against the wood of the hollow tree. "Now why doesn't that reassure me?"

"Why are you afraid of the jungle at night?" His voice was quiet and completely nonjudgmental.

She hadn't meant to let him see her fear, and even though she knew he couldn't see the expression on her face she looked down at Ana. The silence stretched between them, but he didn't say a word. Finally she answered shortly, "I've always been scared of the dark. Being in the jungle, where everything's so alien, just makes it worse."

She didn't think he was going to answer, but after a long time, he said, "I didn't think you were afraid of anything, Lexie. Why the dark?"

Stalling for time, she laid Ana over her shoulder and gently patted her back. He didn't say anything, but she could feel him watching her. Sighing, she said, "Aren't most people afraid of the dark?"

"Some are. But there's usually a reason."

Somehow, in the intimacy of the hollow tree, she suddenly wanted to tell Caine why she was afraid of the dark. She wanted to share the nightmare with him—the one she'd never told anyone, not even her father. Her father would have told her not to be foolish, that it was just a bad dream. Everyone said Caine was just like her father, but somewhere deep down she knew he wouldn't dismiss her fears. Maybe it was because she'd sensed he was a man who hid fears of his own.

"It wasn't long after my mother died," she began in a low, uneven voice. Even thinking about the nightmare made her palms sweat and her muscles tremble. "I woke up from a dream, and it was pitch-dark in my room." Stopping, she drew in a deep, shuddering breath as the horrible memories flooded back. "I'd been having trouble sleeping, and my father had had the maid put up blackout curtains so the light wouldn't bother me in the morning."

Caine slid toward her until he sat beside her, his leg almost touching hers. "What was the dream, Lexie?"

She reached out blindly for his hand, and his fingers curled around hers, warm and reassuring. "I dreamed I was in the coffin with my mother," she said, her voice trembling. "It was dark, and I knew she was dead and I was alive, but they'd closed the lid on top of us. They were going to bury me with her, and I couldn't make anyone hear me and open the lid. I screamed and screamed and pounded on the lid, but no one heard me."

She clung to his hand and stared blindly into the darkness, the paralyzing fear washing over her once again. "I woke up just as they were lowering the coffin into the ground, and I couldn't see a thing. My room was totally black and too warm, and I thought the dream was real."

The remembered panic sickened her again, as it did every time she let herself think about the dream. "For a few seconds, I knew I was awake and I thought it was really happening. I thought I was being buried with my mother."

Swallowing hard, she tried to make her voice sound light. "I know it's stupid, and it was a long time ago, but it's my phobia and there it is. I'm sure one day I'll get over it."

Caine didn't say a thing. Gently taking Ana out of her arms, he laid the child on the ground and pulled her into his arms. "I'm sorry, Lexie," he murmured into her hair. "I had no idea. I wouldn't have made you get into these hollow trees if I had known."

His chest was hard and solid, and his heart beat slowly and reassuringly under her ear. The warmth radiating from him was a welcome contrast to the numbing chill that held her in its grip. Closing her eyes, she wrapped her arms around him.

He pulled her into his lap and held her, rubbing her back and whispering soothing words into her ear. After a long time the trembling slowed, then stopped, and she reluctantly pulled away from him.

"I'm sorry," she said, stiff with discomfort. What on earth would he think of her, falling apart like that? "I'll change Ana so we can go back to sleep."

"It's okay, Lexie," he said, and she had never heard his voice so tender before. "I don't think your fear is silly and I'm not going to tell you to snap out of it. I'll try to make things easier for you at night from now on."

"I didn't tell you because I was whining about our situation," she replied, horrified that he'd misunderstood. "I know we can't change our plans now."

"I never thought you were whining." His voice changed and deepened, and she felt her heart begin to pound. "You've been a real trouper about this whole mess. You've surprised me." The last words were said in a gruff voice, almost as if he was reluctant to admit it.

She lay down and pulled Ana close to her. "I've surprised myself," she said frankly. "I didn't think I would be able to walk into the jungle at night, let alone get into a hollow tree."

"Go back to sleep," he murmured into her ear. "We have a long day ahead of us." Slowly he pulled her next to him and wrapped one arm around her, nestling her into the curve of his body. For an instant she resisted, but she gradually relaxed into the warmth and solid comfort of him. The darkness and fear receded as she closed her eyes and concentrated on how he felt, lying so close to her.

He felt wonderful, she admitted to herself. She was safe and protected, tucked against him with one of his arms curled around her. In fact, she couldn't think of a time when she'd felt safer. Her eyes drifted closed, and just before she fell asleep she wriggled closer to Caine.

The darkness was gone. Her first feeling was relief as she opened her eyes to see the faint light of a jungle dawn illuminating the hollow tree. Even the noises that echoed from outside the tree had become familiar, and therefore almost comforting.

Ana was lying next to her, still asleep. Lexie could roll over and go back to sleep herself—a precious luxury that she hadn't known for the past two months. Her lips curving into a smile even as she let her eyes drift shut, she tried to roll over and found herself unable to move.

Her eyes snapped open again and she looked around wildly. Turning her head, she looked directly into Caine's eyes. He watched her through half-open lids, only half-awake himself.

"Sleep while you can," he rasped, his voice incredibly sexy in the early-morning light. "It won't be long before we'll have to get up."

He had curled one of his arms around her during the night, holding her tightly against him, and his hand covered her belly. Her legs had tangled with his, and now her thigh rested intimately between his. Heat flooded her face as she tried to extricate herself and move away from him.

"Relax." His low voice soothed her, and one of his hands smoothed her hair away from her face. "You'll be more comfortable using me as a pillow."

"I don't want to use you at all," she retorted, trying to push his arm away.

His arm tightened, then he released her so he could roll her over onto her back. "What do you want to do with me, then, Lexie?"

He wasn't half-awake anymore. His blue eyes glittered down at her, hot and aware. She could feel the tension in his muscles where his leg still rested against hers, could feel the effort he made to hold himself in control.

"I don't know," she said slowly, realizing it was the truth. Three days ago, her feelings about Caine O'Roarke had been straightforward and easy to identify. He was the man who'd walked out on her so he could snap to attention for her father; the man who'd left town on her father's orders and never even bothered to say goodbye. Caine was the man who had hurt her so deeply that just thinking about him brought searing pain and a deep, unshakable anger.

But her feelings had shifted almost since the moment he'd walked into her house in Santa Ysabel. They weren't so clear-cut, so black-and-white anymore. Her own reaction to his gesture of comfort yesterday had proved that.

Caine wasn't the easy-to-classify, uncomplicated man she'd assumed him to be. She still had no idea what made him tick, but she knew there were no simplistic explanations. There had been pain in his gaze—hard and desperate and buried deeply— more than once. His reaction to Ana, although it pierced her soul, made her wonder what had caused it.

"I don't know what I want from you, Caine," she repeated, knowing it was the truth. "I don't really know anything about you."

The pain she'd seen before flickered through his eyes briefly and was gone. "There isn't anything to know, Lexie. What you see is what you get."

"Somehow I don't think that's the case," she murmured.

He reached out and cupped her face with his hand. "No?" His eyes pinned her to the ground, his desire plain to read. "Tell me what you see now, and I'll do my best to give it to you."

"I see an enigma," she whispered, watching his eyes darken and smolder.

"I don't think so, Lexie." Slowly he lowered his mouth to hers. "I think what I want right now is crystal clear."

His kiss didn't start out soft and comforting as it had the night before. It was wild and reckless, like the desire she felt raging through him, and it awakened an answering desire in her.

She forgot about the jungle, forgot about the men searching for them, forgot everything but the taste of Caine's mouth on hers and the feel of his hard body pressing her into the dirt and dead leaves they lay on. He reached up to hold her head still for a plundering kiss and she realized, with a shock of excitement, that his hands were trembling.

Tentatively she slid her hands down his back, feeling his corded muscles tense with the effort of holding himself in check. When her hands reached his hips and stilled, he groaned, deep in his throat, and slid his hands down to her hips to pull her closer.

An answering tension gathered in her body, every nerve throbbing to the rhythm of his mouth on hers. One of his hands hadn't stopped at her hip but continued down her leg, finding the incredibly sensitive skin of her inner thigh. Stroking lightly, his fingers slipped beneath the hem of her baggy shorts and crept upward.

She was on fire, her body burning for him. Her mouth stilled on his as she held her breath, anticipating the touch of his fingers at the apex of her thighs. When he cupped her, lightly, within the palm of his hand, she sucked in a trembling breath and clutched his shoulders.

"Yes, sweetheart," he whispered into her ear. "That's what I want. I want you to need me as much as I need you."

She couldn't answer. Turning her head blindly, she searched for his mouth and the dark, intoxicating taste of him. His triumphant groan was smothered as it vibrated into her mouth.

This was what she'd thirsted for for the past eleven months. Caine was the only man who'd ever made her need like this, the only man who'd ever made her feel whole. And in spite of all the reasons that it was folly to get involved with him again, she was powerless right now over the demands of her body.

Caine, she slowly realized, was apparently not quite as swept away. The tension in his body was no longer sexual as he lifted himself off her. The fire in his eyes disappeared, was replaced by the flat, expressionless look she'd begun to hate. Very carefully he eased himself away from her and rolled over onto his side.

As she remembered the previous night, her face began to burn. Had her breasts begun to leak milk again, and had she been so aroused that she hadn't even noticed? A quick check assured her that her blouse was still dry. She turned her head slowly to look at him, and when he saw her gaze he jerked his head in the other direction.

"It sounds like she needs to be fed again."

He was right. Ana was grunting on the ground next to her, and it wouldn't be long before her tiny cries erupted into full-fledged screams. Lexie had been so wrapped up in Caine and what they were doing, she hadn't even noticed.

But Caine had heard. "I didn't realize you were paying such close attention to Ana," she said carefully.

He didn't answer for a while. "I had forgotten all about her," he finally muttered. "Good thing she started fussing when she did. We need to eat, too, and get moving."

In one smooth movement he was on his knees and out the hole in the trunk of the tree. She paused as she unbuttoned her blouse to watch him go. Somehow, hearing Ana cry had stopped his desire cold. Apparently the baby was just as effective as a bucket of cold water would have been.

She couldn't ignore the pain, but she told herself firmly that she could prevent it from happening again. She would just have to make sure that the intimacy of waking up together didn't happen again. From now on she would sleep as far away from Caine as possible. It didn't matter that waking up beside him had made her feel more secure and comforted than she had in a long time. It wasn't worth the heartbreak that would inevitably follow.

The smell of coffee drifted into her hiding place, and her stomach contracted sharply, reminding her how meager her dinner had been the night before and how much her body needed food. Holding Ana against her shoulder, she crawled out into the dim light of the jungle dawn and saw Caine sitting beside a smoldering fire. Two bowls of steaming food sat on the ground next to him.

"Scrambled eggs and bacon," he said, gesturing at the two bowls. "Come and join me."

Her stomach twisted at the thought of eggs, but she knew she had no choice. She had to eat, so she would force them down. Setting Ana on the ground, she picked up the bowl without looking at the food inside. Her stomach quivered when she smelled the eggs, but she tried to ignore it as she glanced over at Caine.

"Did I smell coffee, or was my mind just playing cruel tricks on me?"

He passed her a steaming mug, and she took a sip gratefully. It was burning hot and very strong. If she was lucky, it would numb her mouth so she wouldn't taste the eggs.

Fifteen minutes later she set down her empty bowl and reached for her coffee, taking a deep drink. Her stomach heaved once, but she forbade herself to be sick.

Staring at a piece of peeling bark on the tree in front of her, she waited until she could drink again, then took another gulp of the coffee. The queasiness was passing, but it would be a minute longer before she could trust herself.

"I'm sorry, Lexie," Caine said suddenly.

She looked over at him, hoping she didn't look as green as she felt. "What for?"

"I forgot you didn't like eggs. Why didn't you remind me?"

"It wasn't like we had a whole lot of choice," she said, glancing at his opened backpack. "You had already made it, and if I didn't eat it we would have been short a meal."

"Do you want something else to eat?"

"No, thanks." She shuddered at the thought of putting anything else into her stomach right now. "The eggs are all I can handle."

"We'd better get moving, then."

He stood and began gathering the things that had fallen out of his pack. It was as if he had completely forgotten about what had passed between them just a short time ago inside that tree. Watching him for a moment, she felt something harden inside her. If he could be so casual about it, so could she.

"I'm going to clean up these dishes and get the diapers I left drying last night. Why don't you gather your things together so we can leave when I get back?"

She nodded shortly and looked around for the shawl so she could settle Ana against her chest. He walked away without a backward glance, and after a moment she was alone in the jungle again.

Even in the dim light, it wasn't nearly as scary as it had been during the night. Instead of frightening, even the smell—the damp, moist scent of decay—was beginning to seem familiar.

By the time Caine returned she was sitting propped against the tree, the sling tied across her chest and Ana lying on the ground next to her. The baby was tiny enough that she still spent most of her day sleeping, but she was awake now and Lexie didn't want to confine her to the sling any sooner than necessary.

Caine paused by the tree, and when she glanced up at him she found him staring down at the baby. A look of what could only be described as yearning passed over his face for a moment, then his eyes were shuttered again. He looked at her.

"You ready to go? We need to make some distance today."

Standing, she scooped Ana into her arms and tucked her into the sling, then swung her pack over her shoulders. "We're ready."

He moved behind her and tucked the clean diapers into her pack, then shouldered his own two backpacks. "Let's go, then."

She started after him obediently, wondering about the look she'd surprised on his face. Surely she was mistaken. He'd gone out of his way to avoid having anything to do with his daughter. What she'd thought was yearning was probably just regret—for the accident that had resulted in her birth.

It might have been accidental, but Ana's birth was the best thing that had ever happened to her. Tightening her arm around her daughter, Lexie stared at the back of Caine's head as she battled the tears filling her eyes.

No one—not even Caine—could ever convince her otherwise.

Chapter 8

Lexie took another drink of water from the canteen and replaced it on her pack. There were only a few more mouthfuls left in the bottom of the plastic bottle, and it wouldn't be long before she would have to tell Caine that she needed more.

But that wasn't the problem right now. The problem was her empty stomach and the painful contractions that reminded her it had been too long since she'd had enough to eat.

A vine lying half-buried in the dead leaves caught her foot and she stumbled, catching herself on a sturdy branch. The queasiness she'd felt at breakfast had long since passed, and she'd gone beyond the point of mere hunger hours ago. She knew they would have to stop for lunch soon, and she forced herself to keep walking, to keep putting one foot in front of the other and ignore the dizziness that swirled around her head.

"How are you doing?" Caine stopped abruptly and looked back at her.

"Okay," she managed. "I'm going to need more water soon."

"According to my map, we should be getting close to another stream. We'll stop there for lunch and refill the canteens."

She longed to ask him how long it would be, but realized it didn't matter. They were moving a lot faster than she would have thought herself capable of, but then she'd never been chased by men trying to kill her, either. There was a lot to be said for a little motivation.

Another vine caught her foot, and she stumbled again. This time she went down onto her knees, and Caine spun around.

"What's wrong?" He knelt next to her. "What happened?"

"I just tripped on a vine, that's all," she answered. She stood slowly, holding on to his hand, trying to will the dizziness away. "Maybe I need another drink of water."

What she needed was food. She drank the last of the water in her canteen and screwed the top back on, then wiped her forehead with the tail of her blouse. Her hand was trembling, and she told herself it must be the heat. It had been getting steadily hotter and more humid, and now she felt like she was in a steam bath.

Caine watched her, a hint of uneasiness in his eyes. "Are you sure you're all right?"

"I'm fine," she said, as firmly as she could manage. "I'm just hot and hungry, but I can wait until we find this stream."

He took another look at her, then moved behind her. "You walk in front for a while." His arm rested on her shoulder as he pointed toward a lush patch of green in the distance. "See all those bushes? That should be the stream. Head toward that and you'll be fine."

She wanted to move away from the heat of his arm against her, but didn't have the energy. "I see it."

His arm dropped away and he cleared his throat. "It won't be long before we stop. Are you sure you'll be okay?"

"Positive." She started walking again. Ana was still sound asleep, but she was due to wake up soon. With a little luck, she would stay asleep for just a while longer.

Fortunately there was still very little undergrowth in the jungle. She didn't have the strength to push aside anything heavier than the dead leaves her feet shuffled through. Ana moved and stretched in the shawl across her chest, and Lexie tried to walk a little faster.

After another few minutes she realized they were getting closer to the stream. The bushes were getting thicker and closer together, and the trees were pressing in on her. The bark on several of them loomed in front of her, looking like layers of wide, sharp knives peeling away from the trunk. As she stared at one, mesmerized by the pattern, she lost her balance and began to fall.

She was so dizzy she felt as if she was floating down to the ground in slow motion. Trying to twist sideways so she wouldn't fall on top of Ana, she lurched in the direction of one of the knife trees. Just as she braced herself for the impact, she felt Caine's strong hands catching her.

A sharp, muffled curse exploded from him, then he eased her to the ground. "Lexie," he gasped. "What's wrong? And don't tell me nothing, dammit." His voice was harsh with worry. "You were stumbling all over the path like a damn drunk."

Closing her eyes, she waited until the trees above her stopped spinning around. "Nothing's wrong. I'm just hungry, Caine," she finally said. "It's making me dizzy."

A string of oaths erupted from him. "Why the hell didn't you tell me sooner? I have plenty of food in my pack."

She opened her eyes. "Not enough. I looked last night. You have enough meals for two more days. And I need to eat at least two of those meals at a time, maybe three," she said bluntly.

Rocking back on his heels, he stared at her. "The hell you do. There are supposed to be enough calories in one of those meals for a man my size."

"Maybe so." Her mouth curved upward in a slight smile. "But it doesn't say anything about a nursing woman, does it?"

His gaze drifted down to her breasts, then snapped back to her face. "What do you mean by that?"

"I mean that I need a lot more food." Her voice was patient. "Since Ana was born I've been eating at least twice as much as I normally do, and that's without walking through the jungle all day." She shrugged and looked away. "I figured I could make it until lunch."

"And what were you going to do at lunch? Eat another meal, then start walking again, still hungry?" He sounded angry.

"I'm sorry I fell and slowed us down." Her voice was stiff. "I thought I would eat more nuts with lunch. There's a lot of protein in nuts."

He didn't say a word, and the silence boomed between them in the noisy jungle. When she finally looked at him, he was watching her with an indecipherable look in his eyes. "I'm not angry you slowed us down," he said, but there was still anger in his voice. "I'm angry you didn't say anything to me. Didn't it occur to you that I could get more food?"

"I haven't seen any supermarkets yet. Is there one on your map?" The sharpness of her words barely covered her embarrassment. He was right and she knew it. She should have said something earlier.

Instead of snapping back at her, he angled his body away from her to look around the forest. She was shocked to see the ghost of a grin in his eyes.

"We don't need a supermarket to have a feast for lunch. Let's get you and the kid settled and I'll go shopping."

He reached over with his right hand to pull her to her feet, then stopped. "Do you think you can make it another few yards? I'd rather not leave you here, out in the open."

"Sure," she said immediately. She hoped she was telling the truth. Holding Ana against her with one hand, she put her other hand into Caine's and struggled to her feet.

Her legs felt like two strands of cooked spaghetti, but she fought the dizziness and finally nodded. "I'm fine."

He watched her for a minute, worry in his eyes, then said abruptly, "Give me the kid. You'll have a hard enough time trying to get yourself the next few feet without having to carry her."

Her hand tightened instinctively around Ana, but she knew he was right. Besides, she didn't want to take a chance on hurting the baby if she fell again. She started to untie the shawl, but he shook his head.

"Don't bother with that. I'll just carry her."

Reluctantly she took the sleeping baby out of her makeshift carrier. She cradled Ana close for a moment, then slowly passed her over to Caine and placed her in his arms.

Every muscle in his body looked tense and tight. When he gazed down at his daughter's face a flash of desperate longing appeared in his eyes, but it was gone almost before she saw it. He stared at Ana for a moment, then shifted her into the crook of his elbow. When he glanced up at Lexie, there was nothing in his eyes except a faint shadow of pain. "I'll stay behind you. Just keep going straight ahead."

As she turned to start walking, she noticed that he held Ana with only one arm while the other hung limply at his side. Remembering his sharp, bitten-off curse when he'd grabbed her as she fell and the way he'd angled that side away from her afterward, she stepped around him before he realized what she was doing.

There was a long, ragged gash on the back of his upper arm that oozed a steady stream of bright red blood. She sucked in her breath with a gasp. "Caine! What happened? Why didn't you tell me you were hurt?"

"It's nothing, Lexie. I fell against the tree with the sharp points on its bark."

He tried to turn away from her, but she reached out and held him still, studying the cut. "It doesn't look like nothing to me. What were you planning to do about this, anyway? Just let it bleed?" Her worry made her voice sharper than she'd intended.

"I guess I planned to do the same thing you did when you were hungry—not say anything and hope you wouldn't notice."

She flushed and let go of his arm, reaching for her pack at the same time. "At least I wasn't dripping blood all over myself," she muttered. Pulling out her medical kit, she opened it up and selected a roll of gauze. "I'll wrap it up now so it doesn't get any dirtier, and when we've gotten to where you want to stop, I'll clean it and bandage it."

"That's not necessary," he protested, but she ignored him.

"Don't you know this hot, humid weather encourages infection?" she demanded, watching the wound as she tied the gauze around his arm. Dark red blood soaked through immediately, and she waited, worried, as the entire bandage slowly changed from white to red.

"Put your hand on top of your head," she told him, and to her surprise he obediently rested his left hand on top of his head. "Can you walk like that for a while?"

"If it'll make you happy, I'll walk with one foot on my head, too."

She turned to face him. "You don't have to be sarcastic. I'm worried about that cut."

His face relaxed, and a tender look softened his eyes as he watched her. "I know you are, Lexie, but it's not a big deal. Believe me. I've had worse, and it'll heal just fine."

The tenderness in his eyes was causing a strange sensation in her chest. She turned abruptly away and began walking. "I know it will. But antibiotic ointment and clean bandages won't hurt."

Caine watched Lexie stalk away from him, amazed. She really was worried about an insignificant cut on his arm. But then, he told himself as he began walking behind her, she had no idea that he'd endured far worse in his long, wearing career.

He watched her march along in front of him and wondered when the righteous indignation that was carrying her would begin to fade. He didn't think it would take long, and he was right. They hadn't gone more than fifty feet when she began to slow down.

The undergrowth had gotten more and more lush as they approached the stream. Up until now, they'd been able to walk without clearing a path, but the bushes were beginning to close in and Lexie was obviously losing the fight against them. Looking around, he decided that the little clearing they were in now was as good a place to stop as any.

"Let's stop here," he called to Lexie, and she dropped to the ground immediately. She leaned back against a tree and closed her eyes for a moment, taking a deep, trembling breath. Finally her eyelids fluttered open and she held out her arms for the baby.

He glanced down at the child in his arms, who was still sleeping peacefully. He'd expected her to wake up bawling as soon as he'd taken her from her mother, but instead she'd nestled into the crook of his arm, yawned once, and never opened her eyes.

His arm tightened around the small bundle, and before he could control his reaction a sharp pang of loss stabbed through him. Clenching his teeth, he handed her abruptly to Lexie. Allowing himself to want to hold her was the first step on a very slippery slope—a slope he had no right to even think about, let alone set foot on.

"I'm going to find you something to eat." His words came out more harshly than he'd intended, but he didn't even try to soften them. It would be better for all of them if Lexie continued to think of him as the biggest bastard in the Western Hemisphere.

"What about your arm?" She sounded worried about him, and he turned around to look at her. She held the baby loosely in her arms as she leaned back against the tree again, her eyes closed once more.

"My arm can wait. It doesn't look like your stomach can."

At that she opened her eyes. "A few more minutes won't make much difference," she protested. "At least let me make sure the bleeding's stopped."

"Your hands are shaking so badly that you couldn't do anything for me if you wanted to," he said bluntly. "The first thing you have to do is eat something." He opened his pack and found a bag of trail mix. "Here, try some of this. I'll be back in a little while."

Before she could think of a response he was gone, slipping silently into the green world that surrounded them.

A half hour later he stepped back into the small clearing, worried because he'd been gone so long. Lexie, her eyes closed, leaned up against the same tree, and if it hadn't been for the baby lying on a blanket kicking her arms and legs, and the dirty diaper wrapped in a rubbery leaf, he would have wondered if she'd moved at all.

He watched her for a moment, trying to tell himself the worry he felt was simply irritation that she might have slowed them down. Then he turned away before he could do something really stupid, like bend down and kiss her.

"Lunch will be ready as soon as I get a fire going." His voice was gruff and he didn't wait to see her open her eyes. Scanning the little clearing, he gathered what he needed to start a small fire and prepared the agouti he'd caught.

"Agouti probably isn't the most delectable meat, but it's all I could get quickly."

He heard her stir behind him. "I'm sure it'll be wonderful." She appeared at his side. "What can I do to help?"

"You can sit still and conserve your energy."

He hadn't meant to speak so sharply, and when he saw the hurt, quickly hidden, flash over her face, he gave a vicious jerk to the stick holding their lunch in place over the fire.

"I didn't mean it the way it sounded." She'd turned her back to him, and he could see the tension vibrating in the straight line of her spine. "I'm sorry," he said, more gently. "I only meant that I know what it feels like to be so desperately hungry that you're dizzy and weak."

She faced him then. "But I'll bet you never let anyone else know you were that hungry, did you?"

"What's that supposed to mean?"

Staring at him for a moment, measuring him with her gaze, she said quietly, "It means I feel like a fool for being so stupid. I know I could have hurt myself or Ana, or gotten you hurt worse than I did. I should have said something last night, and I know it."

Slowly he reached out and pulled her to him with his right arm. "It's all right, Lex. Everyone's allowed a couple of screwups. This one is small potatoes."

Her slight weight pressed against him, and he longed to bring his other arm around her and hold her close. To do that, though, would remind her of his injury, and he wanted her to forget all about that. So he sat still, forcing himself to be content with the limited contact.

"How long before lunch is ready?" she asked after a few minutes.

He glanced over at the roasting agouti. "It'll be a little while yet. Why don't I boil some water and we can eat the packaged stuff while we're waiting?"

She moved away, and he could almost imagine that she did so reluctantly. To keep himself from thinking about it, he nodded at the baby. "What about her? Doesn't she need to eat?"

"I fed her while you were gone. I know there isn't anyone around who could hear, but it would make me nervous if she started screaming."

Rather than dwell on the mental picture of Lexie feeding the baby, he focused on the rest of her statement. "Thanks. I doubt very much if there's anyone close enough to hear her, but I'd rather not take any chances."

He could feel Lexie's eyes on him as he turned to check whether the water was boiling yet. After what seemed like a long time she asked softly, "Do you really think they'll chase us through the jungle?"

"I don't know," he said frankly. "First they'd have to find the Jeep and the spot where we went in, then they'd have to track us. That would be a lot easier in the rainy season. Right now, there wouldn't be much for them to see other than some disturbed dead leaves."

He could almost see the tension fade from her body. "So, for now, we're safe?"

"Probably. But we can't count on it. The smart thing for our friend El Cuchillo to do would be to wait for us in Limores. He has to know that's where we're heading, and it would be a lot less work than trying to track us through the jungle. But he seems to be a pretty desperate guy."

There was fear in her eyes as she looked at him. "He does, doesn't he?" she whispered. "Why is he after me? I haven't been out of Santa Ysabel for nine months. Why is he so intent on capturing me?"

"You've been here for ten months. What did you do before you got to Santa Ysabel?"

She shrugged. "Nothing, really. I spent more than a week in Limores, feeling—" She clamped her mouth shut abruptly and looked away from him. Finally she said carefully, "Feeling my way around the city and learning about the country. Then I started to travel. I visited some of the national parks, saw the volcanoes, did the usual tourist things. It was only by chance, really, that I ended up in Santa Ysabel."

"How did you end up there?" he asked softly. He handed her a bowl of rehydrated chili and settled back against a tree.

She stilled and stared at one of the bushes for a long time. Then she slowly relaxed and took a bite of the food, although she didn't turn around and look at him. "I had just planned to stay there for the night, in Maria's inn. The place you were going to stay. When I woke up the next morning I was violently sick. I thought it was something I'd eaten the day before, or that I'd caught some kind of bug."

As he watched her profile, he could see her lips curve up in a slight smile. "Maria and Angelita, one of her daughters-in-law, knew differently. I was the nurse, but they were far wiser in the ways of nature. They fussed over me and took care of me, and made me stay for another day. When I woke up sick the next morning, too, they acted like it was the most natural thing in the world."

Now she really was smiling. "When they realized I didn't know why I was sick, they thought it was hilarious. But they were kind to me. They explained I was sick because I was going to have a baby, and when they saw how shocked I was, they just kind of took over." She shrugged and finally turned to him. "By the time I was feeling better, I'd already been there for over a month. My money had long since run out, but Maria and Angelita and the rest of the people in the village didn't care. They took care of me because I needed help. That was when I began to grow up."

"Is that when you decided to stay?"

Slowly she shook her head. "There never was a day when I said, 'Okay, I'm going to stay here and do something for these people.' It just kind of happened." She gave him a strangely self-conscious half smile. "I was pretty much out of it the first couple of months after I realized I was pregnant. When I started to feel better, I understood what it had meant to the people who were taking care of me. Sometimes they had barely enough for their own families, let alone enough to share with a stranger who had just stumbled onto their village. I realized I couldn't just stay and mooch off them, but I had become very fond of the village and the people. That's when I began to think about what I could do so I could stay."

"I didn't even know you were a nurse, Lexie."

She looked away again. "Like I said before, there were a lot of things you didn't know about me. But as far as being a nurse is concerned, why would you? I wasn't working, and it's not the kind of subject that came up in the nightclubs in Washington where I hung out."

"Why didn't you work as a nurse when you were back in Washington?" he asked, curious. "It must have taken a lot of time and work to get through nursing school."

"It did. And I wanted to work," she answered frankly. "But I was young and stupid. It didn't even occur to me that my family and my father's name would be taken into consideration when I went looking for a job. I was hired by the first hospital I applied to, at a much larger salary than normal for an entry-level nurse. I didn't realize there was anything unusual going on, but it didn't take my 'colleagues' long to enlighten me. When I looked for another job, the same thing happened. I'm still not sure what the hospitals hoped I could do for them, but it was easier not to work at all than face the scorn and gossip that followed me around." She finished the last spoonful of her chili and set the bowl on the ground next to her. "I've since decided that I would much rather give vaccinations in Santa Ysabel than carry bedpans to rich, cranky patients, anyway."

He hated to interrupt the flow of her memories by mentioning their present situation, but he had no choice. "And nothing happened in Santa Ysabel that would explain why El Cuchillo is after you?"

The tension flowed back into her muscles, stiffening her spine again. She glanced over at the baby, resting quietly on the ground and staring up at the tangle of vines above her. Then she looked back at him.

"Nothing that I can remember. Nothing that seemed out of the ordinary, anyway. Most of the people in Santa Ysabel work on the coffee plantations, and one day is very much like another."

He leaned over and looked at the agouti, and decided it was ready to eat. "Then maybe he's going after all Americans this way. Maybe there's nothing unusual about this."

"But you don't think so, do you?" she asked, watching him with shrewd eyes.

He divided the agouti into two pieces and kept one small piece for himself. Giving her the rest, he finally met her eyes. "If he is, the guy's a nutcase. And from everything I've heard, I don't think he is. So I have to assume that he's after you for some particular reason."

She swallowed a piece of steaming meat and looked at him. "Could it have something to do with you? Nothing had happened until you came to Santa Ysabel."

"I suppose it's possible," he said slowly, "but I doubt it. Whatever was going on was set in motion long before I rolled into town. I was only there for the tail end of it. Not even El Cuchillo could have gotten things organized in such a remote village in only a few hours."

She shrugged again, finishing the meat he'd given her. "I don't know what it is, then. I've racked my brain for the past two days, but I don't remember anything."

"It doesn't really matter, anyway," he said as he rose and reached for her bowl. "Whatever the reason, the bottom line is we have to get you out of the country."

She glanced up at him, then let her gaze slide away. "You don't think I'll be safe in Limores?"

He froze, staring down at her. "What?" He couldn't believe what he'd heard.

"I mean, once I'm in Limores, don't you think I'll be safe? It would be a lot harder to find someone in a big city than it would be in a little village."

"I think you're nuts, that's what I think. After busting our butts to get out of here, do you honestly think I'll let you stay in this country?"

"You won't 'let' me do anything," she said, her voice cold. "You have no right to dictate to me. I'll make my own decisions."

Lowering himself until he crouched in front of her, he set the bowls aside and reached for her shoulders. He wanted to shake her until he shook some sense into her, but he curled his fingers into her shoulders instead. "Use your head, Lexie," he said, his voice urgent. "How long do you think it would take this guy to find you in Limores? A week, maybe? Two at the outside? This isn't a game he's playing. For some reason he thinks you're a threat to him, and he has to get rid of you. Look at yourself. You don't even look like a native. How well do you think you would blend in? How many of the people here have blond hair?'' He looked over at the baby. ''And kids with red hair?''

She paled as she glanced at her daughter. ''It would be safer for Ana than trying to sneak out of the country. In a big city, nobody looks that closely at anyone else,'' she muttered. ''Especially a woman with a baby.''

''They'd notice, believe me. And it wouldn't be long before El Cuchillo was knocking at your door. Except he probably wouldn't knock. The guy doesn't strike me as someone with an appreciation for good manners.''

She looked over at the baby again, then turned to him. ''I'll worry about that when we get there.'' Her voice was firm. The discussion was obviously closed. ''Right now, I want to look at your arm.''

He glanced at his arm with surprise. He'd forgotten all about it. ''I'm sure it's fine. I don't feel a thing anymore.''

''If you don't let me take care of it, you'll be feeling it again real soon. Take my word for it.''

She turned and searched through her pack, finally pulling out a small white plastic box. ''Come here and sit down.''

''Don't you have something else to do? Doesn't the kid need anything?''

''Ana is fine right now.'' She slanted him a calculating look. ''What's the matter, Caine? You can face down a jaguar, but not a woman with antibiotic ointment? You're not afraid I'll hurt you, are you?''

''I don't like doctors,'' he muttered, knowing his face was turning red. It was a stupid phobia, but he couldn't help it. Not after what had happened on his last assignment.

''Then you should be fine, because I'm not a doctor. I'm a nurse, remember?''

When had she gotten that grin in her voice? He wanted to insist she leave him alone, that they gather their things and leave, but he knew she wouldn't stand for it. Lexie could be stubborn as hell.

"Oh, all right," he finally growled, sitting down so his injured arm was facing her. Staring at one of the trees, he tried to concentrate on the intricate pattern of swirls in the bark rather than on what she was doing to him.

Her hands were surprisingly gentle on his arm. "I'll have to pull a little for a minute," she said, her voice breathless, as if she was holding back a gasp. "The bandage is stuck to your skin."

He clenched his teeth and stared at the tree, trying to count the whorls in the bark. There was a tiny tug on his skin, then he felt nothing at all. "It'll be worse if you try to go slow. Just get it over with," he said through his teeth.

"It is over." He could hear the hint of laughter in her voice. "The bandage is off and now I'm going to clean it up."

She must have sensed his tension, because she kept up a soothing monologue as she gently bathed the wound with the warm water they had left from their lunch. She told him which animals and birds she'd seen, and how many different kinds of trees and bushes she'd noticed. The whole time, her hands moved lightly against his wound, so lightly that he barely noticed the pain. Or maybe she was hypnotizing him with her soft, musical voice. All he knew was that instead of feeling helpless and out of control, her gentle touch and crooning voice were entangling him in a sensual web from which he had no desire to free himself.

Her hands and voice faltered, then stilled. He heard her take a slow breath, then she said, "I'm going to have to suture this, Caine. It's too deep to just bandage it."

"So do it," he answered roughly.

"The thing is, I don't have any local anesthetic." She took another slow breath. "I have the suture material and needles, but I can't numb it for you."

"Sew it up, Lexie. We need to get moving again."

He felt her hands trembling on his arm, then she took them away. "All right. I'll try to make it as quick as possible."

He didn't look as she fumbled in her box or when he heard the sound of paper being torn. But he couldn't bear not knowing what was going to happen. "What's that noise?"

"It's just the needle and suture material. They come prepackaged in a sterile container." She sounded as eager to talk about the objective details as he was to hear her voice.

Something cool and wet touched his arm, then she said, "I'm all set. Are you ready?"

Her voice trembled just slightly, and he nodded once. "Go ahead."

She touched him tentatively, then suddenly grasped his arm and held him steady. The pain was sharp, but lasted for only a second. It was followed by another sharp, piercing pain that was over just as quickly.

"The first one is in." He heard her swallow. "It looks like it'll take about four more."

He forced himself to look over his shoulder. His gaze caught her eyes and he refused to glance down at the wound. "It wasn't that bad, honey. Go ahead and finish it up. I'll survive." He gave her a crooked smile. "Who knows, maybe the suffering will make me a better person."

The pain came again, short and sharp, and he allowed himself to relax. He'd told her the truth. It wasn't all that bad. He'd survived much worse.

"Will you tell me about it sometime?" she asked softly after the next suture was in place.

"Tell you about what?"

"Whatever happened to you to make you afraid of doctors and medical procedures?"

"I'm not afraid. I just don't like not being in control of my body." His voice was more forceful than he'd intended.

She didn't answer for a long time. Finally she said, "I'm sorry. I shouldn't have asked. I had no right to intrude."

He longed to tell her that he wanted her to have the right, but he couldn't open his mouth. Fear held his jaw clamped shut. The Lexie he'd found here in a South American jungle was as different from the Lexie of Washington as two people could get, and he was frightened of that difference. He'd had his armor firmly in place against that other Lexie, but this one made him feel defenseless. And he didn't like feeling that way.

"Are you just about finished there?" he demanded roughly.

"I'm tying the last stitch." Her voice sounded cool, and he told himself to be thankful. For a while their barriers had been down. She'd told him about her feelings for Santa Ysabel, and she'd uncovered his hidden fear. It was much safer to pretend that neither had ever happened.

She smeared something cool on his arm, then covered it with a bandage. "You're all set," she said, in that same cool, even voice.

"Great. I'll clean up from lunch while you get ready to leave. Do you think you can start walking again?"

"I'm fine," she said briefly. "Completely back to normal. It's amazing what a little food will do."

"Then, let's go."

Chapter 9

Lexie stopped to take another drink from her canteen and wipe her face one more time. As she started walking again, she folded back the edges of the shawl and checked the sleeping Ana carefully. It was getting hotter and hotter, and even though Ana wore nothing more than a diaper, Lexie worried that she would get overheated in the shawl.

"You and the kid ready to take a break?" Caine called back to her.

"We will be soon," she answered, looking down at the baby again. "I'm fine, and she's still asleep. We might as well wait until she wakes up."

"You don't need anything to eat?" Caine persisted.

"No, thank you." She reined in the sharp reply that was prompted by the heat and her weariness and forced herself to voice a civil answer to the question he'd asked too many times that afternoon. "I've been eating the trail mix."

Caine stopped and turned around to face her. "I have to be able to trust you to tell me when you need a break, Lexie. It's going to be harder going from here on in. We're getting to the lower altitudes, and the undergrowth in the forest is going to be a lot thicker. It's also going to be hotter and more humid than it was yesterday and today.'' He glanced toward her canteen. ''Do you need more water?''

''Not yet. How much farther do we have to go?''

''Far enough.'' He didn't stop walking, but he did turn around and give her a reassuring smile. ''Don't worry, we're doing fine. To be honest, I never expected that we'd get this far this quickly. If everything goes well, we should be in Limores in two days.''

''Then what?''

''We'll worry about that when we get there.''

He kept walking steadily, maintaining a pace that wasn't too taxing for her. She watched him for a while as he strode in front of her, completely contained and self-reliant. He seemed to be isolated in a cocoon of his own making. The walls around him were clearly posted with a Do Not Disturb sign. She thought whimsically that there should also be a sign that said, Enter at Your Own Risk. Anyone who tried to get close to Caine O'Roarke was asking for heartbreak.

Two massive tree trunks lay across the path in front of them, and he waited to help her scramble over them. She looked up into the blue sky, squinting at the sudden brightness. The tightly interwoven canopy of massive trees usually shaded the floor of the jungle so completely that little direct sunlight reached it. The two trees that had fallen gave her an unexpected view of the sky and she lingered for a moment, enjoying the sight.

''Come on,'' he said impatiently. ''It's too hot to stand out here in the sun.''

''Don't you have any romance in your soul?'' she demanded. ''We haven't seen the sun for days. I want to appreciate it for a minute.''

''I appreciate how hot it's making me to stand here,'' he said. ''Let's go, Lexie.''

As she moved to follow him, he froze and she almost bumped into him. ''What is it?'' she asked.

''Shh.''

She stood still, straining to listen, but couldn't hear a thing. Then, suddenly, she heard a faint noise in the distance, so faint she wasn't sure it was really there.

Apparently Caine was sure. "Come on," he said, urgency in his voice. Taking her arm, he pulled her with him as he hurried toward the cover of the jungle. By the time they were hidden under the canopy again, the sound was much closer.

She looked over at him. "Is that what I think it is?"

"It's a helicopter." His voice was terse as he looked around. "And it sounds too low."

"Do you think it's someone looking for us?"

"I don't know, but we're not going to take any chances." He looked her over quickly. "Take the kid out of the shawl and give it to me. The material is too bright. I don't want to risk someone spotting us down here."

Her hands shook as she untied the knot that held the shawl in place. Holding Ana with one hand, she handed him the shawl with the other. Quickly he shoved it under his shirt where it was hidden from view, then he looked at her again.

"Your shirt," he said flatly. "It's too red. Take it off."

Without a word she pulled the red blouse over her head and handed it to him, and he tucked it under his shirt with her shawl. His gaze flickered over her again, impersonal and frighteningly calculating. "You should be all right now. Everything else will blend in with the dirt and the leaves."

She felt vulnerable and exposed, sitting so close to Caine wearing only a bra. He didn't even seem to notice. He was too busy scanning the skies for signs of the helicopter.

The noise was coming closer and closer. It sounded as if the aircraft was almost skimming the tops of the trees, and suddenly she was frightened. They were crouched in a thick clump of bushes at the base of an enormous tree, but she was sure whoever was in the helicopter would spot them easily. Holding Ana more tightly, she tensed to get up and run, knowing there had to be someplace else to hide where they would be more protected.

Caine gripped her arm, holding her still. "Don't!" he shouted over the whop-whop of the helicopter's rotors. "They'll see you in a second if you move. Just hide your face and hold still."

The sound of the helicopter drowned out all other noises, and she could feel the air stir around her as the aircraft passed over their heads. Covering Ana's ears with her hands, Lexie kept her face pressed between her knees and waited for the helicopter to pass.

She didn't move until the sound of the rotors beating had faded far into the distance. When she could barely hear the helicopter, she raised her head and looked over at Caine. He crouched, perfectly still, and scanned the surrounding jungle, his eyes constantly moving.

His tense watchfulness, the readiness she sensed in him, frightened her almost as much as the helicopter had. "What is it?" she asked. Her voice sounded as if it was stuck in her throat.

"Nothing, yet. I just want to make sure." He didn't look at her, just kept watching the jungle.

"Sure of what?" She swallowed hard.

"I want to be sure that the helicopter wasn't a smoke screen. I don't want to start walking again and step right into a trap. I want to be sure that whoever sent that helicopter over our heads doesn't also have someone planted in the jungle ahead of us who's just waiting for us to assume that since the helicopter's gone, everything's safe."

She stared at him, amazed. "Isn't that awfully convoluted? Is El Cuchillo really that clever?"

"You tell me. I just got to this country a few days ago, and I'm not the one he's looking for. Judging by the number of men and weapons he had waiting for you on the road, I'd say he was at least that desperate."

A chill crept up her spine and she shivered in the steamy heat. "What do we do now, then?"

"We wait here for a while." He turned and looked at her, and his face was expressionless except for the hard glitter in his eyes. "I'm real good at waiting. I hope you are, too."

She shivered again. "Can I at least have my blouse back?"

He looked at her again, and this time he seemed to notice that she wasn't wearing anything except her white cotton bra. For just a moment, awareness flared in his eyes and an answering warmth unfurled inside her. Then he looked away, and without a word he pulled her shirt out from under his and handed it to her.

As she tugged the blouse over her head his scent surrounded her. Musky and potent, it wrapped around her senses like a silken rope, drawing tighter with every breath she took. Inhaling deeply, she looked toward him, feeling her head spin.

He was still motionless, staring out into the jungle with an unnerving intensity. As far as she could tell, everything was back to normal in the green sea in front of her. The birds squawked in the canopy above them, the monkeys screeched and the hundreds of different insects hummed and droned around them. It didn't sound any different than it had for the past two days; but still, Caine didn't move.

She was stiff from sitting motionless by the time he turned to her once more. "I don't see or hear anything unusual. We can start walking again."

Gathering Ana closer, she slowly stood, stretching protesting joints. "What if the helicopter comes back?"

"If it had seen anything, it would have been back before this. I think we can assume it didn't spot us." He swung his large pack on his back with ease, then turned to help her with her tiny one. "On the other hand, if it was El Cuchillo looking for us, he's not about to give up. From now on, no fires at night. We'll have to stop earlier in the day to cook the food, and we'll have to be ready to start walking again at first light. And no more standing in the open, enjoying the sun."

"Don't worry," she muttered, reaching for the shawl he held out. "I don't want to see the sky again for a long time."

Knotting the shawl around her neck, she tried to ignore the fact that it, too, smelled like Caine. She didn't even want to think about the fact that she was carrying his daughter—the child he didn't want to acknowledge—in a scarf that was permeated with his scent. It was too bitter an irony.

Caine moved faster now, and she had to push herself to keep up. He hadn't had to use the machete yet to cut their way through the increasingly dense undergrowth, but vines and trailing branches reached out and grabbed at her with every step. When Caine stopped and pulled the map out of his pocket, she found she was almost panting from the heat and the effort to keep up.

"Another mile or so and we're going to stop for the night," he said abruptly. "Can you keep up this pace for another mile?"

"Of course," she answered immediately. Fear, she'd found, was a powerful inducement. All she wanted was the safety and anonymity of Limores, where she could hide in the tangle of narrow streets and busy lives. If she had to exhaust herself racing through the jungle to get there, so be it. "I'll keep going for as long as we have to."

His eyes softened with admiration, then he nodded. "With any luck, we'll reach a decent-size river in another mile or so. That's where we'll stop for the night."

Eating another handful of the trail mix he'd found in the bottom of his pack, she nodded. "I'm fine, Caine. Go ahead."

He paused, then said too quickly, "Why don't you let me take the kid? You look like you could use a break."

Her heart leaped in her chest, but she ignored it. He wasn't offering because he wanted to spend time with Ana. It was merely because he thought they would move faster. "Thanks, but you might need your hands free to use your machete. I'll be fine since we're stopping soon."

Caine pushed ahead through the bushes, shoving the vines to one side and ignoring the ache around his heart. Lexie was right. It was foolish of him to think about carrying the kid. He couldn't hold on to her and use his machete at the same time, and right now he should be worrying only about getting to Limores. His gut told him they didn't have any time to spare.

The helicopter worried him. If it was El Cuchillo, it meant the rebel leader wanted Lexie far too much. If he was desperate enough to send a helicopter searching the jungle when he must know the chances of finding her that way were slim at best, it meant he had one hell of a reason for capturing her. And whatever that reason, it was going to make getting out of San Rafael a tough job.

He glanced back over his shoulder and found Lexie close behind him. The baby was apparently still asleep, and he forced himself to look away from the bundle that bounced gently against Lexie's chest and concentrate on Lexie. She stumbled once as he watched, then caught herself and hurried to catch up to him.

Once again, admiration surged through him for the woman who followed him. He'd kept up a killing pace, but not once had she complained or told him to go slower. Her pinched face and the black circles under her eyes spoke eloquently of her exhaustion from the brutal trek, but instead of railing at him she just kept stubbornly on. His Lexie was turning out to be one hell of a woman.

The thought jolted him. She wasn't "his" Lexie anymore. Hell, she never had been. In order to give yourself to someone, you had to know who you were in the first place. And by her own admission, Lexie hadn't discovered that until she'd landed in Santa Ysabel.

No, he and Lexie had had nothing between them but a powerful physical attraction. Maybe that was still there, but now there was something even more powerful standing between them. The baby might be small and helpless, but she represented an insurmountable barrier.

He stole a look over his shoulder at the exact moment when Lexie smoothed the shawl away from the baby's face. The kid's tiny mouth was pursed and moving in a sucking motion, and Caine felt a treacherous warmth encircle his heart. The next moment Lexie eased the shawl back into place, hiding the baby again, and he looked away feeling that something precious had been taken from him.

Don't be a sentimental fool, he told himself savagely. He didn't want to be able to see the kid's face. He didn't want to look at the fuzz of her red hair and wonder if it would be curly or straight. He couldn't bear the pain of knowing that he had no idea how to be a father, of knowing that he didn't dare try to learn.

"Caine?"

Lexie sounded worried, and he spun around immediately. "What's wrong?"

"Nothing's wrong, but I'm going to need to stop and feed Ana soon." She surveyed the solid wall of green that surrounded them and licked her lips once. "This doesn't look like the kind of place you'd want to stop."

"It isn't." He looked around himself and compressed his lips. "Can you wait for another fifteen minutes?"

"I'll try." From the tone of her voice she wasn't hopeful, but he turned and started forward again.

"We'll go for as long as we can, then we'll stop. I'd rather be delayed while you feed her than have her screaming. We still don't know if there's anyone else around."

"I know," she said in a small voice. "I won't let her cry."

He glanced back at her worried face. "I know you won't, Lexie." His voice was soft. "You're doing a great job. Don't worry if we have to stop. It'll be all right."

A few minutes later he heard a grunt from behind them, but no hungry screams followed and he assumed that Lexie had been able to soothe the kid to sleep again. Finally, after another ten minutes, he spotted the glint of water ahead of them. Closing his eyes in a prayer of relief, he turned around to tell Lexie.

She had fallen several steps behind him again, and he immediately saw why. She was feeding the baby as she walked, just as she'd done the day before.

It took only a few strides to reach her. "I told you we could stop," he said, more roughly than he'd intended. "Why are you doing that?"

She looked up, and he could see the strain of fear in her eyes. "Fifteen minutes might make a difference," she whispered. "We don't know what's going to happen. Why take a chance on stopping?"

He stared at her for a long time, then slowly shook his head. "You're something else, Lexie. Where was all this steel when you were living in Washington?"

"In Washington I didn't need it," she retorted. "In fact, it would have made life with my father intolerable."

"Then why didn't you move out?"

She shrugged her shoulders and looked away. "Because it was easier not to. It was easier to go along with him than stand up for myself. And whenever he talked me out of doing something I wanted to do, he made it sound like the only reasonable or sensible thing to do."

Caine thought of the man who had been his boss and his mentor for more years than he cared to count, and understood what she meant. James Hollister had a way of wearing down even the most determined person. It was what made him so powerful, and so successful. As his own child, she must have found it almost impossible to fight.

Lexie rebuttoned her shirt and straightened the shawl, and as he watched her he said abruptly, "Give me the kid. Your back must be uncomfortable after feeding her while you were walking."

She glanced up at him, surprised. "How do you know that?"

"I've watched you when you feed her. You're always careful to lean up against a tree or a stump, and you always use your pack to support your arm. Both your back and your arm must be aching by now."

Slowly she reached into her shawl and handed him the baby. "It's almost frightening how observant you are. Do you always notice everything?"

He shrugged, trying to concentrate on her question and not on the sweet weight of the child lying in the crook of his arm. "I have to. Noticing everything around me can mean the difference between living and dying."

He began to walk again. "Caine," she called out to him.

She sounded hesitant. "What?"

"She needs to be burped. Why don't you let me do that, then you can carry her."

He saw the way her arms were trembling slightly as they hung at her sides, and he shook his head. "I'll do it. Just tell me how."

She gave him an uncertain smile, as if she didn't believe he was serious. "Hold her up against your shoulder and pat her on the back. When she burps, you're all set."

He looked down at the baby in his arms. To his surprise, she wasn't sleeping. She returned his gaze with a serious stare of her own. She appeared to be examining him, and he wondered for a moment what her verdict would be.

The next instant he felt as if he'd been poleaxed. She smiled up at him, her whole body wriggling with joy. He couldn't have moved if his life depended on it. All he could do was stand there, his heart turning over in his chest, as the baby grinned up at him.

"Do you want me to do it?" Lexie's voice came from behind him.

"Do what?" He sounded dazed.

"Burp her."

Slowly he shook his head. "She smiled at me," he whispered, unable to keep the wonder out of his voice. He looked up and stared at Lexie. "She looked at me and she smiled."

Lexie's face softened and she smiled mistily at him, including him in her joy and love for her child. "Why shouldn't she? You're her daddy."

A fist reached out and squeezed his heart, crushing it to bits. "I'm her father, Lexie. There's a big difference." Unable to look at Lexie and the pain he knew he would see in her gaze, he blindly lifted the baby to his shoulder and patted her on her back. He felt awkward and uncomfortable as he waited for the burp Lexie had assured him would come.

Finally he heard it—a deep rumbling he couldn't believe had come from such a small body. Immediately afterward he felt something warm and wet on his shoulder, and he craned his neck to see what it was.

"I'm sorry, Caine." Lexie's voice was stiff behind him. "She spat up on your shoulder. I should have warned you that happens sometimes."

"Don't worry about it," he muttered. Awkwardly he lowered the baby until she rested in the crook of his arm. He warned himself not to do it, told himself he was just asking for more pain, but he couldn't resist looking at her. When she caught his eye she smiled again, this time waving her tiny arms and legs with glee. For a moment he allowed himself to watch her, then he tore his gaze away and looked blindly toward the river ahead of them.

It took another ten minutes to reach it. By the time they got there, the baby had fallen asleep in his arms, and he looked down at her with relief. He wouldn't have to worry about any heart-stealing smiles for a little while, anyway.

When he found a small clearing that was completely covered by the canopy of huge trees above them, he stopped and turned to Lexie. "This looks like as good a place as any. Why don't you take her and stay here while I look around? I'll be back in a few minutes."

As Lexie held out her arms for the sleeping baby, Caine stole a look at her face. He expected her to look angry, or at least hurt. Instead, when their eyes met he saw a sad understanding in them that scared him far more than Lexie's fury would have. He didn't want her understanding him. He wanted her to keep her distance.

"Where are you going?" she asked in a soft voice.

"I want to see if there's anywhere with better cover for us to spend the night. I also want to make sure no one else has been around here lately."

"All right." Without another word she slid to the ground. Balancing the baby on her knees, she untied the shawl from around her neck and spread it on the ground. Then, after laying the baby on the shawl, Lexie leaned back against the tree and closed her eyes.

Caine watched her for a moment longer, then slipped away through the trees. He had work to do. He couldn't stand around mooning over what couldn't be.

By the time Caine returned, Lexie's arms had almost stopped trembling, and she was beginning to feel hungry. When he stepped silently into the clearing, carrying what looked like another agouti, she smiled wearily at him.

"How did you know I was getting hungry?"

"A lucky guess." He laid the agouti on the ground and began to gather material for a fire.

Glancing at the sky nervously, she asked, "I thought we couldn't have any more fires." She looked at the agouti longingly.

"We can't have any fires at night. They'll be as obvious as a neon light to anyone looking for us. As long as it's daylight, though, we can take a chance." He looked over at her and continued frankly, "I'd prefer not to light one, but we don't have any choice. You have to eat in order to keep going. As long as we do it quickly, before the sun starts to go down, I think we'll be all right."

She watched unhappily as he started the fire and prepared their food. He was right. There was no way she could continue without eating, and there was no way she was going to eat raw meat.

The fire blazed hotter than the one they'd had earlier, and the agouti cooked much more quickly. As soon as it was finished and the water for their dehydrated meals had boiled, Caine doused the fire and covered it with dirt to stop it from smoking.

They ate in silence. She wondered what he was thinking, but from the way he avoided looking in Ana's direction, she was afraid she knew. For some reason he'd convinced himself that he wanted no part of his daughter. She had no idea why, but from the wonder on his face when Ana had smiled at him, she suspected that it was becoming harder and harder for him to keep his distance.

Since she'd seen that wonder this afternoon, all her anger at him for rejecting Ana had disappeared. Now she felt only sorrow and regret, both for his loss and for his stubbornness in insisting on maintaining his distance.

"Why don't you bring the kid and come down to the river with me while I clean the dishes?" His voice interrupted her thoughts, and she looked up at him, startled, as he continued, "You can wash her diapers afterward."

"All right," she said immediately, reaching for the shawl so she could carry both Ana and the load of dirty diapers down to the river.

She heard the river before she saw it, and her pulse quickened at the soft gurgling sound. It really was a river, and not just a trickle of muddy water. When she stepped through the last of the bushes screening it from view, she stopped and caught her breath.

The water was the color of weak tea, but it was clear enough to see almost to the bottom. As she stared at it, she could almost feel its cool smoothness flowing over her hot, sticky skin.

She turned impulsively to Caine. "After we finish cleaning up, can I take a bath?"

He had already begun to wash the dishes, and he looked up at her and shrugged. "Sure. This water's too shallow for crocodiles."

"Will you watch Ana for me?"

He stilled for a moment, then shrugged again. "I guess so."

She moved downstream a few feet, then squatted on the edge of the river and carefully removed Ana from the shawl. Laying the baby on the ground, she began washing the pile of soiled diapers. As she finished them, one by one, she wrung them out and hung them over the branches of a bush to dry.

By the time she was done she felt hotter and stickier than ever. She looked over at Caine and noticed the stain on the back of his shirt where Ana had spat up on him. Without stopping to think, she called out to him, "Why don't you give me your shirt and I'll wash it for you? That way it'll be clean in the morning."

"Thanks, but don't bother. It's fine."

"I'm afraid it might begin to stink before the morning. Ana spat up on it, remember?"

His shoulders tensed, then he turned to her. "I'd forgotten about that." Slowly he began to unbutton his shirt. "Thanks for reminding me."

"You're welcome." She sat, mesmerized, as he pulled the shirt off and tossed it over to her. She had told herself she'd forgotten how he looked, but realized as she watched him that every detail was branded on her soul.

From broad shoulders his torso tapered to a narrow waist and hips. Even though he was whipcord lean, she could see his muscles flex and ripple every time he moved. The thatch of dark blond hair on his chest arrowed down his flat belly to disappear under the waistband of his cotton pants.

When she forced her gaze back up to his face, she realized he'd been watching her. Her cheeks burning, she turned jerkily back toward the river and blindly dipped the shirt into the water. What was the matter with her, anyway? Her heart was pounding like a drum and her hands were trembling so hard she had trouble holding on to the shirt. Why was she blushing like a schoolgirl, for heaven's sake? She'd seen half-naked men before. And she'd seen Caine a lot more than half naked.

She didn't dare look over at him, but she could feel his gaze on her, watching as she washed his shirt. When she found herself smoothing her hand down the back of it, she twisted it sharply to wring it out and flapped it open with a crack, then dropped it onto the bush to dry.

Wiping her still-shaking hands on her shorts, she stood and faced him. "I'd like to take a bath now," she managed to say.

"Fine. I'll keep an eye on the kid."

She waited for him to pick up Ana and leave, but he merely strolled over and sat down close to her, leaning against one of the rocks that lined the stream.

"What are you doing?" she demanded, although she had a feeling she already knew.

"Watching the kid. What does it look like I'm doing?"

"I can't take a bath with you sitting right there," she said, appalled.

"That's up to you. Take it or leave it, Lexie. I'm not leaving you down here alone. There may not be crocodiles in that river, but there are plenty of other things to worry about."

She stared at him for a moment, trying to decide if he was bluffing. She realized almost immediately that he wasn't. Caine didn't have any need to bluff. He simply gave you the options.

The river beckoned, cool and inviting, and she turned away from him abruptly. "I'll trust you to be a gentleman and not watch me."

"I've seen it all before, Lexie." His voice was low and shockingly intimate. "You know that as well as I do."

Crouching behind a bush and feeling like a complete idiot for trying to conceal herself, she unfastened her shorts and unbuttoned her blouse with hands that shook. The water was dark enough that once she was in the river, it wouldn't matter if he watched her or not. All he would see was the top of her head.

Slipping off her bra and panties, she crouched naked on the riverbank, welcoming the air on her skin, as she quickly rinsed out her underwear. Hanging the flimsy garments on the bush to dry, she stepped into the water and was relieved to feel a rocky bottom under her feet. Pushing away from the edge, she let the water flow over her hot body.

Nothing had felt this good in a long, long time. The water was like cool silk wrapping around her. When she dipped her head in and let the smooth current wash the sweat and grime out of her hair, it seemed as if gentle fingers massaged her scalp. She floated in the river, feeling the dappled sunlight caress her, and relaxed for the first time since Caine had walked through her door in Santa Ysabel.

At the thought of Caine she raised her head and looked over toward where he sat with Ana. She wasn't surprised to find him watching her intently.

"I thought you promised not to watch me."

He shook his head. "You said you'd trust I was a gentleman and not look. I've never been a gentleman, Lexie, and I never will be. You should know that by now."

She paddled over to the river's edge and hauled herself onto the bank, squeezing the water out of her hair. As she was looking around and realizing she didn't have anything to dry herself with, she heard Caine approaching.

"You can use this to dry yourself off." He handed her one of his clean shirts, and she snatched it out of his hand and held it in front of her.

His eyes gleamed with amusement and something darker and hotter. "You're a lot more modest than you used to be," he said in a husky voice. "You used to enjoy flaunting your body in front of me. Remember all those short, low-cut dresses you used to wear?" He nodded at the shirt that barely skimmed her thighs. "My shirt covers up more than they did."

"This isn't Washington, and things have changed." She hated the breathless tone of her voice. Watching the way Caine's eyes narrowed, she knew he'd noticed it.

"Some things never change, Lexie." Without taking a step toward her, he reached out and brushed her wet hair away from her face, tucking it behind her ear. It was a surprisingly sweet gesture, and she blinked as he turned away from her.

"You looked like you were having a good time in the river. I think I'll take a swim, too." He turned back to her as he unbuttoned his pants and slowly pulled down the zipper. "And you can watch all you want."

Chapter 10

"No, thank you," she said tartly, holding on to the shirt more tightly. "I've seen all I care to see."

He shrugged. "Suit yourself." He began to lower his light cotton pants and she hastily turned away from him.

"Your back is still wet, Lexie," he said from behind her, and she could hear the mocking grin in his voice. "Want me to dry it for you?"

Scrambling to pull the shirt around her, she noticed that her hands were trembling again. Would Caine always have this effect on her? she wondered with a stab of pain. For eleven months she'd tried to convince herself that she'd gotten over him, but in a couple of days he'd managed to knock down all her defenses. He didn't even have to touch her before she started shaking. Just the sound of his voice was enough.

Tugging the edges of the shirt together with a jerk, she searched blindly for the buttons through the haze of tears in her eyes. Caring about Caine was the surest way she knew to heartbreak, but she couldn't seem to stop herself. Inside his tough, hard shell was a man who desperately needed to be loved.

The question was whether or not he *wanted* to be loved. Her hands dropped to her sides and she turned toward the river. He lay floating on the water, completely unconcerned about whether or not she was watching. He made no secret of the fact that he wanted *her,* but that wasn't the same thing at all. She'd found that out the hard way.

He flipped over in the water and the shadow of his narrow hips and taut buttocks flashed in the mottled sunlight. Heat gathered, heavy and throbbing, in her abdomen. She watched him for a moment, unable to tear her gaze away, then she forced herself to lower her eyes. She'd spent the last eleven months struggling to gain control over her life and her emotions, and she wasn't about to relinquish that control now, especially to Caine O'Roarke.

She wasn't a teenager anymore, to be controlled by lust and impulse, and she had living, breathing proof of what happened when you allowed your hormones to rule your brain. She looked over at Ana, sleeping peacefully under the bush, and a spring of fierce maternal love and protectiveness welled up inside her. Watching the face of her child, she vowed that she would never lose control of herself like that again. She couldn't afford to.

She picked up the sleeping baby and headed toward the clearing when she heard Caine getting out of the water. Keeping her back turned, she bent and kissed Ana's head as she hurried away from him.

Caine said from behind her, "What's the matter, Lexie? Afraid to look?" The teasing tone made her begin to ache all over again, and she struggled to keep herself from giving in to it.

She stopped but didn't turn around. "Is it so inconceivable to you that I'm not interested in looking?"

"Yes, it's inconceivable, Lexie." His voice was very soft behind her, and incredibly seductive. "You're just as interested as I am. You try harder to hide it, that's all."

She spun around, not caring that he stood in front of her, stark naked. "You don't want me, Caine, not really. You want my body and that's all. And I'm not interested in sex for sex's sake."

"Are you sure that's all I want, Lexie?" His voice was low and intense. "Do you know me that well?"

"Well enough," she retorted. "I know you're not interested in the baggage that comes along with me, and that's all I care about."

Slowly, almost as if against his will, his gaze lowered to rest on the sleeping baby in her arms. He stared at her for a long time, until he finally looked up at Lexie once more, his eyes blank. "Don't bring the kid into this," he said, and his voice was flat and expressionless. "This is between you and me."

She closed her eyes, the pain almost too much to bear. "No, it's not, Caine. That's the whole point. Ana isn't an inconvenience that will magically disappear when you want her to. She's here, and she'll be a part of my life forever. A major part of my life."

He turned away and pulled his cotton pants over his still-damp legs, his movements jerky. "I'm not what she needs, Lexie. I'm not cut out to be a father. She's better off if she never even gets to know me."

She stared at him, shocked. "How can you say such a thing? How could you even begin to imagine that she'd be better off without you in her life? Even if—" She stopped and swallowed painfully, then began again, "Even if her parents aren't together, she'll want to know her father."

"We don't always get what we want in life, Lexie. Don't you know that by now?" Without looking at her he grabbed his shoes and socks and sat down to put them on. "Take my word for it, she'll be better off without me."

"I won't take your word for it," she cried passionately. "I accepted long ago that you couldn't make a commitment to me, but this is an innocent child we're talking about. All a child wants is a father who will love her. Even you could give her that, Caine. Dammit, I know you can."

"You don't know anything about it, Lexie." He finished tying his shoes, then stood, staring down at her, his face harsh and closed.

She opened her mouth to challenge him again, but the pain she glimpsed lurking far below the cold surface of his eyes held her silent. Finally she quietly said, "If you ever want to tell me about it, I'd be happy to listen to you." Then she turned and walked back to the clearing, holding Ana tightly against her chest.

He didn't follow her for a long time. When he did come silently into the clearing, he put the dishes back into his pack and pulled out a small green nylon package. He was careful not to look at either her or Ana.

As he began to unravel the package, she realized it was a tent. "We're not going to look for a hollow tree tonight?" she asked, keeping her voice neutral and polite.

He shook his head. "I already did. There isn't one close enough to the river, and I don't want to backtrack just for the sake of better cover. The tent is small, but you won't have to worry." He turned away and jerked open the fluttering nylon. "I'll be a gentleman."

"I never doubted that for a moment, Caine," she said gently. "That wasn't what I was worried about."

"What are you worried about, then?"

Telling herself to be a grown-up about it, she looked around the tiny clearing. The sun hung low through the trees, and even though it wasn't close to totally dark yet, she could imagine what it would be like, out in the open, with nothing around her but the blackness. "I was scared of the hollow trees at first," she said slowly. "They were so dark and so enclosed. But at least they were some protection against the darkness outside. Sleeping in a tent seems so vulnerable, somehow."

He turned to her. "I'll be there with you, Lexie," he said steadily. "Nothing will happen. We'll be safe."

Nodding, she turned away to fuss with the shirt she'd put on Ana. "I know. You think I'm being stupid and silly, and I am. But I'll deal with it. I'm not about to let my phobia get in the way of what we have to do."

His hands came down on her shoulders, surprising her with their gentleness. "I know you can deal with it, Lexie. But you don't have to deal with it alone. I'm here to help you."

Turning around slowly, she looked up at him in the deepening gloom. "There are things you don't have to deal with alone, either, Caine," she whispered. Reaching out, she touched his face in a brief caress, then let her hand drop. "Think about it."

She turned away and bent down to Ana again, but she felt
him standing motionless behind her. She ached to put her arms
around him, to comfort him, but she knew she didn't dare. If
she did, he would just retreat again.

"We have to get up early tomorrow morning," he said behind her, and his voice was brusque. "You should go to sleep
now."

"I'm going to wake her up and feed her again, then I will."

"Why don't you just let her sleep until she wakes up, and
then feed her?"

Settling herself against a tree, she gave him a tired smile.
"Because I know that she'd wake up in an hour or so, just as I
was getting into a deep sleep. If I feed her now, she might sleep
for four or five hours before she wakes up again."

He frowned down at them, but he didn't move away. "I
thought babies were supposed to sleep all the time. How come
she's awake so much?"

Lexie leaned back against the tree and watched him as Ana
started to eat. He was careful not to let his gaze slip below her
face, but at least he wasn't turning away as he had at first. "She
has to sleep a lot, but she needs to eat a lot, too. She wakes up
when she's hungry."

He stood watching her for a moment, then suddenly stepped
aside as if he remembered what he was doing. "I'll get the tent
ready," he muttered.

Twenty minutes later Ana was fed and changed and it was
almost completely dark in the little clearing. After squatting in
the doorway of the tent for a few minutes, Caine had come
back out and sat down next to her. He hadn't looked at either
her or Ana, but she was grateful for his presence.

"She's asleep," Lexie whispered as she looked around at the
blackness closing in on her. "Can we go in the tent now?"

"Yeah." He stood and helped her to her feet. "Go on in and
make yourself comfortable. I'll make sure everything is se-
cured out here."

Lexie glanced over at the tent that was almost invisible
against the background of dark trees and bushes. It looked way
too small for two adults and a baby, but it would have to do.

Walking carefully across the clearing, she stooped down at the doorway and peered inside.

They would fit, but it would be close quarters tonight. As she thought about Caine lying next to her, near enough for her to feel his heat, sensation shivered through her belly. In spite of everything, she couldn't deny the fact that he touched her in some place deep inside that no other man had ever reached.

She wouldn't think about that tonight. She couldn't. Suddenly so tired she could barely keep her eyes open, she crawled into the tent and carefully laid Ana down. Then, curling up next to her, she closed her eyes and waited for sleep to come.

Even though she was exhausted, she didn't fall asleep right away. She found herself listening for Caine out in the jungle. His footsteps moved back and forth through the clearing, until finally they stopped at the door to the tent.

She felt him waiting there, and she realized he was looking to see if she was asleep. It would be better to let him think so, she told herself. It would take away some of the awkwardness they were both bound to feel. So she lay motionless on her side, her eyes tightly closed, as she waited for him to crawl in next to her.

"Stop worrying about it." His voice floated over to her, soft and amused. "I'm not going to jump your bones tonight, Lexie."

Her eyes flew open and she saw him watching her. "I never thought you were. I just thought it would be more comfortable for both of us if we could pretend I was asleep."

"I can take the heat," he murmured as he slid in beside her. "Can't you?"

"Of course." But she couldn't, she realized. Every cell in her body was aware of how close he was lying to her. His scent surrounded her, sharp and clean and intoxicating. If she moved just a little, she would be in his arms. She closed her eyes as the trembling started, deep inside her.

"Then there's no problem. Good night, Lexie."

"Good night," she murmured.

He rolled over, facing his back to hers, and didn't move. As she lay beside him, so close that the heat from his body warmed her, she longed to slide closer and curl herself around him. Not only would she be taking comfort for herself, but she had a feeling she would be giving it, too. She and Caine were alone in this green world, completely cut off and isolated. And he had his demons, too. As she wondered what had happened to him to make him fear getting involved with Ana, her eyelids grew heavy and she slipped into sleep.

She woke suddenly and looked around wildly in the darkness, her heart pounding in her chest. Ana was still asleep, but she sensed Caine's wakefulness next to her.

"What's wrong?" she whispered.

"Nothing. Go back to sleep."

"Something woke me up," she insisted.

"There was some thunder, higher up in the mountains. You probably heard it."

He had turned to face her, and she stared at the pale slash of his face in the darkness. "Thunder? How come?"

She felt his shrug rather than saw it. "I don't know. It must be raining up there."

"But the rainy season isn't supposed to start for another three or four weeks. It can't be raining."

"I guess someone forgot to tell the rain god." He sighed and his voice gentled. "Go back to sleep, Lex. We can't do anything about it, anyway."

She knew what the rainy season was like, had experienced the mud and the mire, and could only imagine how much more difficult it would make their trek through the jungle. "How are we going to walk through the jungle if it starts to rain down here?"

"In two days we should be in Limores," he said softly. "With any luck, the rain will hold off for that long. And if it doesn't, it'll just take us longer. Besides, if it makes you feel any better, it'll affect El Cuchillo, too. In fact, it might even help us."

"What do you mean?"

"We're two people and a baby, and we're on foot. He's got a lot of men and jeeps and equipment to worry about. While they're getting stuck in the mud and trying to figure out where it's safe to drive, we might be able to slip past them and into Limores. So maybe we should pray for rain."

At some point during the day she had managed to push all thoughts of El Cuchillo out of her head. Now they came flooding back, and she wondered what or who would be waiting for them in Limores. This tent, which just a couple of hours ago had seemed so vulnerable and unprotected, suddenly felt like a haven that she didn't want to leave.

"Caine?" she said in a small voice.

"Hmm."

"Would you hold me?"

She felt him tense next to her, and finally he asked carefully, "How come?"

"For comfort, I guess." Her voice sounded forlorn, and she wished she could call the words back, but it was too late.

It didn't seem to matter, anyway, because without a word Caine reached out and pulled her close, holding her snuggled against him as if they were two spoons. The muscles in his chest and legs were tense, and she felt the unmistakable proof of his arousal nestled against her hips.

"Sorry, Lexie," he murmured into her ear, his warm breath caressing the side of her neck. "That's what you do to me, and I'm not going to try and hide it. But I know that's not why you wanted me to hold you, so go ahead and fall asleep." She thought she felt his lips brush her hair, then she gave in to the sleep pulling her into oblivion.

The sound of Ana snuffling in the darkness woke her again, and she opened her eyes to find that she'd turned sometime while she slept and had wrapped her arms around Caine. One of her legs had crept between his, and her knee rested against a vulnerable part of his anatomy.

"Just don't make any sudden moves," he said into her ear as he eased away from her. "I assume that means the kid needs to be fed?"

She nodded and reached for Ana. "It feels like she's slept longer than she usually does at night."

He swung himself into a sitting position in the tent. When she felt his hands on her arms she turned around to look at him, but he was pulling her against him. "Use me as your tree trunk," he murmured.

He had pulled her between his legs, and as she leaned against him he rested his hands on her shoulders to steady her. It felt so right, so natural to share the intimate nighttime feeding with him this way. As she unbuttoned her blouse and lifted Ana to her breast, she relaxed against him, letting him take her full weight.

"How do you know she slept longer than usual?" His whisper rustled through her hair and stirred the heat inside her.

"Because my breasts are more full of milk than usual," she whispered back. There was no reason to use such hushed tones, she knew, but somehow the fragile intimacy of the situation seemed to require it.

"You can feel the milk in your breasts?" He sounded incredulous.

Slowly she took his hand and brought it to the breast Ana hadn't yet nursed at. "Feel how heavy it is?"

Hesitantly he cupped her in his hand for a moment, then his fingers slowly began to explore her heavy curves through the sturdy cotton of her bra. She closed her eyes as licks of fire raced through her. When he carefully touched her nipple with one finger, she couldn't control the shudder that she knew he felt.

Pressed against him the way she was, she couldn't help but feel his reaction to her, too. Closing her eyes, she moved closer and felt his hand tighten on her breast for just a moment.

Ana began fussing then, and Lexie knew she was still hungry. Bringing her hand up to close over Caine's, she slowly pushed aside the bra that covered her full, throbbing breast. She heard him suck in his breath as her naked breast fell into his palm.

She was helpless to move while he circled her taut nipple with one finger. When he tugged at it, she heard herself moaning softly. Then Ana grunted again, and she felt a wetness slide down her breast and drip onto his hand.

She moved to pull his hand away, but he stopped her. "What happened?" He tugged softly at her earlobe as he whispered the words, and she felt herself shudder in response.

"It's the milk. That happens sometimes."

"When you're feeding her?"

"Then, and also..."

"Also when, Lexie?" His fingers glided across her nipple again, and again she felt herself shudder, felt the heat throbbing lower in her belly.

"When I'm aroused," she whispered, wanting to twist around and press herself close to him. But Ana whimpered again, and she was forced to shift her to her other arm and gently take Caine's hand away.

He waited while Ana began nursing, then his other hand came around and found her other breast. Holding it in his palm, he murmured, "Is that what happened last night?"

She nodded slowly. "It startled me. I wasn't expecting it, and I didn't know how it would make you feel."

He pressed closer to her, and the heat of his arousal burned into her, even through her clothes. "How do you think it's making me feel?"

"Caine," she whispered in a shaky voice as he gently kneaded her nipple. His lips glided over her neck, and his tongue traced small circles below her ear.

"Can you tell how it's making me feel?" he murmured into her ear.

She nodded slowly. "The way I feel," she said, half turning in his arms so her lips could find his.

"Lex..." His mouth feathered over hers, barely skimming it while his tongue traced the outline of her lips. Hot, aching need swelled inside her, pounding with the heavy rhythm of her heart. Holding Ana tightly in one arm, she lay sprawled against him helplessly while his hand caressed her breast.

When his other hand slipped down to rest on the inside of her thigh she jumped, startled. His fingers trailed fire wherever they touched, and even through the cotton of her shorts she felt his burning heat. She knew he could feel her tremble at his touch, but she didn't care. No one else had ever affected her like this, and she knew with a flash of insight that no one else ever would.

Ana squirmed in her arms, startling her out of her sensual daze, and she looked down at her. The baby had finished eating and was falling asleep. Ignoring her body's protests, Lexie leaned forward, tearing herself away from Caine's heat, and set

Ana on the floor. She snuffled once, drew her legs closer to her tiny body, and closed her eyes again.

Caine's hands slid down her arms and slowly, inexorably, pulled her back against him. She tried to turn around and face him, but he gently held her in place, her back pressing against his chest. His arousal burned into the cleft of her buttocks, making her start trembling all over again.

To her surprise, he didn't move to touch her or kiss her again. Crossing his arms over her chest, he held her against him for a moment. The tenseness of his thighs and the hardness of his arms against her told her the depth of his struggle to hold himself in check. When she tried to turn in his arms again, he held her more tightly.

"Don't turn around, unless you're very sure this is what you want," he whispered into her ear. "If it's not, we'll just sit here for a few minutes, then lie down and go back to sleep."

Immediately she tried to turn around but he wouldn't let her. "I want you to be sure, Lexie." His breath caressed the damp spot on her neck where he'd kissed her earlier, and she shivered. "Really sure. I don't want you to have any regrets when the sun comes up."

He was forcing her to make a decision, and for a moment she stiffened with resentment. Making love with Caine would have been so much easier to dismiss in the morning if they'd both been carried away by lust during the night. But he was deliberately forcing her to confront her feelings.

For the space of several heartbeats she was terrified and she wanted to pull away from him. Then gradually she relaxed again. Tonight, it didn't matter that he wouldn't allow himself to care about her, or Ana. It didn't matter that he surrounded himself with fences so high that it was almost impossible to scale them. What mattered was the pain she'd seen in his eyes earlier when they talked about Ana, and the need he couldn't disguise right now. What mattered was that Caine was the man who had touched her soul and left a mark that couldn't be erased, no matter how hard she'd tried.

For the first time since finding out she was pregnant with Ana, she didn't think about the consequences of what she did. She didn't think about tomorrow, or what was going to happen then. She wanted Caine tonight more than she'd ever wanted anything in her life, and he wanted her. That was enough.

Pushing against his arms, she eased herself away from his body. From the way his muscles stiffened as his arms fell away from her, she knew he assumed she had come to her senses. Slowly she turned and faced him. "I want you, Caine," she whispered. "Make love with me. Please."

His hands came up to grip her shoulders, not to pull her close but to hold her away as he stared at her. All she could see in the darkness was the pale shadow of his face. "Are you sure, Lexie?" His low voice was fierce in the confines of the tent. "Very sure?"

"Yes," she answered steadily. "I'm sure. I don't think I've ever wanted anything as much as I want you right now."

His breath shivered out in a sigh when he pulled her against him. As he held her tightly, she realized his arms were trembling. Then she didn't notice anything else as his mouth took hers in a fierce kiss.

It wasn't anything like the gentle caress earlier. This was a kiss of possession, of passion running hot and deep. His desire was like an irresistible current, swirling around her and pulling her under into the dark, hot depths below. Her hand was trapped between their bodies, and she felt the beating of his heart against it. Her body's demands seemed to throb in time with the pounding of his pulse under her fingers.

His hands fumbled with the blouse she wore. She hadn't buttoned it after feeding Ana, but he had trouble pulling it off her shoulders. She shrugged out of it, and the bra that was also unfastened. Then she reached for the shirt he wore.

She'd managed to tug it halfway over his head when her fingernails scraped over his flat nipples. Sucking in his breath, he ripped the shirt the rest of the way off and pulled her against him. Her breasts flattened against his chest, the soft mat of hair tickling her sensitive nipples.

"I wish we could light the lantern," he murmured into her ear. "I want to look at you, to see if my memory was as good as the reality."

"Did you think about me?" she whispered, hating the wistfulness in her voice, but needing to know.

"Every day and every night." His voice was rough and hoarse, and his hands moved on her back. "Thinking about you was the only thing that got me through."

"Through what?"

His arms tightened around her. "Not tonight. I don't want to think about anything but you tonight." He bent and kissed her again, and his hands slipped under the waistband of her shorts. "Tonight I don't want to think about anything besides how you feel—" his fingers danced over her hips "—and how you taste—" his mouth dipped to the hollow in front of her collarbone "—and how you make me feel."

He shifted and she could feel the heat of him, burning into her. "Caine..." Her voice trembled in the still air and she reached blindly for him. Their mouths met in an explosive kiss—one that had her aching for his touch, for the feel of him wrapped around her and buried inside her.

Lowering her to the floor, he swept her shorts down her legs, then sat up long enough to pull off his own thin cotton pants. When he lay back down, he pulled her gently against him, then bent to take one nipple into his mouth.

Sensations cascaded through her, making her arch helplessly against him. He slid his hand along her thigh until he reached the spot where her legs met, and he gently cupped her in his palm. Her shivering cries were swallowed by his mouth covering hers.

The thrust of his tongue into her mouth was matched by the stroking of his hand farther down. All she could do was hold on to him as she felt the trembling start, deep inside.

"Caine," she panted. "I need you. Please..."

"I'm sorry, Lex," he muttered as he lowered himself between her legs. "I wanted to go slow, to take all night to make love to you. But I can't. I'm going to explode with wanting you." As he eased into her, he murmured into her ear, "I'll do better next time, I promise."

"Caine!" Her hands dug into his back as he began to move slowly inside her. His whole body shook with the effort he made to hold himself in check and go slowly. Sensation spiraled more tightly inside her, and suddenly she surged against him, wanting all of him.

With a groan he arched above her, then they were locked together in a heated, frenzied haze of passion. When she flew off the peak he was with her, holding her so tightly she could barely breathe, his trembling matching her own.

As her heart rate slowly returned to normal she turned her head and nuzzled his neck. His face was buried in her hair, his arms still wrapped around her as if he would never let her go. When her lips traced a pattern below his ear, he tightened his grip on her for a moment, then suddenly rolled over, carrying her with him.

"We're not exactly lying on a bed of roses, here," he whispered, smoothing her hair away from her face and running one hand gently down her back. "I'm a better mattress for you than the ground."

"You certainly feel better," she murmured, nestling closer to him. The hard planes of his body felt wonderful against her softer curves, and she sighed as she trailed her fingers down his side.

She stopped abruptly as she found a small, hard, raised bump on his skin. As her fingers explored it, she realized there was another one close by, and another near that. Running her hand lightly over his skin, she found that his side and abdomen were covered with the small, irregular lumps.

"Are these insect bites?" she asked, ignoring the fact that he'd stiffened when she'd found them.

"No, they're not." His voice was abrupt.

"What are they, then?" Her fingers brushed over another one and lingered, smoothing his skin.

His arms tightened around her, then he gently reached down and pulled her hand away from his side. "Let's just say they're a legacy from my last job." He raised her hand to his mouth and pressed a kiss into her palm.

"What...?" she began to ask, but he laid his fingers against her lips. In the darkness she could feel him shake his head.

"Not tonight, Lexie. I don't want to talk about it now. I promise I'll tell you all about it sometime, but not now."

He had tensed in the last few moments, and slowly she nodded. As curious as she was, she didn't want anything to spoil the magic of this night. And to prod him to talk about the marks on his skin would do just that. The tenseness that had filled him when she'd asked about the bumps was all the proof she needed.

"I can wait," she whispered. She raised her hand to let her fingers tangle in his hair, and felt him slowly relax. "Besides," she murmured into his ear, "there are a lot more interesting things to talk about."

His hand trailed down her back and lingered at her hip. "Such as?"

She touched his earlobe with her tongue, then rolled off him to snuggle against his side. "Oh, like what good books you've read lately, for instance." She grinned into the darkness as she felt his thunderstruck reaction to her words.

"What the hell is that supposed to mean?"

"Aren't those the kinds of things you're supposed to talk about on a first date?" She tried to keep the laughter out of her voice, but she couldn't keep the smile off her face when he turned to her.

"This is hardly our first date, Lexie." She trailed her fingers over his face and could feel the slight upward curve of his lips. "And even if it was, I'd say we've gotten past the favorite-book-and-movie conversation."

His hand swept down her chest and splayed flat on her abdomen, an unconsciously possessive gesture that started the heat inside all over again.

"It feels like a first date, Caine," she whispered, and all of a sudden she wasn't laughing anymore. "I feel like a completely different person than I was eleven months ago."

"You are, Lexie. So maybe you're right." He lifted his hand from her belly and slid it lower, and she arched into him. "And if that's the case, maybe I'd better stop right now."

"How come?" she managed to say, unable to concentrate on what he was saying.

"Because you know what they say. 'Once is a mistake, twice is a habit.'"

She turned on her side and slipped one of her legs between his. "Then here's to old habits," she whispered, and raised her head to kiss him.

Chapter 11

Caine awoke slowly, wondering why he felt so damned good. A heavy languor enveloped him, making him reluctant to open his eyes or move his arms and legs.

Someone moved against him, snuggling closer to his chest, and the memories came flooding back. Lexie. He reached out for her instinctively, pulling her harder against him, feeling himself stirring with need for her.

"Mmm, good morning to you, too," she whispered against his chest. He could swear he felt her mouth curve up in a smile. "I guess this means I wasn't dreaming last night."

"Why don't we find out for sure?" he asked, his low voice cracking with sleep and sudden, flaring desire. Rolling over onto his elbows, he looked down at her, trapped between his arms, and watched awareness heat her eyes.

"If once is a mistake and twice is a habit, what's three times?" she whispered, watching him, her enormous eyes darkened with passion.

"Inevitable as the sunrise," he answered as he reached down and kissed her. She wrapped her arms around his neck to pull him closer, and he felt himself being swept up into the vortex of passion again, helpless to stop himself. All Lexie had to do was look at him, let alone touch him, and he was lost.

Except that he didn't feel lost; he felt as if he'd come home. When he skimmed his hand down her side, feeling her skin heat and soften with desire, she moved against him as if this dance was intimately familiar to her. Opening to him, she lay beneath him trustingly, gathering him close and wrapping her arms around him as if they belonged together. And as he closed his eyes, in a moment suspended in time, he allowed himself to think so, too.

Unlike during the night, when their lovemaking had been hot and frantic and driven, they went slowly in the semidarkness of the dawn. He stroked her, kissed her, tasted every inch of her, until she was sobbing his name and he was gripping the material of the tent so hard he thought he would rip a piece out of it. When he could no longer control his body, when every inch of him was in an aching, throbbing agony of need, he finally eased into her.

She arched her back and met him in the air, but he refused to let himself go and moved inside her slowly and deliberately. He wanted this to last forever, but when she suddenly cried out his name and convulsed around him, his control snapped.

Feeling her delicate contractions caress him intimately wrung a hoarse cry from him, and he wrapped his arms around her and held her against him. He drove into her frantically, wanting to bury himself inside her so deeply that she would never be able to release him. Dimly he was aware that she had wrapped her legs around him in an attempt to draw him closer.

He was swept over the edge of the abyss and fell through the air, holding on to her, crying her name. He felt shudders racking him, and he wasn't sure if they were his or hers. As he slowly settled to the earth again, he realized that she was holding him every bit as tightly as he held her. When he lifted his head to brush a kiss along her cheek, he tasted the salty trail of her tears.

Lifting himself above her with an effort, he stared down at her, trying to see her clearly in the too-dim light. "What's wrong? Did I hurt you, Lex?" he whispered.

She shook her head slowly and opened her eyes. He knew she was smiling. "Nothing's wrong. Just the opposite, in fact." She pulled him down to her again. "Don't tell me we have to go now. I want to hold you for a little while longer."

He rolled over, holding her close, until he was lying on his back and she was nestled against him. "I couldn't get up now if I wanted to."

He swept his hand down her back until it rested on her hip, and he told himself they could lie like this for a few minutes. As her lips brushed his neck, he inhaled her soft scent and closed his eyes. For a few minutes, he could savor her.

Caine awoke abruptly when he heard the noise. Although it came from far in the distance, his whole body tensed as he struggled to identify it. As it got closer, he realized with a jolt of icy fear that it was the same sound they'd heard yesterday—the coarse whop-whop of helicopter blades.

Lexie raised her head from his chest and looked at him with half-opened eyes. "What is it?" she whispered.

As he stared at her, the fear congealed in his gut. He shouldn't be able to see her this clearly in the tent. The next second he realized why. It was daylight. Dawn had long since passed, and the gloomy light of the jungle floor by day had filled their tent.

"Damn it!" He slid Lexie aside and ripped open the zippered door. Poking his head out, he saw by the position of the sun that it had been light for at least two hours, maybe more. And the helicopter was getting closer.

Lexie had picked up the baby and sat with her back to him, nursing. Momentary tenderness flooded him when he realized she was shy about sitting naked in front of him, even after what had happened between them during the night. Then, forcing those distracting thoughts out of his mind, he zipped the tent again and reached for his clothes.

"The helicopter's back," he said, in what he hoped was a matter-of-fact voice. There was no reason to alarm her unnecessarily. "Once it's gone, we'll get dressed and leave."

She turned and looked at him over her shoulder. He could see the fear she tried to hide, and it made him want to reach out and pull her into his arms. "Will they be able to see the tent?"

"I don't think so." He prayed it was the truth. "It should blend in with the trees and bushes. As long as we don't move out of it, we'll be fine."

She watched him for a moment, as if trying to decide whether or not he was telling her the truth, then she nodded. "I'll finish with Ana as fast as I can."

The helicopter seemed to linger in the air above them for longer than it had yesterday, but Caine told himself it was just his imagination. And his nerves. Lexie's head was bent low over the baby, and he could hear her murmured words of reassurance to the kid. He wished he felt half as confident as she sounded.

Finally the helicopter's noise began to fade, and he eased out a long breath. "Get ready to leave," he said as he unzipped the tent. "We'll have breakfast after we've gotten away from here."

"We'll be ready in five minutes," she answered.

Out of the corner of his eye he saw a flash of white, and he turned to see her fastening her bra. Desire stirred through him again, shocking him with its intensity when he should be thinking only about how to get the three of them to safety. Pushing his way out of the tent, he moved to gather their packs as he tried to push the memory of her soft, naked skin out of his mind.

A few minutes later she crawled out of the tent, holding the baby in one hand and a wad of white material in the other. Her face was as white as the cloth she held, and she looked at him with stricken eyes.

"What's wrong?" He dropped the pack he was holding and grabbed her upper arms. "What happened, Lexie?"

"Oh, Caine." She bit her lip and turned away, but not before he saw her lip trembling. "I'm so sorry."

"Sorry about what, Lex? What happened?"

Slowly she turned back to face him. "Remember those diapers I washed in the river yesterday? I hung them over a bush to dry, and I never went back to get them. They're still there."

"Still there?" he repeated stupidly, feeling sudden panic twist his gut. "The diapers are still draped over that bush by the river?"

She nodded. "I figured I could leave them until we left this morning and give them plenty of time to dry." Her mouth trembled again, with fear, and she bit down on her lip. "I didn't think about the helicopter coming back."

"I thought we'd be gone by now." He looked over at the tent again, and memories of what had delayed them swirled around him. When he looked over at her, he saw that she understood what he was thinking.

Fear and regret filled her face. "We should have been. I'm sorry, Caine," she whispered.

In two steps he was in front of her. "Don't ever say that." His voice was fierce. "There were two of us in that tent. Hell, blame me if you need to blame someone. I should have known better. But don't tell me you're sorry."

"I'm not sorry it happened, Caine. Don't ever think that. But if I hadn't fallen back asleep..." Her voice trailed off as she gestured around. "If I had been thinking, this wouldn't have happened."

"I wasn't thinking, either," he said gently. "Now, let's get those diapers and get out of here."

She looked at him for a moment, as if seeking reassurance that their slip wasn't too serious, and he bent down and kissed her, hard and quick. Then he turned away and reached for the tent. He was frantic to put some distance between them and this spot, but he couldn't force himself to tell Lexie his fears. She had enough to worry about.

By the time he had taken down the tent and rolled it up, she had the baby settled in the shawl and her pack hanging on her back. She was just leaving the clearing when he noticed what she was doing.

"Where are you going?"

"To get the diapers, of course. Where else would I be going?"

"Wait a minute and I'll go with you. We'll get them on our way."

She waited patiently while he shoved the tent into his pack and swung it onto his back. Then he stepped to the edge of the little clearing and examined it with a critical eye. He had no doubt that El Cuchillo's men would be here soon, and he wanted to make sure there was no trace of their presence.

He spotted the little mound of earth and dead leaves where they'd buried the remains of the agouti they'd eaten yesterday. Digging it up, he flung the bones and pelt as far into the jungle as he could. Then he filled the hole, being careful to smooth it over with his foot so the ground looked undisturbed. When he looked up, Lexie was watching him with a frightened expression on her face.

"You think they're going to come here looking for us, don't you?" she whispered.

"They might," he said evenly. "I think they'll have a hard time getting here, but we can't take any chances. I don't want to leave any evidence that we were here."

"I never would have thought of that," she said, gesturing to the spot where he'd dug up the bones. "What have you been through, to think that way?" Her face looked stricken.

"This is what I do, Lexie," he said, trying not to frighten her. "I was trained to think this way." He looked around one more time to make sure he'd taken care of everything, then looked back at her. "Let's go."

He led the way down to the river, and he could feel her right behind him. When they got to the place where she'd washed the diapers, he saw they were still draped over one of the bushes, bright white in the early-morning sun. They would have stood out like beacons of light against the dark green of the jungle and the brown of the river.

Instinctively he scanned the horizon. He heard nothing but the normal jungle sounds. He couldn't see far over the canopy of trees, but nothing appeared out of place. But if his gut feeling about this El Cuchillo character was right, and he wanted Lexie as badly as Caine thought he did, that wouldn't last for long. They needed to put as much distance between themselves and this place as they could.

"Turn around," he told Lexie as he grabbed the diapers off the bush. "I'll stick these in your pack for you."

"Do you think we should leave a couple, to make them think they didn't have anything to do with us?" she asked.

He stared at her, surprised and impressed by her suggestion. "I hadn't thought of that," he said slowly. "It might not be a bad idea. If they flew over here and saw the white spots again, they might assume it was flowers or something else that belonged here."

She nodded, some hope creeping back into her face. "That's what I thought."

He stared at the last two diapers, still lying on top of the bush, and finally shook his head. "We can't take the chance. I'm tempted, but I don't know enough about this guy to assess what his reaction would be. Maybe he would assume that it didn't mean anything and go away, but maybe he would try to get a better look. If he got close enough to see they were diapers, then he'd know for sure we'd been here. No." He grabbed the last two diapers from the bush and shoved them into her pack. "We have to take them. Hey," he said, turning her around and forcing a smile onto his face, "this guy may not remember where he saw them. From the air, everything in the jungle looks the same."

"But we can't take that chance, can we?" she asked in a low voice.

The smile faded from his face. "No, we can't. So let's go."

Three hours later they staggered to a stop and threw themselves onto the ground between the buttresses at the base of a huge tree. Lexie glanced over at Caine, who for once looked as tired as she felt. "Thank you for stopping," she said, reaching into the shawl to remove Ana. "I wasn't looking forward to feeding her while we walked."

"We've come a long way in three hours." He spoke without opening his eyes. "And there's been no sign of anyone looking for us. I think we're safe for now."

Lexie opened her shirt and began to nurse Ana, glad that Caine's eyes were still closed and telling herself that she was being ridiculous for feeling that way. After what had happened between them the night before, she certainly had no physical secrets from him.

Except that last night they couldn't see anything. All the knowledge they had about each other had been gained only through touching, smelling and tasting. Her cheeks warmed as she thought about all the exploring she'd done. Her fingertips knew every part of him intimately, and she knew that his fingers held the same knowledge of her. But it wasn't the same as sitting in front of him half-naked in the light of day.

He would avoid looking at her if he could, a tiny, bitter voice reminded her. He always did while she was nursing Ana. Lexie looked at the small head covered with red down and felt the pain well up again—pain that she had managed to banish from her mind during those hours with Caine. It didn't matter that she had found something rare and wonderful last night with him. If he couldn't accept Ana, and love her unconditionally, they had no future.

"I'm going to fix breakfast," he said, breaking into her thoughts.

"Can we afford to take the time?" She glanced around nervously. "Wouldn't it be better if we kept going?"

"Probably. But we both need to eat to do that. And we're getting to the hottest part of the day. We might as well stop now."

"I didn't know there was a hottest part of the day in here," she muttered, buttoning her shirt. Laying Ana on her shawl on the ground, she stood, trying to find even a slight breeze.

"I figured you'd be used to the jungle by now." Caine looked up from the tiny fire he'd started, a small grin on his face. "After ten months of San Rafael, I thought you'd be as adapted as a native San Rafaelite."

"I didn't live down here in the swamps," she retorted. "It never got this hot up in the mountains."

"Surely you must have visited the rain forest, though." He stopped working on the fire and turned to look at her. "At least you had to pass through it to get up into the mountains."

"I passed through what the tourists see. I visited the national parks, where all the buildings that give you information about the rain forest are air-conditioned. Then I drove down paved roads, in my air-conditioned car, to look at the sights. That was it."

He rocked back on his heels and stared at her. "Come on, Lexie. Are you telling me that once you got to Santa Ysabel you never left?"

Shrugging, she sat back down next to Ana. "Once I got there, I was too sick to go anywhere for a while. And when I started feeling better, I was too busy working."

He continued to stare at her, then to her surprise he left the pan of water heating on the fire and came over to sit next to her. "You were sick because you were pregnant, weren't you?"

Slowly she looked at him. "Yes."

"Tell me what it was like, being pregnant."

Shocked by his request, she stared at him. Finally she said, "Are you sure you want to know? Up until now, you've been doing your best to avoid knowing anything."

He nodded. "If it happened to you, I want to know," he said simply.

Looking down at Ana, who was wide-awake and watching her, she chose her words carefully. "I was pretty sick for the first three months. I couldn't eat anything except rice for a long time." She stared down at Ana, remembering those frightening days. Forcing herself to smile, she continued, "Fortunately, there was no shortage of rice in Santa Ysabel."

"Why did you stay in that primitive village, Lexie? You can afford the best medical care in the world."

It sounded as if the words were torn out of him, and she looked at him in surprise. "All a doctor would have done is pat my hand and tell me it was all in my head. There's nothing anyone can do for morning sickness except get through it. At least Maria and Angelita understood what was wrong." She watched him for a moment. "Why are you so upset about it, Caine? It's a normal part of pregnancy."

"You shouldn't have had to suffer through it alone," he muttered. "You should have had friends around you, people who cared about you."

"I did," she answered gently. "Angelita and Maria are the best friends I've ever had."

"I should have been there, dammit." The words were almost whispered, and his voice was filled with anguish.

For just a moment she opened her mouth to agree with him, to tell him that all she'd dreamed about during those frightening months had been his return. Then she slowly closed her mouth, biting her lip. He had been the one to leave without a word to her. Just because he felt guilty now, after hearing about the first miserable months she'd spent in Santa Ysabel, didn't change anything. She didn't want his guilt. She wanted—

She stopped, shocked. She'd been about to say she wanted his love, but that wasn't possible. Caine was exactly the kind of man she'd been trying to escape her whole life—a man like her father. It had taken her twenty-six years to break free of him, and she wasn't about to hand control of her life over to another man who was cast from the same mold. She had to make that clear.

"But you weren't there, Caine." A niggling inner voice told her that she was being unfair. He hadn't known about her pregnancy because she hadn't told him. But then, she thought sadly, she wouldn't have been able to tell him even if she'd wanted to. She'd had no idea where he was.

Even now, thinking about it was like having someone thrust a knife into her heart. Refusing to give in to the pain, she looked over to where the water was just beginning to boil. She had other things to worry about right now, anyway. Like staying alive long enough to have the luxury to think about the kind of man Caine was.

"Shouldn't we be cooking the food?" She couldn't believe how calm and cool her voice sounded. She'd been afraid all her inner turmoil would be reflected in the words she spoke.

Caine looked over at the small fire, then leaned over and grabbed two pouches of dehydrated food. "Yeah. As much as I'd like to let you rest for a while, I think we'd be better off covering more ground this afternoon."

He didn't sound like a man who was agonizing over the fact that he'd abandoned the woman who was pregnant with his child, she told herself brutally. And she wasn't about to agonize over him, either. Glancing at Ana one more time and seeing that she was still content on the shawl, Lexie reached into his pack and brought out the aluminum pans and silverware. She could be as casual about this as he was.

By the time they'd finished their quick meal, sweat poured down her back and matted her hair to her head. Eating warm food hadn't helped her body adjust to the hot, humid conditions in the rain forest. Wiping the sweat from her forehead, she watched Caine destroy the evidence of their small fire and wondered where she was going to get the energy to keep walking.

She stood, struggling to tie the shawl around her neck, and she felt Caine's hands on her shoulders. "Turn around," he said. "I'll do it for you."

"You don't have to," she replied, her voice stiff. "I can get it."

"I know you can, Lexie, but you don't have to. I can do it for you." He sounded infinitely patient, as if he'd read her mind and was determined to convince her that he hadn't dismissed her from his thoughts.

"I can manage on my own, Caine." Her words were hard and brittle, and his hands stilled for a moment as they tied a knot in the shawl at the back of her neck. Then, with what felt like a lingering caress, he stepped back and slid her pack onto her shoulders.

"I know you can manage on your own, Lexie." As she turned to face him, she saw the pain in his eyes that he hid a fraction of a second too late. "You've managed a lot of things on your own lately that you shouldn't have had to. But the rest of this trip isn't going to be a picnic, and we'll need each other to make it. You'll need me, and I'll need you."

He glanced at Ana, once again resting in the shawl, and his eyes were unreadable. "In fact, why don't you let me take her for a while?"

She shook her head too quickly. "She's fine." When she saw the hurt momentarily flash in his eyes, guilt stabbed at her. "All right," she said, her voice abrupt. "I guess it would help if you carried her."

Lexie watched as he rearranged the packs on his back, then took Ana from her and tied the shawl around his neck. Before he started forward, he looked over his shoulder at her. "Thank you," he said quietly. "We can't afford for either of us to get too tired." As he spoke, she saw his hand linger over Ana, lying against his chest. Without another word he headed into the jungle again.

She stared after him for a moment, her heart twisting in her chest. How had they gotten to this, after the magic of the previous night? What had happened to open up this chasm between them?

She was as much to blame as he was, she admitted, following behind him. More, probably. She was the one who couldn't let go of the past, who couldn't forget her fear and terror when she'd found out that she was going to have a baby, alone, in a foreign country. His questions about her pregnancy had stirred all those old fears.

Caine was right. If they were going to survive this trek through the jungle and the cat-and-mouse game they were playing with El Cuchillo and his men, she was going to have to forget about the past—at least temporarily. And she could do it.

She looked ahead at Ana, swaying gently against Caine's chest. She had the best reason in the world right in front of her.

They didn't stop again until the sun hung low in the sky and Lexie was almost dizzy from the heat and hunger. Every inch of her clothing was soaked with sweat, and the pack and Ana's shawl were beginning to chafe her skin. She had taken Ana back the first time she had to be nursed, letting the baby eat as they walked. She'd nursed her twice more without stopping and changed her diaper three times, stumbling along each time until Caine had waited for the minute it had taken to get the baby clean and dry again.

When he stopped in front of her now, she almost walked right into him. She had passed tired long ago, and was almost beyond exhaustion. Reaching out to steady her, he looked down at her with unreadable eyes.

"There's another river coming up, a big one, and I think we should stop here for the night. We need to eat something before it gets any darker, and I don't think we're up to getting across that river right now."

She licked her lips, which felt dry in spite of the humidity that hung in the air. "Are you sure it's safe? Are you sure we've gone far enough?"

His eyes softened. "We've walked a long way today. If I'm reading this map correctly, we should get to Limores sometime tomorrow."

She closed her eyes as relief flooded her. "Thank goodness. I'm not sure how much farther I can walk."

"You can walk as far as you have to, Lexie."

At the odd note in his voice she opened her eyes. The way he was looking at her made the color creep up her neck, and she knew it wasn't from the heat that surrounded them.

"Why are you looking at me like that?" she whispered.

He never took his eyes off her. "How am I looking at you?"

"Like...like..." She shrugged and turned away. "Like I've done something special, or something."

"Because you have," he whispered again. "I've worked with men who were trained to do this who couldn't have kept up the pace you did today. You're all heart, Lex. All heart and courage, and I'll die myself before I let anyone capture you."

Slowly she turned to face him. The sun shone low through the trees, and one beam of sunlight surrounded his head. His dark blond hair, matted to his head with sweat, seemed to pulse with life. The light softened the hard features of his face, and for a moment his eyes glowed with an emotion that made her breath catch in her chest.

Then the shutters came down again, and he turned abruptly away. "Why don't you rest for a while and I'll find something to eat." Without waiting for her answer, he slipped past some trailing liana vines and disappeared.

Sliding the pack off her back, she looked around. They had stopped in another small clearing, this one scarcely bigger than a closet. Towering trees soared above her, the canopy of their leaves so dense that even at high noon no sunlight would penetrate to this small patch of ground. That was good, she told herself. That meant that no one in a helicopter would be able to see them, either.

Quickly she woke Ana and nursed her before Caine returned. She told herself it was so she would be free to help him fix dinner, but she knew the real reason was his continuing reluctance to show any interest in Ana. It was just too painful to see him try to look anywhere but at the baby while she was nursing.

By the time he returned carrying another agouti and some small red fruits, she had finished feeding Ana and changed her diaper. Ana was once again content to lie on her shawl and watch the trees above them, and Lexie said a prayer of thanks for her baby's easygoing disposition the last few days. Easygoing as long as she was fed on time, she corrected herself, looking over at her daughter and feeling herself smiling. Ana always seemed to do that to her.

"I didn't start a fire," Lexie apologized, looking over at Caine. "I fed Ana instead."

"Just as well." He laid the agouti and the fruits on the ground, and began to gather what he needed. "I don't want to make any more sounds than we have to."

"Why don't I go and fill the canteens and clean her diapers before we eat? She'll be fine there for a while."

"All right." He didn't look up from the fire he was coaxing to life from a small pile of dead leaves and branches. "Take the water purifier, though, and purify the water before you put it in the canteen."

"Uh, do you want to show me how to do that?"

He looked at her and gave her a rueful smile. "I forgot you don't know how a lot of this works." Reaching into his pack, he pulled out a long narrow tube and handed it to her. "Fill up a pan with water first, then pour it into this tube. Let it run from the tube into the canteen. That's all there is to it."

He flashed her a quick grin that took her breath away. "And purify the water before you clean the diapers."

"Aye, aye, captain," she said, saluting, but she did it with a grin. The smile slowly left his face and his eyes turned dark and smoky as she stood. She could feel his gaze on her as she left the clearing and walked toward the river, following his careful directions.

When she reached the bank of the river she stopped, awestruck. Sunlight shimmered off the water, reflecting back into her face, and she shaded her eyes as she looked out over the broad expanse of the river. The wide ribbon of brown seemed to be moving sluggishly, and she thought longingly of how good the water would feel against her hot, sticky skin. But it would be stupid to go in without Caine nearby, so she squatted down at the river's edge with a sigh. If they finished dinner before it got dark, maybe she could take a bath later.

Setting the diapers wrapped in the huge, rubbery green leaves carefully on a rock, she bent over and dipped out a panful of water. She poured it into the purification tube, and watched as it ran down through the layers of what looked like dirt and grit and began to trickle out the bottom. Holding the canteen to the bottom of the tube, she listened with satisfaction as she heard the water pinging against the bottom of the canteen.

It took two pans of water to fill one canteen. She'd filled two of them and was working on the third when she bent over the river to dip out another pan of water. Just as she was leaning out over the water, her arm extended, something screeched in her ear.

Startled, she looked around in time to see a flash of blue and yellow as a macaw swooped past her. The sudden movement threw her off-balance, and as she struggled to right herself she felt herself falling toward the water. The next instant she felt herself go under, and as she kicked frantically to reach the surface, something grabbed her leg. Then the current caught her, and she was sucked below the surface of the muddy, brown water.

Chapter 12

Just when her lungs felt as if they would burst, her head broke free of the water. Gasping for breath, she tugged at whatever had caught her leg, but it wouldn't give. She tried to reach for one of the bushes at the edge of the river, but the current was frighteningly strong. It pulled her inexorably away from the bank, and only the grip on her leg kept her from being swept down river.

"Caine," she called, but she knew her voice was too weak to reach him. Coughing and sputtering as the current pulled her under again, she sucked in a deep breath as soon as she surfaced and shouted desperately, "Caine!"

The current swung her around suddenly and slammed her into a rock hidden beneath the surface of the river. A scream was torn from her throat, and she barely got her mouth closed in time as she was sucked underwater once more. She smashed into the rock again as she struggled to reach the surface. When her head broke free she saw their canteens and the water-purification tube sitting peacefully on the rock where she'd left them just moments ago, but there was no sign of Caine. Battling the panic and the water, she was fighting to stay afloat when she was pulled under again.

Caine looked up sharply from the fire that was just beginning to glow red underneath the leaves. He'd heard something other than the normal jungle sounds, and he sat still as a stone, straining to identify it. When it came again, a little stronger than before, he felt the hair rise on the back of his neck. He couldn't make out the words, but it sounded like Lexie's voice.

Pausing only long enough to grab the baby, he bolted toward the river. When he got there, he saw the canteens and the water tube sitting on a rock, but there was no sign of Lexie. Setting the baby down, he frantically scanned the riverbank, wondering why she might have wandered off.

Something splashed in the water in front of him. His gut clenched into a giant fist as he saw Lexie breaking the surface of the muddy water in front of him, and thrashing weakly.

"Lexie!"

She opened her eyes and he saw a spark of hope leap into them. "I'm caught," she gasped. "My foot."

Throwing himself down on the edge of the river, he stretched out for her hand. "Can you reach me?" He forced himself to keep his voice calm and steady.

She struggled against the current that tried to pull her away, but he could see she was getting weaker. "A few more inches, Lex," he coaxed, trying to keep the desperation out of his voice. "Come on, you can do it."

He strained to reach her, pushing himself even farther off the bank until he was in danger of falling in with her. Water swirled around her, tugging at her with invisible fingers, trying to pry her loose from whatever held her trapped. He could see her fight against it, trying to push her way through the muddy brown water to reach his hand.

Easing himself farther off the bank, he suddenly lunged toward her. He saw the exhaustion in her face, knew she couldn't stay afloat much longer. And he was afraid that if he went in after her, they would both be swept down the river.

His hand brushed her fingertips for one agonizing second, then she was wrenched away from him as if by a giant, invisible hand. He was going to lose her. Frantically he looked around, searching for a stick or a vine lying on the ground.

Something protruded from underneath a bush, and he scrambled over to yank it out. It was a piece of dead vine barely two feet long, dry and brittle. He refused to think about the fact that it might not work.

Throwing himself back on the bank of the river, he held the vine out to Lexie. "Grab on to this!" he shouted, and said a prayer of thanks as her fingers closed around the dry, dusty vine. Slowly he began to pull her closer, mentally willing the rotting branch to stay intact.

As she drew within reach of his hand, he heard the vine rustling and crackling and knew that it was falling apart. He lunged off the bank, managing to grab her wrist just as the piece of vine disintegrated in his hand. Fear washed over her face, and he stretched out to extend his other hand to her. "I've got you, Lexie," he said in a soothing voice. "Just grab on and I'll pull you in."

He could see the huge effort it took for her to reach out and take hold of his other hand. He had to get her out of the water before the last reserves of her energy were used up. Glancing backward, he managed to hook one foot around the base of a jungle plant as he began to slowly pull her toward him.

Whatever had hold of her leg didn't want to give it up, but he pulled slowly and steadily until she was half lying on the bank of the river. Then he let her go, and as she lay gasping and coughing on the rocks, he reached into the water to see what held her foot.

It was a vine, made tough and inflexible by its immersion in the water. Pulling his knife from its sheath in his boot, he hacked at the stubborn strands until the last of them finally separated and he pulled her foot free.

She had turned her head to watch him, and when he closed the knife and slid it back into his pocket, she rolled over onto her back and shut her eyes.

"Thank you," she whispered. She lay on the river's edge, one foot still submerged, small rivulets of brown water running from her body like tiny streams etching a path in the mud.

He reached out and touched her soaking-wet hair, stroking it tentatively. "Lexie, look at me."

She opened her eyes slowly and tried to smile at him. "Don't worry, I'm still alive."

Cupping her face in his hand, he studied her, as if her face, pale and white beneath the dirt from the river, could tell him how badly she'd been injured. "Did you swallow a lot of the water?"

"I don't think so." Her voice came out as a harsh rasp. "I tried to keep my mouth shut."

He swept his hands down her body until he reached the foot that had been trapped in the vine. Staring at it for a moment, he finally reached out to touch it, afraid of what he might find. "How about your foot?" he managed to ask in a normal voice. "Did you hurt it when you were thrashing around?"

Experimentally she moved the ankle joint, first sideways, then back and forth. She shook her head. "It feels okay. A little sore, but I don't think anything's damaged."

"Anything hurt anywhere else?"

He could see her gather her strength, and before he could tell her to lie still, she tried to sit up. Wincing, she managed to make it, but she reached around to massage her back. "There were some rocks under the water. I must have hurt my back on them."

"Let me see." He pulled her blouse up. Several red welts crisscrossed her back, and he suspected that by the morning they would be livid bruises. Gently lowering her shirt, he said matter-of-factly, "Looks like you're right. That must have been quite a ride."

She nodded, then began to shake. Turning blindly, she reached out for him and buried her head in his shoulder. "I thought I was going to die, Caine." Her hands trembled where they gripped his shirt, and convulsive shudders racked her body. "I was so scared."

He drew her into his arms and held her close. "It's okay to be scared, Lex. It's all over now and you're going to be fine. It's okay." He stroked her back and held her close, trying to keep his eyes closed. Calling himself a perverted jerk, he tried to ignore the fact that he could see her bra, see the dark outline of her nipples through the wet material. He forced himself to keep his touch comforting, when he ached to reach out for her, to turn her fear-induced shudders into the trembling of passion.

Shifting slightly so she wouldn't feel his reaction to her, he reached up and smoothed her hair away from her face. He was disgusted to notice that his hand was shaking, too. There hadn't been many times when he'd sat with a woman and tried to comfort her. Hell, there hadn't been many times when he'd *wanted* to. But he wanted to now, and he was determined to do it right.

Before he could control his body's reaction to having Lexie in his arms, she stirred and looked up at him. "Kiss me, Caine," she whispered. "I need to taste you, to feel you."

Bending down, he lightly brushed his lips over hers in a fleeting caress, then tucked her head into his shoulder again. She struggled to free herself. "That's not what I meant. I want you to kiss me, Caine, really kiss me. Like you did last night."

He stared at her, cursing his body's throbbing reaction to her words and trying desperately to control himself. She stared back, and the embers of desire he saw smoldering in the depths of her dark blue eyes made him groan. "Lexie, I'm trying to do the right thing, here. You need to be comforted and taken care of, not kissed senseless."

Her gaze softened, and for a moment her eyes lit with a deep tenderness. Then she slowly pulled his head down to hers and took his mouth.

The hunger he could feel in her fueled his own desire, and he felt all his self-imposed barriers crumbling. When her lips opened slightly beneath his, he groaned and swept his tongue into her mouth.

Weaving his hands through her hair, he held her close as he tasted the dark sweetness of her. She shifted in his arms, pressing closer to him, and he groaned again as her rump brushed against him.

He let his hand slide down her neck until it lay against the wet fabric of her blouse. As his fingers splayed over her chest, he could feel her skin warming under his hand. Finally, unable to resist for another second, he slowly reached for the buttons on her blouse and undid them, one by one.

She shuddered when he brushed the damp material aside and cupped one lush breast in his hand. When he slid his fingers inside her bra, she arched against his hand and murmured something, deep in her throat.

The small sound was enough to push him over the edge. Lowering her to the ground, he began to pull the blouse off her shoulders. He'd managed to get it half off her when he realized she was wincing in pain.

His hands stilled immediately as desire left his body with a rush. "Oh, God, Lex, I'm sorry," he whispered, appalled at himself. "I forgot all about your back."

She smiled up at him. "It's all right. I did, too."

She reached for him, but he gathered both her hands into his and brought them to his lips. Lingering over them, inhaling her scent, which somehow managed to overpower the smell of the river, he finally looked down at her and bent to kiss her lips.

"I'm going to carry you back to the clearing," he said. "You need to rest and eat something, then go to sleep. As much as I don't want to stop, you don't need to make love on the rocky edge of the river."

She opened her mouth to answer him, but he put his fingers on her lips. "You've just been through a dangerous experience, Lexie. It's normal to want to reassure yourself that you're alive afterward, and sex is a good way of doing that."

She stared at him for a moment, then finally she smiled. The tenderness in her gaze made him yearn for something that he knew he would never have, and he had to close his eyes to stop himself from reaching for her.

"You're wrong, you know," she said, and her voice was soft and low. "I wasn't trying to reassure myself that I was alive. I know that very well. I was trying to reassure myself that I hadn't lost you."

He was swept by a need so profound and deep that he knew if he looked at her he would blurt it out. He wanted to hold her close, tell her that she could never lose him because he belonged to her, heart and soul. But he kept his eyes closed and clamped his mouth shut, because he knew it could never be.

After a few minutes he heard her stirring, and he reluctantly opened his eyes. She'd seen the baby lying on her shawl not far from the river, and she was trying to reach her.

"The kid is fine," he told Lexie, scooping her up into his arms. "I'll take you back, then come for her."

"No," she said sharply. "I don't want to leave her down here alone. Put her into my arms and I'll carry her back with us."

He did as she asked, then carried her the short distance to the clearing. It was getting late, but it was still light enough to make a fire without the smoke betraying their position. Setting Lexie and the baby down next to the trunk of a huge tree, he tried to concentrate on getting dinner fixed.

By the time the agouti was ready and the hot water had been poured into the pouches of dehydrated food, Lexie was sound asleep. The baby was still lying on her lap, her head supported by one of Lexie's arms, but she looked damned precarious. He stared at the two of them, wondering what to do. He needed to wake Lexie for dinner, but he was afraid that if he startled her, the kid would roll off her lap onto the ground.

Finally, gritting his teeth, he picked up the baby and looked around for the shawl. When it was nowhere in sight, he realized he must have left it down at the river. Holding the baby in the crook of one arm, just the way Lexie had done, he started to walk down toward the water.

He remembered too vividly the first time he'd held the kid. The memory of her smiles still stabbed at him whenever he thought about it, piercing him with a sharp, deep pain that penetrated to his soul. It didn't mean anything, he told himself. A kid this age would probably smile at anyone. Still, as they walked through the jungle, he couldn't stop himself from glancing down at her again.

She was looking around, and if he didn't know better he would say she was cataloging everything she saw. Her serious gaze drifted from the trees to the vines, then fixed on the enormous flowers that seemed to grow right out of the trunks of the trees.

"Pretty impressive, aren't they?" he heard himself say to her. As soon as the words were out of his mouth he called himself a fool for talking to a baby, but to his surprise she looked up at him, apparently startled by the sound of his voice. As she stared at him, her mouth curled up into a smile, and while he watched, fascinated, she began to wriggle in the whole-body grin he was beginning to recognize.

"Hey, do I look like a comedian?" he growled down at her. To his delight, she opened her mouth and a noise that sounded suspiciously like a giggle emerged. Her arms and legs whirled like four little windmills and her grin threatened to split her face.

"Shows what you know," he muttered, feeling a fist reach out and smash into his heart. He knew better than to let this tiny baby sneak in under his defenses. He had nothing to give her except heartache. But he had no choice tonight, he told himself. Lexie needed to rest, to recuperate from her near drowning. There was no one but him to take care of the kid. Just because he held her for a few hours and talked to her didn't mean he was tied to her for life.

Scooping up the shawl from the place he'd left it earlier, he draped it over his shoulder and headed back to the clearing. Every time he looked down at the kid he found her studying him, and even though he warned himself to ignore it, he felt his heart soften each time he caught her eye and she smiled.

No wonder parents were so loopy about their kids, he thought, catching her eye again and feeling himself smiling back at her. They were damned close to impossible to resist.

He set the shawl on the ground and gently laid the baby on top of it, then touched Lexie lightly on the shoulder. "Time to wake up, honey. You have to eat something."

She opened her eyes and stared at him. He could see the effort it took for her to focus on him. "Ana?" she asked groggily.

"Right next to you. She's fine."

Pushing herself into a more upright position, she looked around at the lengthening shadows in the clearing. "How long was I asleep?"

"Not long enough. While you're eating I'm going to put up the tent so you can go right to sleep."

"I have to take care of Ana."

"Feed her, then let me take care of the rest. What else is there, anyway?"

She looked up at him quickly, and an odd expression flared in her eyes. "I have to change her diaper, for one thing, and clean her up. She's sweating so much that she'll get a rash if I'm not careful."

"I'll take care of it," he repeated, wondering how on earth to change a diaper.

"Are you sure?" She looked at him doubtfully, but she could barely keep her eyes open.

"Positive. How tough can it be to change a diaper and clean a kid?"

It wasn't tough at all, he realized a while later. Lexie had finished eating and then fed the baby. She'd barely had enough strength to hold the kid up, and when she'd finished and laid the baby back down on the shawl, Caine had picked her up and carried her into the tent.

"Go to sleep," he told to her. "I'll take care of everything."

She murmured something about diapers and her backpack, but she was asleep before she'd finished. Caine backed out of the tent and looked over to where the kid lay on the shawl.

Not just a kid, he reminded himself. *His* kid. His heart twisted at the thought, leaving him with an ache in his chest. He stared at her for another moment, then looked around for Lexie's backpack.

Rummaging inside it, he brushed against a flat object as his hand closed around what he presumed was a clean diaper. As he pulled the diaper out of the bag, the package shifted again and his hand stilled. It had to be the packet of pictures that Lexie had insisted he get from her house, the pictures of the baby as a newborn.

He hesitated, his fingers touching the cool paper, then slowly withdrew his hand. Looking at those pictures was just asking for trouble. He didn't need to see what his daughter looked like when she was born. He could see her now just fine. How much could a kid change in two months, anyway?

Pulling Lexie's pack shut with a snap, he turned to the baby. There was still some water left from dinner, and by now it had cooled to the temperature of bathwater. Gently he unwrapped her diaper, being careful to notice how it was put together. Then he pulled her shirt over her head.

She looked so small and defenseless, lying naked on the shawl in front of him. Her legs and arms continued to wave around, but without her clothes he could see how tiny and fragile she really was.

A fierce surge of protectiveness swept over him. He had never really thought about her as an entity separate from Lexie before—she was always just a package that came with her mother, something extra to worry about. Now he looked at her and saw an individual; a miniature human being who, for some reason, had decided that she trusted him.

He watched her as he dampened one of his T-shirts and carefully wiped her down. Her eyes widened in surprise at the feel of the water, and she tensed for a second. Then, as if she recognized the sensation, she relaxed again. When he looked at her face, she gave him another hundred-watt smile.

Rocking back on his heels, he just stared at her. It couldn't happen, he told himself desperately. He couldn't be a father to this child. It would just bring sorrow and heartache down on her. His ex-wife had been so certain of it that she'd—

He shut his mind down, refusing to think about the past. Even without those memories, he knew damn well he wasn't father material. He had no idea what a father was supposed to do. All he knew was what they *weren't* supposed to do; and that couldn't ever be enough.

He quickly finished cleaning the baby and wrapped a fresh diaper around her. It seemed as if it could wrap around her tiny body twice. Refusing to think about her anymore, he put her shirt back on and washed and wrung out his T-shirt. Hanging it over a bush to dry during the night, he carried the baby into the tent and laid her down next to her mother.

Stretching out beside Lexie, he pulled her body against his. There would be no repeat tonight of the passion they had shared the previous evening, but he could give her the comfort of his arms. As he snuggled her against him, his hand brushed over the baby. He froze, then slowly pulled her next to Lexie.

When he finally fell asleep, his hand was curled around Ana as he held her close to her mother.

Lexie awakened abruptly from a deep sleep to the familiar sound of Ana snuffling in the darkness. Without opening her eyes she reached out for the baby, expecting Ana to be right next to her. When she couldn't find her, she opened her eyes and struggled to sit up.

Every muscle in her back screamed in pain, and Lexie had to bite her lip to keep from crying out. She must have made some slight sound, because Caine rolled over beside her and said, "What's wrong?"

"Nothing." Taking a deep breath, she slowly eased herself upright. "I'm just a little sore, that's all. I'd forgotten about yesterday."

Swinging himself into a sitting position, he reached out for her and gently pulled her back against him. "Remember how we did this last time she woke up? Hold on and I'll get her for you."

As she relaxed against Caine's solid strength, she vaguely recalled waking up sometime during the night to feed Ana. He'd held her against him then, too. And if her mind wasn't playing tricks on her, she also remembered that he'd practically held Ana to her breast. She swallowed and looked around for the baby. Obviously she'd been too tired to pay attention to what had been going on.

Ana wasn't anywhere in sight, and as the panic started to rise, Caine's voice murmured behind her. The low, rumbling tenderness was something she'd never heard in his voice before. As she sat frozen, listening to him, he laid Ana in her arms.

"Can you hold her all right?"

"I...I think so," she managed to say. She wished desperately that there was some light in the tent. She needed to see Caine's face.

As Ana settled against her and began nursing, Lexie half twisted toward Caine. "What happened during the night?" she whispered.

In the darkness she felt his shrug. "You were sleeping like the dead. When An—the kid started to whimper, you didn't wake up, so finally I held her for you while she nursed. I think you fell asleep again before she was even finished.''

Shifting Ana to her other arm, she waited for a moment, then said, ''When I woke up this time, she wasn't next to me.''

She could feel him squirm behind her. ''Yeah,'' he finally said. ''I had her next to me. I figured you needed your sleep.''

Her throat swelled as she stared blindly down at Ana in her arms. What had happened while she slept yesterday afternoon and evening? He had almost called Ana by her name. What magic had occurred to put that note of tenderness and wonder in Caine's voice when he talked about her child? *Their child,* she reminded herself, as one tear rolled down her face and fell onto her hand.

His hands slid up her arms as she leaned against him, and slowly and gently he began to massage her shoulders. ''I bet you hurt like hell, don't you?'' he murmured into her ear.

She wanted to tell him that she'd never felt better in her life, but she knew he wasn't ready to talk about whatever was happening between him and Ana. So she said softly, ''I have had better mornings, I guess.''

His hands moved to her back, and she closed her eyes and let her aching muscles savor his touch. ''I hate to sound single-minded, but do you think you'll be able to walk this morning?'' he asked.

''Yes, I will.'' She didn't even hesitate before she answered. Her muscles might ache, but if they stayed where they were, it would be too easy for the rebel leader to track them down. Their only hope of safety was in getting to Limores.

His hands tightened on her shoulders for an instant and he bent and kissed the back of her neck. Then he released her. ''You're a hell of a woman, Lexie.''

The emotion in his voice made her shiver, but before she could answer he had unzipped the tent and crawled out into the predawn darkness. As she laid Ana down on the ground and rebuttoned her blouse, now stiff with dried mud, she heard him rustling around outside. It would take him only a few minutes to pack everything and they would be ready to leave.

Every muscle in her body seemed to shriek with pain as she tried to lift Ana into her arms. Closing her eyes, she gathered her strength and tried again. Her body protesting, she slid toward the door of the tent and wondered how she was going to stand without stumbling. .

Before she had to try, Caine was there. "Give her to me," he said, bending to take Ana from her arms. In the dim light of dawn she saw him lay the baby on her shawl, then he came back to her. "Hold on to me and pull yourself up."

She couldn't have stood any other way, and she suspected he knew it. When she was finally standing, she slowly straightened and tried to ignore the pain that shot across her back and down her legs.

"You hurt, don't you?"

Caine stood next to her, watching her with worried eyes.

"Yes, I do," she said frankly. "But I'm sure it'll get better when we start to move." She tried a weak smile. "Don't coaches always tell their players to walk it off?"

Caine looked around the clearing, then back at her. She could see the indecision in his eyes. "Maybe we could stay here for another day. By tomorrow you'll probably feel a little better."

"By tomorrow, I want to be sitting in the biggest bathtub in Limores," she answered, looking around for her pack. "We can't afford to stay here for another day, and you know it."

"We haven't seen another helicopter," he said, and she wondered which of them he was trying to convince.

Staring at him, she said softly, "Is that good or bad?"

"Dammit, Lexie, I don't want to force you to walk. I know how you must feel." He turned around abruptly and gave the string on his backpack a vicious jerk.

"You're not forcing me to do anything. I know as well as you that we have to get to Limores as fast as we can. Tell me the truth. Why do you think we haven't seen another helicopter?"

His hands stilled on the pack and he was silent for a moment. Then he stood and turned around. "I'm going to tell you straight, because you deserve to know. You're a lot tougher than I ever would have guessed. I wish to hell we had seen another helicopter. In fact, the more choppers, the better. It would have meant he wasn't sure what he saw, or that he was trying to pinpoint our location. The fact that we haven't seen or heard another one is not a good sign."

"What do you think it means?" she whispered.

"I think it means that they know exactly where we are, and they're waiting for us to come out of the jungle. I think it means that they're between us and Limores, and they know they have us trapped."

Feeling oddly detached from the fear she knew should be consuming her, she asked, "So, what do we do?"

"The only thing we can do. Get to Limores as fast as we can, and hope like hell we can think of some way to get around them, if they're waiting for us."

Bending slowly to pick up Ana, she said, "Then what are we waiting for? Let's go."

His hand on her arm stopped her. "Don't, Lexie. You're going to have a hard enough time walking today without trying to carry anything. I'll get the packs and the kid. You worry about yourself."

"You can't take everything," she protested. "You don't even have room for everything."

"Yeah, I do. Most of our food is gone, so I could put your small pack and my small pack inside the larger one. That makes one pack for my back and one kid for my chest." As he spoke he hefted the pack onto his back and then bent down for Ana.

"Are you sure?" she asked as she watched him.

"It's the only thing that makes sense." His voice was gentle. "There's no way you can carry her today. You're just too sore. This'll work fine."

He raised his hands to massage her shoulders again, and she had to stop herself from flinching. He was right. Her back was too sore to bear even the small weight of Ana, let alone her pack. "All right, let's go." She twisted to look at him. "But how are we going to get across the river?"

His mouth tightened momentarily, then he looked away from her. "While you were sleeping yesterday I found a place where the river narrows quite a bit. That's why there was such a powerful undertow. I think we can swing across on vines. Let's go give it a try."

She looked at him, horrified, but he had already started to walk, so she fell in behind him, steadfastly ignoring the pain in her back and her ankle.

It seemed like only a few minutes before they stopped at the river's edge.

She stared at the spot where he wanted to cross and swallowed hard. "You think we can swing across this?"

"I'm sure of it. It isn't as far as it looks."

He laid Ana on the ground with gentle hands, then swung his pack off. "I'm going to try it first. If I make it all right, I'll come back and get you and the kid."

"What if you don't make it?"

"Then I'll be taking a bath this morning." He flashed her a grin, then grabbed a thick vine that hung over the placid water. He might joke about taking a bath, but she knew how the currents swirled beneath that calm surface.

She held her breath as he took a running jump and sailed over to the other side of the river. He made it look easy, but her heart began to pound as she watched him return.

"I'm going to take the pack over first, then I'll take the kid. All right?"

She nodded numbly and watched as he swung easily across the river with the pack on his back. He made it look like a Huckleberry Finn type of adventure, rather than the desperate scramble for their lives that it really was.

She couldn't bear to watch as he swung across the water with Ana in his arms, and she couldn't bear to look away. He made it across in one smooth jump, and the next moment he was back, standing expectantly in front of her. "Ready?"

"Are you sure that vine will hold both of us?" she asked, staring at it as it swung gently in the air.

"Nope." He grabbed it and gave it a tug. "Would you rather go alone?"

Measuring the distance between the two shores, she finally shook her head. "I don't think I could jump that far."

"Okay, then, it looks like we're a pair. Hold on to me."

She had barely tightened her arms around his neck when he leaped into the air. The vine dipped sickeningly under their combined weight, and her toes brushed the surface of the water, but in a few seconds they were standing on the opposite bank of the river, watching the vine snap back to its original position.

He grinned at her again. "That was an invigorating way to start the morning. We'll have to do it again sometime."

"I'll put it on my list of things to do," she muttered.

Scooping up his pack, he adjusted it on his back, then picked Ana up and tied the shawl around his neck. "Ready?" he asked.

When she nodded, he said, "Let's go."

Chapter 13

Her head spinning, Lexie stumbled and barely stopped herself from falling by grabbing on to a thick vine. Sharp splinters stabbed into her palm and the muscles in her back burned with the strain of holding herself upright. It was late afternoon, and they had been walking forever. The only time they had stopped was when Ana needed to eat, and Caine had given Lexie trail mix and nuts while she nursed the baby.

Her stomach growled, but Lexie was too tired to even think about eating. All she could do was concentrate on putting one foot in front of the other. It took all her energy to block out the pain from her sore and aching body.

Spears of white-hot fire stabbed down her back with every step she took. When she tried to raise her hand to wipe away the sweat that trickled into her eyes, her shoulders tightened and the muscles knotted and throbbed. Even holding Ana to nurse was an agony.

But she knew she had no choice. The closer they got to Limores, the more acute the danger. They didn't dare stop so she could rest. And she was afraid that if they did stop, she wouldn't be able to move again.

She knew Caine was in front of her only because she could hear the dead leaves on the jungle floor crunching under his boots and the cracking of the branches he pushed out of the way. She hadn't looked up at him for a long time, let alone talked to him. She didn't dare raise her eyes from the ground. Even watching constantly, she couldn't stop herself from tripping over the smallest root or branch in her way.

Without warning she bumped into something hard and solid. As her breath whooshed out of her, she looked up and realized it was Caine. He'd stopped dead in his tracks and stood frozen, listening.

She was too numb to do anything more than stand behind him and wait until he was ready to move on. Vaguely she wondered if he'd heard another helicopter, and what it would mean. If they had to stop and hide, she wasn't sure if she would be able to stand afterward and keep moving. Only the realization that all their lives could depend on it had kept her going this long.

Caine turned abruptly and looked around. Seeing one of the huge kapok trees over to their left, he led her toward it. "I want you to stay here for a while with the kid and our pack," he said in a low voice. "I heard something ahead of us, and I need to check it out before we go any farther."

"You mean it wasn't a helicopter you heard?" she asked as she stumbled along behind him.

He shook his head. "No. I'm not sure what it was, but I don't want to take any chances." They'd reached the base of the enormous tree, and he led her into the shelter of the wide buttresses at the base of its trunk. "You need to sit down for a while, anyway, and the kid probably needs to eat. Stay here until I come back."

Then he disappeared into the jungle like a wraith. Slowly she sank to the ground, her back rubbing against the smooth bark of the tree. Caine was right. Ana would be hungry very soon, and she probably needed to be changed right now. Gathering her strength, Lexie reached for the backpack and pulled out a diaper.

* * *

Someone was shaking her shoulder and calling her name. The voice was too insistent, and she closed her eyes more tightly and willed him to disappear.

"Lexie, wake up," someone said sharply, and she dragged her eyes open and looked up into Caine's worried face.

"I am awake," she croaked. Struggling to sit up, she almost cried out loud when her muscles screamed a protest. He must have seen the pain in her face, because strong hands lifted her smoothly and a warm arm surrounded her to hold her steady.

"Where's Ana?" she cried, looking around frantically.

"Right beside you," Caine soothed. "She's sleeping, too."

Once she saw the baby, asleep on her shawl next to her leg, Lexie relaxed and looked around. The sun hung low in the trees, but there was an odd glow to the sky that made her grasp Caine's hand and sit up straighter.

"What's that?" she whispered.

"What?" He twisted around to look in the direction she was facing.

"That...that light in the sky. Is there a fire in front of us?"

His arm tightened around her, then he smiled down at her. "That's Limores. It's the light from the city being reflected into the sky," he explained.

Hope surged in her heart. "We're that close?" she whispered.

"Yeah, we are. That's the good news."

She looked over at him sharply, hope crashing and burning inside her. "What's the bad news?"

His mouth tightened, and his arm dropped away from her shoulder. "The bad news is that rebel troops have set up roadblocks on every route into the city that I can see. They're searching every car and truck that's headed there. There's no way we're going to be able to catch a ride."

The last cobwebs of sleep disappeared as she looked up at the sky. "You were gone a long time. Did you figure out another way to get there?"

He turned to stare at her, an odd expression on his face. "You sound like you're sure I have."

She looked at him, meeting his gaze and not turning away. Something moved inside her—a tenderness that slowly grew and blossomed in her heart. "I think you can do anything you want to do. If there's a way into Limores, I think you know what it is."

Something flickered in his eyes and he started to reach for her, but then he looked away. "I have an idea," he said gruffly. "I don't know if it'll work or not, but at this point I don't think we have much choice."

"What do we have to do?" she asked as she started to gather their belongings and stuff them into the pack.

"You're ready to go? Just like that, without hearing any of the details?" He sounded incredulous.

She stopped packing and looked at him. "I trust you," she said simply. "If you say this is our only chance, I believe you." She tried to smile and failed miserably. "And based on past experience, I'm quite sure that you'll tell me exactly what to do."

He reached for her and gently pulled her close. "No one has ever trusted me like that, Lexie. Ever. It's enough to make me scared spitless."

"Why?"

"Because I'm afraid I'll fail you. I'm afraid my plan won't work."

"If it doesn't work, it won't be your fault," she murmured against his shoulder. "It'll be El Cuchillo's fault. Besides—" she lifted her head and gave him a weary grin "—I thought Caine O'Roarke was invincible."

"I wish," he muttered. Slowly he lowered his head and kissed her. It was a kiss of promise, a pledge of faith. Whatever happened, she knew, he would do his best to protect her and Ana.

He stood and looked around. "We're not going anywhere until it gets dark. We might as well finish the trail mix and the nuts while we wait."

The nap she'd taken had made her feel better, she realized. She even felt hungry. Reaching into the pack, she pulled out the two bags of snacks and divided them carefully into two portions. Then she handed one to Caine and began eating the other one. After a moment, he sat down next to her and ate, too.

* * *

The moon was a sliver of light in the black sky and the sounds of the jungle surrounded them. Caine looked down at the woman who slept at his side, reluctant to wake her up. As soon as they'd finished their small meal she'd fallen asleep, and he'd sat and watched her as the sun set.

He still couldn't believe that she'd managed to walk as far as she had today. He'd seen her rubbing her back when she thought he wasn't looking, and he'd heard her stumbling behind him. He'd ached to turn around and catch her in his arms, to ease her to the ground and massage her aching muscles while she slept. But he knew he didn't dare.

Their lives depended on getting into Limores, then staying hidden until he could arrange transport out of the country. Every delay, every stop they made, gave the rebel leader more time to organize his search and tighten the noose around the city. The roadside checks Caine had seen during the day had been somewhat cursory, although more troops had arrived while he'd watched. He guessed that El Cuchillo had calculated that it would take them longer than this to reach Limores, and that he wouldn't really step up his checking until tomorrow and the next day.

With any other woman besides Lexie, it would have taken a hell of a lot longer to get here. He couldn't think of another person, man or woman, who would have kept on walking without one word of complaint after what had happened to her yesterday.

He ached as he remembered what she'd said after he'd pulled her out of the water. She'd wanted him to kiss her, not so that she could reassure herself that she was alive, but so that she could reassure herself that she hadn't lost him.

Eleven months ago, he would have given anything to hear Lexie say those words. Hell, who was he trying to fool? He wanted even more badly to believe them now. But it wasn't so simple anymore. He glanced over at the sleeping baby. She might be tiny, but she packed a hell of a wallop—one that he wasn't sure he would ever be able to deal with.

As he watched the baby sleep, he noticed that she was beginning to stir. Just as well, he told himself. He was starting to get sentimental, sitting out here in the moonlight next to Lexie. It was time they got moving, anyway.

"Wake up, Lexie," he whispered.

She woke up a lot more quickly than she had when he'd returned that afternoon. Stretching once, she opened her eyes and looked around. He saw the flash of fear, quickly controlled, when she saw it was dark. Then she looked for the baby.

"I think she's getting hungry," he murmured.

Lexie nodded. "It's time she was fed."

Caine closed his eyes as memories of the night in the tent swept over him. He remembered in vivid detail how she'd held his hands to her breasts, letting him feel their weight filled with milk. And he remembered how she'd trembled against him when he'd slipped his hands under her bra and felt her satiny-smooth skin.

All his senses were unbearably sharp. He heard the rustling of the material as she opened her blouse, heard the tiny sucking sounds the baby made as she ate. He could even smell Lexie's scent, sweet and warm, on the slight breeze.

"Caine," she said, and he turned to look at her. Even though the moon was only a small sliver in the sky, its light seemed to shine on her breasts, turning them a pearly white.

"What?" he asked hoarsely.

"Can you tell me what we have to do?"

"Do?" He stared at her breasts, able to think only about how much he needed her and how it would feel to reach out and touch her now.

"Caine?"

He tore his gaze away from her breasts and looked up at her face. Even in the dim light he could see she was blushing. "Sorry," he muttered.

"Don't be." Her voice was a whisper on the breeze. "I . . . I like it when you look at me."

He closed his eyes as fierce need almost overwhelmed him. He wanted to take her right now, to drive himself so deeply inside her that neither of them would know where he ended and she began. But he forced himself to sit motionless, teeth clenched, until the desire had receded to a throbbing memory. Getting into Limores alive was more important right now.

"I'm sorry, Lexie. As much as I want you, this isn't the time or place. Finish with the kid, and I'll tell you what we're going to do as we walk." He silently shouldered the pack as he watched her change the baby's diaper, then settle the kid in the shawl. He didn't protest when she tied the shawl around her neck. The kid needed to be kept quiet, and she was better equipped to do that than he was. Besides, he needed his hands free. Just in case.

He began walking at an angle parallel to the city. "The jungle ends suddenly, about fifty yards in front of us," he said in a low voice. "It looks like they just hack it away when they want to build more houses on the edge of Limores. There's a major road to the right, and it's swarming with soldiers. We're going to walk about a half mile to the left, to where I saw a cornfield this afternoon."

"How is a cornfield going to help us?"

"They can't be guarding every row of corn," he answered. "On the other side of the field the houses begin, and we're going to crawl through the corn until we get to those houses. I'm sure El Cuchillo has some men around those houses, but once we're in the town our chances improve." He tossed a grim smile over his shoulder at her. "My specialty is blending into the shadows."

"You'll get us into the town safely, Caine. I'm sure of it."

"I wish I was as sure," he muttered, stopping abruptly. The moonlight silvered the pale rows of corn just ahead of them. The ears had been harvested long ago, and only the dry and shriveled stalks remained. It would have been better to find a field of thick, green, growing plants that could have hidden them more completely, but beggars couldn't be choosers.

He could feel Lexie watching him, waiting for him to say something, but he stared into the distance at the houses on the other side of the field. They were there somewhere, the soldiers who had been commanded to capture them. Or had they merely been told to stop them, whatever it took? He looked over at Lexie, holding the baby against her chest, and shivered. What was he leading her into?

"We're going to walk between the rows of corn. When I put out my hand, you stop, no matter what. If there's a place where the corn isn't higher than your head, you stoop or crawl."

He reached down to be sure his knife was in place inside his boot, then took her hand and walked into the field of dry cornstalks. The broad leaves rustled in the breeze, making it hard to hear anything else. Lexie walked along carefully in the row next to him, looking up from time to time to make sure that the stalks were higher than she was.

They were almost to the end of the field when a dog started barking. Caine motioned for her to drop to the ground, and they squatted in the dirt and waited.

A light came on in the nearest house, and a man's voice yelled at the dog to be quiet. When the dog didn't stop, a door slammed and the same man's voice grumbled as he seemed to get closer.

"Damned worthless mutt. Some watchdog you are, barking at a lousy cat. Get in here and be quiet before you wake the whole neighborhood." A door slammed again, and then the light went out.

He looked over at Lexie and gave her a faint grin. She tried to smile back at him, but her face was strained. "It's okay," he said, scarcely breathing the words. "We'll give him a few minutes to go back to sleep, then we'll keep going."

She nodded and shifted the baby in her arms. Caine waited twice as long as he thought necessary, then started to move again.

When they were at last near the end of the field, he stood for a long time scanning the houses around them. There was no sign of soldiers, no evidence of anyone waiting and watching. He wished there had been. At least then, they would have known where the danger was.

Finally he knew they had to move. He touched Lexie's arm and they glided silently out of the protection of the cornfield and into the deep shadows next to another house. The mud brick felt cool against his back as he plastered himself against it, listening for any sounds that shouldn't be there. He didn't hear a thing.

At first he moved them cautiously and slowly through the villages ringing the city of Limores, expecting to see a soldier at every corner. But as they approached the center of Limores itself he began to relax. There were people in the streets here, some hurrying home after working late, some laughing and talking and obviously out to have a good time. They stopped clinging to the shadows and began walking freely along the streets, Caine slinging one arm over Lexie's shoulder. When she looked up at him, fear in her face, he tried to reassure her with a squeeze to the shoulder.

He could feel her trembling, so he finally backed her up against a wall on a dark street and bent over her. To an on-looker, he would simply be a man who couldn't wait until he got home to kiss his sweetheart.

"It's all right," he whispered into her ear. "We'd look more suspicious around here if we were skulking down the alleys. We blend right in with all the other people."

She held on to his arms with a desperate grip. "Why haven't we seen any soldiers?"

"I don't know." He didn't want to admit how much that worried him. "But let's not worry about it now. We only have a little way to go—maybe another half mile. Can you make it that far?"

She nodded and shifted the baby in her shawl. When she reached up to arrange the knot on her shoulder, he saw her wince. He longed to reach out and take the baby, but knew he didn't dare.

"I want to carry her for you, but I can't." He leaned closer as if to kiss her neck. "It would be noticed right away. Men don't carry babies in this part of the world."

She nodded again. "I know. I can do it."

He wanted to sweep her into his arms and carry her the rest of the way. Hell, he wanted to rush her to the airport and take the first plane out of Limores. But he knew that wasn't possible. The airport was the first place El Cuchillo would look for them.

As he pushed away from the warmth of her body she looked up at him. "Do you know where we're going?"

He nodded. "I checked the city out before I left for Santa Ysabel. I found a place that I think will be okay."

Lexie glanced around as Caine started walking again. They were leaving the fashionable part of the city, with its fancy shops and restaurants and the crowds of people on the street. This part of Limores wasn't nearly so prosperous, and she looked around nervously as they turned a corner. This was more like a slum, with people huddled asleep in doorways and small, run-down shacks lining the street.

Dark shapes flitted in and out of the shadows, startling Lexie every time she saw one out of the corner of her eye—people on missions as secretive as theirs, she assumed, but that didn't re-assure her. She didn't want to think about the reasons for people to be on the street this late in this section of town.

A darkened building loomed ahead, and suddenly Caine drew her into the shadows at the side of a vacant house. Leaning against the wall for support, she tried to focus on him instead of their surroundings.

To her surprise he pulled the pack off his back and rummaged in the bottom of it. When he removed his hand, she saw a key on a rusted ring.

"What on earth is that for?" she breathed.

He flashed her a grin. "It's our room key. I told you I'd checked the place out when I first got here."

"You got a room?" She stared at him. "In this part of town?"

"Nobody asks too many questions around here. Especially if you pay your money up front and make it clear you want some privacy. They respect only two things in places like this, money and strength. I made sure they saw I had both."

She took a deep breath. "So what now?"

"I'm going in to check and make sure the room hasn't been disturbed. I'll be right back."

"You're not leaving me here alone." She grabbed his arm. "I'm coming with you."

"I want to make sure it's safe first."

Pulling him around to face her, she said, incredulous, "You think it's safe for me to stand around out here by myself? You're nuts if you think I'm going to do that."

His eyes narrowed, then he looked over her shoulder and his mouth tightened. "You're right. Let's go." But instead of walking away, he pressed her into the building and bent to kiss her.

"Shh," he whispered. "Someone's watching."

He brushed his lips over hers, and she felt herself begin to melt. It was all a show, she knew that, but she couldn't stop herself from responding. Caine's muscles were rock hard, and she knew that he was concentrating on whoever was behind them and not on her. It didn't seem to make any difference. When he touched her, she forgot about everything except him.

Caine raised his head and slid his arm around her, urging her away from the wall. To anyone watching them, they would simply be an eager couple who couldn't wait to get to their room in the motel. As they walked slowly toward the decrepit building, she could feel Caine's watchfulness and she saw him looking carefully around the almost-deserted streets.

She slowed down as they reached the door to the large building Caine had pointed out, but he tightened his grip on her shoulder and kept going. Maybe he hadn't meant they were staying in this building, she thought. It didn't look much like any motel or inn she'd ever seen, anyway.

The front was painted mud brick, but the paint had begun peeling years ago. Now there were only irregular blotches of some dark color left on the building, surrounded by curls of weathered paint. The windows had shutters, but most of them hung crooked, missing a nail or two. No lights were visible in any of the windows. Altogether, the building looked dark and menacing.

They sauntered around a corner, then Caine began to walk faster, leading her to the back of the building. Opening a door, he pulled her inside, then eased it shut.

They stood in the darkness for what seemed like a long time. She didn't hear anything outside the door, and finally Caine took her hand and led her up a rickety flight of stairs. Her eyes had adjusted to the darkness by now, but she was still barely able to see the steps in front of her.

"Why don't they have lights on these stairs?" she whispered.

He looked over at her and his lips curled up in a faint smile. "Usually they do. I took care of that before I left. I knew nobody would bother fixing it for a while."

He had planned such a small detail that far in advance? She stared at him as they entered a long, narrow hallway. Bare, low-watt lightbulbs hung from the ceiling, swaying slightly as they passed. The doors all had numbers on them, and they all stayed firmly closed. Caine had apparently been right when he'd said this was the kind of place where everyone minded his own business.

When they got to the last door in the hall, Caine placed her against the wall and motioned for her to be still. He scanned the doorway, looking for something, and after a few minutes he nodded once. Fitting the key into the lock, he eased open the door and stood watching the room for a moment.

When he disappeared inside the room without turning on the lights, she hugged Ana closer and looked nervously up and down the dingy hallway. Caine might be just around the corner, but she didn't like standing out here by herself. She was just about to go into the room after him when he appeared in the doorway and motioned her inside.

Once the door was closed he turned on an overhead light. It was just as dim as the ones in the hallway, but at least it illuminated the room. The shutters on the windows were tightly closed, so no light could shine through to the outside.

The room had one double bed and an old, scratched dresser. Above the dresser hung a mirror with wavy, pockmarked glass, and a straw mat covered the floor. As she was looking around the room, Caine opened the other door in the room.

"It may not be the Ritz," he said, giving her a smile that made her legs weaken, "but it does have indoor plumbing."

The tiny bathroom was no bigger than a closet, but it had a white tin shower stall in one corner. "I'm afraid you'll have to wait until we get back to Washington for your bath, but go ahead and take a shower.''

She looked over at him sharply at the mention of Washington and opened her mouth to reply. But then she looked at the shower again and decided that the argument could wait. Washing off the river mud couldn't.

''A shower would be heaven,'' she said fervently. Walking over to the bed, she untied the shawl and laid the sleeping Ana carefully on top of the old but clean bedspread. Her muscles screamed in protest as she bent over, but she gritted her teeth and thought about streams of hot water pounding down on her aching back.

Opening her backpack, she found a clean T-shirt and took it into the bathroom with her. When she turned on the water and felt the warm steam drift over her face, she exhaled softly and closed her eyes as she stepped under the stinging needles of the spray.

When she emerged from the bathroom she saw Caine leaning back against the headboard of the bed, wearing nothing but his shorts. When he looked over at her, she was suddenly too conscious of the T-shirt that scarcely reached the middle of her thighs. As she stood frozen in the doorway of the bathroom, he slowly sat up and swung off the bed.

''I thought I'd take a shower, too. Did you leave me any hot water?''

She nodded as she watched him come closer to her. His legs were just as long as she remembered; sleek and firmly muscled and covered with fine golden hair. The mat of dark blond hair on his chest covered taut, lean muscles that glided under smooth skin as he moved toward her. When he stopped in front of her she realized she'd been staring at him.

Heat flared in her face as she tried to step around him. He put his arms on the doorframe on either side of her, trapping her. ''Hey,'' he said softly, ''it's okay. I like it when you look at me.''

Hearing her own words echoed back at her in his husky, sexy voice made her start to quiver. Caine stared at her for a moment, his blue eyes darkening, then he lowered his mouth to hers. His kiss was a promise, a taste of things to come. Then he stepped back and watched as she moved away on legs that suddenly felt weak and wobbly.

"The bed's not much. It's about what you'd expect in a dump like this." His lips curved upward. "But it's better than the floor of the jungle."

He disappeared into the bathroom and shut the door quietly behind him. The next moment she heard the shower come on.

She heard a whimper from the floor, and looked down to see Ana at her feet. Her heart contracted as she saw that Caine had taken one of the dresser drawers and filled it with his shirts, then placed Ana inside it. Leaning over, she picked the baby up and fed her. The shower was still going when she laid the sleeping child back in her makeshift bed.

Pulling back the covers of the bed, she slid between the sheets and closed her eyes at the blissful pleasure. Caine would be finished with his shower in a minute, she told herself. In the meantime, she would enjoy the sensation of lying in a bed again.

Lexie rolled over and bumped into something solid and warm. Something that moved as she leaned closer to it. Her eyes flew open and she saw Caine smiling down at her.

"Good morning, Sleeping Beauty," he murmured. "I was afraid someone had put a spell on you and I was going to have to kiss you to get you to wake up."

"Would it really take a spell to make you kiss me?"

He leaned over her, staring into her eyes. "I'm already under one," he whispered. "I think I was from the first moment I saw you."

"Caine," she murmured, reaching for him. "I think I fell asleep last night while you were still taking your shower."

He gathered her close and held on to her. "You were sawing logs when I walked out of the bathroom." Leaning back, he looked at her and smiled again. "I doubt if I would have been able to wake you up if I'd set off a stick of dynamite in the room."

"I'm sorry." She pushed a lock of his tawny hair off his face.

"Don't be," he said as he brushed a kiss over her mouth. "I still can't believe you were able to walk this far. You had to hurt like hell yesterday."

Moving her legs experimentally, she was pleased to find that they hurt less than they had the day before. "I did, but it feels a little better today." She grinned up at him. "Unless you have another jungle I have to walk through."

His smile faded. "No more jungles. I'm going out later to check out the situation, but the bathroom there is as far as you have to go today. You and the kid deserve to take it easy for a while."

"What about you?" she whispered. "You walked as far as I did."

"But I'm used to it. Besides, we have to get out of Limores, and the sooner the better. With any luck, we can be on a plane out of here before our friend El Cuchillo even knows you made it to the city."

She remembered his words from the night before, about going back to Washington. "We need to talk about that, Caine. About where we're going to go."

Brushing his mouth over hers, he said, "We will. Right now there are other things I'd like to discuss."

"Such as . . ."

He froze, then rolled over to lie next to her. "Such as feeding the kid."

Lexie heard the whimpering from beside the bed and slowly sat up. For the first time since Ana had been born she didn't welcome having to feed her. She wished the baby could have slept for a while longer.

Picking her up, she cradled her in one arm and reached to pull up her shirt. Then she froze. She'd completely forgotten that all she wore was a pair of panties and a T-shirt. Caine was sitting right next to her, and she couldn't bring herself to bare her entire body to his gaze. With a fiery blush, she pulled the bedclothes up to her waist before lifting one side of the shirt.

She could feel Caine's eyes on her, but she refused to look up at him. Slowly he reached out and touched one finger to the side of her breast, sending a bolt of sensation through her.

"You're beautiful, you know," he murmured, in a voice filled with wonder.

As she laid Ana over her shoulder to burp her, she glanced at Caine. He was propped up on one elbow, watching her, with a tender expression on his face. "I've never seen anyone so beautiful. Inside or out."

She blushed again, then turned to lay Ana back into her bed. Caine stopped her with one hand on her arm. "Let me do that. Your muscles are probably still sore."

He took Ana out of her arms and placed her gently in the nest of shirts he'd made for her the night before. Then he sat back up and looked at her. Lexie could see the heat of desire in his eyes, feel the tautness in his muscles. As she watched him, an answering flame burst to life inside her, and she held out her arms to him.

Chapter 14

"I wish you had woken me up last night," she whispered as he pressed her down into the lumpy mattress.

"Don't worry, I'll make up for it today," he murmured into her ear, lightly biting her lobe.

Sensation shimmered through her body, winging along her nerves and heating her blood. She turned blindly toward him, needing to feel his mouth on hers, aching to taste him. His lips brushed gently over hers, but when she tentatively touched her tongue to his lower lip, his arms suddenly tightened around her.

His kiss changed from gentle and tender to hard and almost desperate in the space of a heartbeat. He rocked his lips against hers as he dragged his hands through her hair, straining to hold her closer. She struggled to free her hands, trapped against his chest, and he lifted his head to look at her, puzzled.

She curled one hand around his neck and burrowed the other into his hair. Clean and soft, it slipped through her fingers like spun silk. When she drew him closer again, he groaned, deep in his throat, and pulled her on top of him.

"Lexie," he whispered, his voice harsh with the struggle for control, "do you have any idea how much I want you?"

She looked down at him, and tenderness warred with desire in her heart. "I hope it's as much as I want you," she answered. She spread her hands on his chest, feeling the wiry hair curl around her fingers, and began to trace its path down his chest and stomach.

"I think I can guarantee that." Catching her hands, he brought them to his mouth and kissed each of her palms, then gently bit down on one of her fingers, his teeth barely skimming her. As he sucked on her finger, drawing it more deeply into the warm velvet of his mouth, she felt heat gather deep in her belly. It pooled and spread, making hidden parts of her ache for him.

"Caine!" She shuddered as she looked down at him. His eyes were hooded, glittering with passion and need barely held in check. As he stared back at her, he released her finger and slowly reached up to touch her breasts.

She felt the heat creeping into her cheeks as he cupped their heavy weight in his palms and let his gaze caress her for a long time. Finally he looked up at her and said, "I didn't think it was possible for you to be any more beautiful than you were before I left, but I was wrong." Pulling her down against him, he murmured into her ear, "And now I know it isn't just skin-deep, either."

She could feel his heart beating, fast and hard, against hers. Suddenly he rolled her over and rose above her. As he watched her, he lowered his head to one breast and drew the nipple into his mouth. Waves of sensation rippled through her, making her clench around him. When he reached down to touch her, skimming his fingers over the tangle of hair at the apex of her thighs, she cried out his name.

Opening her eyes to look at him, she saw sweat beading on his forehead and his jaw clenched in an effort to control his passion. When she slid her hands down his back to cup his taut buttocks in her palms, she felt him quivering above her.

"I need you, Caine," she whispered, trying to draw him closer.

"Not yet. I want to make this last forever." He touched her again, and she arched against him.

"I can't wait for forever," she cried. "Please, Caine!"

Reaching around, she touched the hard, hot length of him, cradling him in her palm. "Stop, Lexie," he groaned as he thrust against her hand. "If you touch me like that, I'll..." He groaned again as she fluttered her fingers over him.

Suddenly he surged against her, his control snapped. Again arching up to meet him, she whispered his name as he plunged into her. When he lifted her hips to meet his thrusts, she curled her legs around him and tried to pull him closer. Their sweat-slicked bodies slid together and apart, each time drawing her nearer to the edge.

It felt as if something exploded inside her. She clung to Caine and sobbed his name as spasms rocked her. The next moment she felt him stiffen and cry out, then he buried his face in her neck. His ragged breathing caressed her neck and made her hair flutter around her face. He whispered something to her, but all she could hear was her name, repeated over and over.

They lay together for a long time, until their breathing had returned to normal and the sweat had dried on their bodies. Finally he loosened his grip on her and raised his head to gaze down at her.

He watched her with a look in his eyes she'd never seen there before. It made her feel treasured, and when he reached out and brushed the hair out of her face she held his hand to her mouth and kissed him.

"Are you all right?" he asked.

"I've never been better in my life," she said softly.

To her surprise, a dull red washed over his cheeks. "That's not what I meant. Do your back and legs still hurt?"

"Oh." Tentatively she moved her legs again, and stretched her spine. "They still hurt, but I'll survive." She looked at him, wondering what was going on in his head. "How about you? You walked just as far as I did."

"I'm fine. Like I told you, I'm used to it."

For a moment she thought he was going to get out of the bed and pretend that nothing had happened, but then he lay back down next to her and pulled her close. She snuggled into his shoulder and closed her eyes, content to feel him underneath her and hear the steady beat of his heart.

"I'm going to leave in a while to see what I can find out. I'll bring back something to eat, but is there anything else you or the kid need?"

A chill swept over her, reminding her that paradise was only an illusion, after all. Slowly she raised her head to look at him. "Why do you always call her the kid?" she asked softly. "Her name is Ana. Why won't you call her by her name?"

Caine looked down at the woman clasped in his arms, his heart breaking at the hurt on her face. He resisted the urge to leap out of the bed and run away from her and the question that evoked so much pain. Instead, he pulled her closer, tucked her head under his chin, and stared at the wall for a long time.

Finally he eased his grip on her and rolled over to sit up against the headboard. "I can't be a father to her," he whispered, and it felt as if his soul were being flailed with every word he spoke. "I can't do it."

She slowly sat up next to him and took his hand. "Yes, you can. You can be as much a part of her life as you want to be. I'll admit that at first I wanted to keep her all for myself, but now I know that isn't fair. Whatever happens between us has nothing to do with your relationship with Ana."

"You don't understand, Lexie." The words tore at him, clawing and scratching. "It's not that I don't want to have anything to do with her. I don't know anything about being a father. All I know is how not to be one. I can't bear the thought of using an innocent child as my guinea pig."

"What do you think any parent does? Children don't come into the world with an instruction manual. It's always a learn-as-you-go proposition."

He turned to look at her, desperate to make her see the truth. "You don't know anything about me, Lexie. Not really. You don't know how I grew up. Did you know my mother died when I was born, and my father hated me for it? Did you know that he started drinking, and when he got drunk enough he would remember why I was there and my mother wasn't? Do you know what he did when he remembered?"

She reached out to hold him, but he ignored her, staring at the wall, remembering things he had tried to bury long ago. "He couldn't bear to look at me. I could see it in his face, every time he noticed me. When I got older, and harder to ignore, he started to use his fists on me. I guess he figured that if he hit me hard enough and long enough, eventually I would go away. He was right. I left when I was sixteen and I never looked back.''

''Caine.'' He heard her voice, soft and full of pain, but still he ignored her. Now that he had started, it was as if he'd lanced a festering wound and all the poison had to come boiling out. He had to make her see what kind of man her baby had for a father.

''I thought it wouldn't matter—that once I was away from him I could live a normal life like any other man. I joined the army, and when I got out your father hired me. I had a job I was good at, and I even got married.''

She made a surprised noise, and he glanced over at her. ''It didn't last long. I didn't really love her, and I think I even knew it at the time. But I wanted a normal family so badly that I was willing to settle for anything I could get.''

He stopped abruptly, remembering what came next. Even after more than ten years, the pain was still a raw spot on his heart. He glanced over at Lexie, dreading the pity he knew he would find there. Her face was pale and her eyes were full of pain—for him, he realized with a jolt of surprise. And he didn't see a shred of pity in her gaze.

''Just because your marriage didn't work out doesn't mean that you can't be a father, Caine.'' She laid one hand on his arm.

Staring down at her hand, small and delicate against the bronzed skin of his arm, he wished that he didn't have to tell her the rest. He wanted with his whole soul to bury the rest of the story, to pretend that everything could be all right for them. But he couldn't bear it if he made a mistake and his daughter paid the price. His daughter. The pain of those words propelled his story.

''My marriage didn't just 'not work out,' Lexie. It was blown apart.'' He took a deep, shuddering breath. He'd never told another living soul about what had really happened. ''I was working for your father at the time, and he sent me away on an assignment. My marriage was already shaky, and I was glad to get away. I figured that it would give both of us time to think about what to do.''

She slipped her hand into his, and he curled his fingers around hers tightly. "When I got back, my wife was packing to leave. She'd decided that she'd had enough, that she wanted out of the marriage. I didn't feel anything but relief. It had been a mistake from the start. But then she told me something else.''

He stopped, remembering, unable to speak over the pain. "What happened, Caine?" he heard her whisper.

"She told me that she'd had an abortion while I was gone.'' He tried to keep the agony out of his voice, but didn't succeed. "She'd found out she was pregnant right after I left, and didn't even hesitate to end it. She told me she didn't want me as a father to any kids she might have, that some people just weren't meant to be parents and I was one of them. I had a bad temper, she said, and she was afraid of what I might do to her or the kid.''

He looked at Lexie. "I never hurt her, Lexie. Never. I never even threatened to.'' He closed his eyes. "I hadn't told her about my father, but somehow she knew. She knew what I had come from, she could see it in me. And maybe she was right.'' Opening his eyes, he said, "Can't you see that I could never take that chance? If I ever hurt that baby, I wouldn't be able to live with myself.''

"Oh, Caine.'' Her voice was an agonized whisper, and he felt her hand on his face, resting against his cheek. "You're no more capable of hurting Ana than . . . than I am. I would stake my life on it.'' She turned his face so she could look at him. "Or hers.''

"You haven't thought about what you're saying,'' he answered roughly. He couldn't bear to let himself begin to believe her. "How can you take that kind of chance?''

Her response was immediate. "How can you believe what that . . . that bitch told you? She was right when she said some people aren't meant to be parents, but she was talking about herself, not you. Anyone who could do something like that without even telling you first that she was pregnant with your child doesn't deserve to have children. And she certainly isn't what I'd call a reliable judge of character.''

He almost smiled at the fierceness of her words. He had known she would be a tiger, leaping to defend someone she cared about. But it didn't change anything. "Even if you are, I'm not willing to take that chance, Lexie."

"There is no chance to take," she insisted. "I've seen you under the worst possible conditions the last few days. You took care of me, and you were gentle with Ana." When he flashed her a surprised look, she smiled tenderly at him. "Do you think I didn't notice the way you handled her when you were forced to? You held her like she was fragile and precious. I saw your face when she smiled at you. You would make a wonderful father, Caine. I know you would."

He slid out of bed. He couldn't bear it anymore. She was holding out to him the one thing he'd always secretly wanted more than anything in the world, and he couldn't have it. He couldn't allow himself to have it. "We don't have time to argue about this now, Lexie," he said, refusing to look at the baby lying in the dresser drawer on the floor as he rummaged in his pack for his last set of clean clothes. "I need to get going. I'm sure you're hungry, and I have to make some contacts."

She pulled up the white sheet, covering her breasts as she watched him get dressed. For a moment, seeing her slide modestly between the sheets, he wanted to forget about food, forget about getting out of Limores and just climb back into bed with her. He wanted to think of nothing but Lexie, to lose himself in her sweetness. But he couldn't do that. He had a job to do, so he turned his back and pulled on his clothes.

Pausing at the door, he said softly, "Go back to sleep for a while. You might as well get some rest while you can. But whatever you do, don't leave the room and don't let anyone in. I'll be back as soon as I can."

Lexie watched him slip out of the room, closing the door softly behind him. She stared at it for a long time after he'd disappeared, aching inside for the vulnerable child and young man he'd been, for the pain he'd kept hidden for so many years.

A beam of light had managed to find its way through the shutters and it bathed the side of the bed where Caine had lain in a golden glow. A soft smile flitted over her mouth. Caine was going to make a wonderful father. She had meant every word when she'd told him she would trust him with her life and Ana's. Now, all she had to do was convince him.

Sliding farther down into the bed, she felt her eyes closing and she gave herself up to the arms of sleep.

The voice calling her name seemed to come from a long way off, dragging her from the depths of a dream. She groaned and rolled over, burying her face in the pillow, trying to recapture the shimmering vision already dancing out of reach. It was no use.

"Lexie, wake up," the voice said again, and the dream retreated permanently into the mists. "I brought you something to eat."

The smell of french fries reached her, and she opened her eyes. Caine stood over the bed, holding a paper bag with a familiar logo on it.

"There's one of those in Limores?" she asked, sitting up and clutching the sheet to her breasts. Her voice sounded both sleepy and incredulous, but her stomach was reminding her how long it had been since she'd eaten. Reaching for the bag, pulling out the red container of french fries and the cheeseburger wrapped in yellow paper, she realized she was ravenous. "How did you know what I liked?"

"Lucky guess," he answered with a shrug. "I figured that after a few days of that dehydrated stuff we've been eating, anything would taste good."

"Don't forget the agouti," she reminded him with a grin, taking a bite of the cheeseburger. The familiar taste made her close her eyes and savor every bite.

"That's my specialty you're talking about," he warned, a smile twitching the corners of his mouth.

"And it was wonderful." She ate a french fry and grinned at him again. "But nothing can beat a greasy fry."

"How did you survive for all that time in Santa Ysabel? I didn't see any fast-food outlets up there," he teased.

"Willpower." She took another bite and closed her eyes again. Caine was right. After the food she'd been eating for the past few days, this humble cheeseburger and fries tasted like manna from heaven.

When she'd finished, she looked at him expectantly, wrapping the sheet around herself. "So, what did you find out? Do you know how we're going to get out of Limores?"

He stared at her for a moment, then turned abruptly and walked over to her pack. Rummaging around in it, he pulled out a handful of clothes and gave them to her, then turned around to face the wall. "Here, why don't you put these on? It'll be easier to have a conversation if I'm not wondering when that sheet is going to fall down."

"Oh." She could feel her face flame, even though he wasn't looking at her. "I was so excited to eat, I didn't even think about—"

"It's okay, Lexie." His voice softened. "Believe me, I prefer the view the way it is, but we have to think about getting out of here. And it'll be a lot easier for me to concentrate if I'm not thinking about joining you in that bed."

Scrambling out of bed, she threw her clothes on before he could turn around and see her. She knew it was silly, after what they had shared, but she still felt self-conscious about Caine seeing her naked. It was because of Ana, she knew, and what the pregnancy had done to her body. Her abdomen was flattening out again, slowly but surely, and the stretch marks were already beginning to fade to faint, silvery lines, but she was still too aware of them. And vain enough that she didn't want Caine to see them.

"You can turn around now," she said, pulling the sheets back over the bed, as if that somehow could make both of them forget what had happened there earlier in the morning. Caine was right. This wasn't the time to be daydreaming about making love.

"What did you find out?" she asked, glancing down at Ana. The baby was still sound asleep.

"Why we didn't see any soldiers after we got past the roadblocks, for one thing," he answered, his voice grim. "They're all at the docks and the airport. He's even got some of them at the train station, and I'd have to be really desperate to use the San Rafael trains."

A shiver of fear crept up her spine at the grimness of his face. "What are we going to do?" Her voice was barely louder than a whisper.

"Our best chance is on a plane. That'll get us out of here the fastest. Unfortunately, El Cuchillo thinks so, too. There are soldiers swarming all over out there, both at the ticket windows and at the planes themselves. There's no way we could sneak past them."

"What about in a disguise? I could dye my hair and we could get some old clothes that the peasants would wear. Maybe that would fool them."

He shook his head. "Any group of two adults and a baby is going to be checked with a magnifying glass. We certainly can't use our own passports, and we don't have any other papers that would pass inspection. Given a few days I could get some, but we don't have a few days. No, we can't get on a plane that way."

"How about a boat? There must be plenty of small boats that could take us to another city where there wouldn't be as much scrutiny."

Slowly he shook his head. "I thought of that, too, but it's too risky. We'd be too vulnerable on a boat." He watched her for a while, and she thought he looked unsure of himself. "I do have an idea, but I'm not sure how you'll feel about it."

Hope flickered in her chest and caught hold. "What?" she asked eagerly.

"It involves a plane," he said slowly, pacing the room. "I've got some contacts here in Limores, and they could do it for us." He stopped in front of her and took her hands. "If we had any other options, I wouldn't even mention it. But right now, we don't."

"What is it, Caine?" He looked so worried that the hope slowly died, and was replaced by fear.

Holding on to her hands, he watched her for a moment. Finally he sank down on the bed next to her, gripping her hands tightly. "They're not watching the cargo planes nearly as closely as the passenger planes. Other than checking the pilots, they're not bothering with them." His eyes on her face were intent.

Suddenly she realized what he was saying, and she closed her eyes and swallowed as a wave of nausea swept over her. Faintly she said, "If we hide in a box, you think we can get onto a plane without being caught."

Tightening his grip on her hands, he said, "It's up to you, Lexie. I know how you feel about enclosed places and this would be a hell of a lot more real than any nightmare. It would only be until we were off the ground, but if you don't think you could handle it, I understand. We'll find another way."

Nausea threatened again, but when she looked at Caine and saw the concern on his face, she swallowed hard, forcing it away. He was willing to forgo their easiest and safest way out of this country because of her phobia, and she wouldn't let him do it.

"I won't like it, but I can do it." She licked her suddenly dry lips. "You risked your life to get me this far. I'm not about to wimp out on you now."

A look of pride flashed across his face. "You're something else, Lexie," he said. Brushing her hair back from her face, he murmured, "I'll make it as easy for you as I can. I've already talked to one of my contacts here, and he can get us on a plane for Washington tonight. By tomorrow morning, you'll be home."

Home. Slowly she leaned away from him. "I don't want to go back to Washington. I thought you understood that."

"I know you don't, but this is just for a while. Just until I can be sure you're safe, and that El Cuchillo isn't going to come after you."

"Why would he come after me?" she protested. "He just wants me out of the country."

He looked at her, his mouth a tight line. "I'm not so sure, Lex. For someone who just wants you gone, he's going to an awful lot of trouble to keep you from leaving. You can bet your ass that all those soldiers at the airport aren't there just to escort you onto a plane."

She paled. "You think this is personal, don't you?" As she thought about El Cuchillo's relentless pursuit, she stared at Caine with horror. "Why?" she whispered. "What could he possibly want with me?"

"I have no idea. And I don't intend to stick around Limores long enough to find out."

Standing, she moved away from him and stared at the dust motes dancing in the beam of light from the broken shutter. "Pick anyplace else in the world and I'll go there. But I won't go back to Washington."

"Why not?"

She heard the exasperation in his voice, but she didn't turn around. "I can't. I'm afraid, Caine. Afraid that if I go back, I'll fall into the same relationship with my father again. Afraid that he'll try to run my life, and that I'll let him. It's a lot easier to drift along, letting other people make the decisions for you. I know. I did it for twenty-six years, and I don't want to do it again."

"I'm not saying you have to live there for the rest of your life, dammit. If there's going to be trouble, I just want it to be on my turf. I'm not asking you to submit to your father again."

She turned around then and gave him a weary smile. "It's not that easy, Caine, but I don't expect you to understand. You're just like my father in a lot of ways. You don't take no for an answer. You would never allow anyone to manipulate you like that. But I'm not as strong as you. Old habits are hard to break, and I'm afraid that I wouldn't be able to stand up to him."

He stood and walked over to her, cupping her face in his hands. The expression on his face was tender. "You are one of the strongest people I know, Lexie Hollister. You're more than a match for your father or anyone else. I'd back you every time."

She gave him a shaky smile. "Thank you for saying that. But I can't take that chance. Not until I feel more confident about myself. Please, promise me that we won't go back to Washington."

He stared at her for a long time. Finally, his hands dropped away from her face and he stepped back. Deep, searing pain flashed in his eyes, then the shutters came down. "All right, Lexie, I promise." He turned away, heading for the door. "I have to go and make the final arrangements. Stay here and be ready to leave when I get back."

He stopped at the door and turned around. "What should I bring you back to eat?"

He looked at her as if it was her last meal, she thought uneasily. She told him the first dish that came to mind and he nodded. Opening his mouth to say something else, he stared at her again for a moment before quietly slipping out the door.

She watched him go, then turned and reached for Ana. The baby needed to be fed and bathed before they left, and she had no idea how long he would be.

Late-afternoon shadows were creeping across the bed when Caine slipped back into the room. Lexie had opened the shutters a crack, just enough to let some light in. She and the baby were sound asleep on the bed, Lexie's arm curled protectively around the kid. He watched them for a moment, his heart turning over in his chest, then he set the bag containing their food on the dresser and quietly pulled the shutters closed.

Would she ever forgive him? he wondered as he watched her sleep. He wasn't sure, but he knew he couldn't let it matter. He'd walked around Limores for a couple of hours, trying to decide what to do, but in the end he'd known he had no choice. Her life and the kid's were the pawns in a deadly game, and he didn't even know the rules. He had to protect them—even if Lexie never forgave him.

Forcing the grim thoughts away, he spoke softly to Lexie, trying to waken her without startling her. Finally she rolled over and opened her eyes, looking up at him. His stomach clenched into a tight knot of desire when she gave him a sleepy smile, full of invitation.

"Hi." Her voice was low and husky, and made him remember other times when she'd sounded like that.

"Hi, yourself." He forced himself to smile. "I hope you're hungry. I got enough food to feed the French army."

"That sounds like it might barely be enough." Swinging her legs over the side of the bed, she saw the bag and her eyes lit up. "I'm famished."

They ate for a while in silence, until finally she slowed down. "Is everything set for tonight?"

She didn't look at him, but he saw the sudden tenseness in her hands and for a moment he thought she knew. Then he realized she was thinking about the crate they would have to hide in.

"We're set. We'll leave here after dark and go to a warehouse. There'll be a box waiting, and one of my contacts." He looked up at her, catching her eye. "I've arranged it so that we're both in the same box," he said gently. "I thought that might be easier for you."

She nodded and tried to smile. Her mouth quivered at the corners, and he wanted to tell her to forget it, that they would find another way out of the country, but he knew he couldn't. More and more soldiers were pouring into Limores, and they had to get out tonight.

"Finish your dinner, and then maybe you should feed the kid again."

She pushed away the cardboard container. "I'm full. I'll take care of Ana now." Getting up too quickly, she stumbled over the straw mat on the floor, then caught herself and walked over to the bed.

He hated himself for forcing her to do this. Her dread was a throbbing presence in the room, coiling around his throat until he felt he was choking. Shoving his food away, he went into the bathroom and closed the door. He couldn't bear to watch for another instant as her fingers, clumsy from fear, fumbled with the buttons on her blouse. Her hair had swung over her face as she bent her head, but he didn't have to see the expression in her eyes. He knew it would be sheer, unadulterated terror.

He shut his mind to her fear, to everything but what would happen if El Cuchillo caught them. It was the only thing he could allow himself to think about. If he thought about what he was going to make her do, he wouldn't be able to go through with it.

Forty-five minutes later they stood outside a darkened warehouse in one of Limores's more dilapidated neighborhoods. They'd passed the occasional person on the street, but everyone minded his own business around here, especially after dark. Nobody had appeared to notice them.

He looked around one more time, cataloging all the hiding places he'd checked earlier in the day. He was almost certain that no one was watching them. Pulling the heavy door open only far enough for them to slip through, he urged Lexie into the warehouse, then eased the door shut.

One bare lightbulb hung from the ceiling in a corner, and he took Lexie's hand as he walked toward it. The sweltering heat of the day had eased a little at dusk, but it was still hot. Lexie's hand was ice-cold, and she clung to him with a desperate grip. Again, revulsion for what he had to force her to do rose up in his throat, and he wanted to stop and tell her there was another way.

He knew there wasn't, and he kept on walking.

They stopped before a large wooden crate. The lid stood off to one side, propped against the wall. Several pillows and blankets lined the inside of the crate, and a canteen of water sat in one corner.

"All the comforts of home," he heard her say.

He turned to look at her, and found she was staring into the crate. Pulling gently on her hand, he tried to turn her away from it. "It's not too late to change your mind, you know. There's always another way."

It looked as if she struggled to tear her gaze away from the box. Finally she looked at him, and beneath the fear that glazed her eyes he could see the determination. "No. I can do this, Caine. I know I can."

"I'm sure of it," he said gently, another wave of admiration for her flooding through his chest. "But if it's really too much for you, we'll find something else."

"Don't worry, I won't flip out on you halfway to the airport." Beneath the false bravado he felt her terror building. As she turned away, he saw her hand tremble as she clutched the shawl holding the baby.

"Let's go, Lexie." He grabbed her hand and tried to pull her toward the door. "I'll think of something else."

She stared at him, hope and fear mixed on her face. But before she could answer, a figure silently emerged from between the tall piles of boxes that lined the walls.

The man standing at the other side of the crate was careful to stay in the shadows. "All set, Smith?" he asked in a guttural voice.

Caine opened his mouth to tell the contact that they'd changed their minds, but before he could speak, Lexie clambered over the side of the crate and settled herself in a corner. "We're ready," she said in a shaky voice.

"Lexie—" he began.

"Hurry up and get in, Caine. We don't want to miss the plane."

He stared at her for a long moment, but seeing the resolve in her eyes he finally sighed and climbed in. The man next to them immediately grasped the lid and lowered it into place.

Caine slid over next to Lexie, pulling her against him and wrapping his arms around her as the box was plunged into darkness. She made one tiny sound, then buried her face in his shoulder.

Chapter 15

Lexie fought her terror as the crate lifted into the air, swung gently from side to side, then settled onto something solid. A moment later an engine started, and they began to move.

Caine's heart beat steadily against her cheek. She kept her eyes tightly closed and her face pressed into his shoulder as cold sweat trickled down her back and sides. The grip she had on his arm would probably cause bruises tomorrow, but she couldn't let go. She was holding herself together by a single, frayed thread, and that thread was attached to Caine.

"Are you all right?" she heard him whisper next to her.

She nodded, afraid that if she opened her mouth she would sob with fear. He moved, and she clutched at him frantically.

"It's okay, Lex," he murmured into her ear. "I won't let you go."

She could feel him sliding her over his leg and nestling her onto his lap. "I've got you," he said, stroking her hair. "It'll take about ten more minutes to get to the airport, and we should be in the air a half hour after that. We tried to wait until the last possible moment to leave."

He kept up a soothing monologue until the truck shuddered to a halt. Then, bending closer to her ear, he breathed, "I have to be quiet now. We can't take a chance on someone hearing voices from this crate." He smoothed his hand down her back and side, again and again, until he touched the shawl. His hand stilled.

"What about her?" he whispered. "Is she asleep?"

Lexie nodded again, then whispered back, "She should be fine until we're in the air." Her throat felt swollen and tight, and she had to force the words out.

Suddenly they were swinging through the air, and she fell away from Caine as the box tilted to one side. She bit on her lip, trying to stifle the scream that tried to escape, and scrabbled frantically in the darkness as she reached for him.

His strong hands grasped her arms and he pulled her back against him. This time he braced her between his legs, then lowered his head and brushed his mouth over her cheek.

She clung to him, trying to let him banish the nightmare that filled her head. His mouth drifted toward her ear, and he breathed, "It's all right, Lex, I'm here. It won't be much longer."

The crate bumped against something and shuddered to a halt, and the next moment she could feel them sliding across a floor. She heard voices, muffled and indistinct. Then they bumped into something else and stopped. Caine must have sensed her question, because he put his mouth against her ear again and said, "We're on the plane now. Almost there."

She nodded once, jerkily, and shifted Ana in her arms. Then, searching for Caine's hand in the darkness, she grasped it as she tried to listen to the voices coming from outside the crate. She couldn't make out the words, but the effort distracted her from the blackness that enfolded them.

Suddenly Caine stiffened. She felt all his muscles tense, and he eased her away from him and pressed his ear against the wood of their prison. The voices had suddenly gotten louder, and even inside the wooden crate she could feel their anger.

Terror filled her again, but this time it was fear of being caught. They couldn't have gotten this far only to be stopped minutes before they would have been free, she thought with despair.

She reached out for Caine, needing to hold on to him. He took her hand, but didn't move away from the side of the crate. After a moment, he dropped her hand and she felt him reach for his boot. Fear clawed at her as she heard the quiet hiss of his knife sliding out of its sheath.

The voices were suddenly louder and closer. Her heart began to pound, and she was sure anyone within a ten-foot radius of the crate could hear it booming against her chest. Blood roared in her ears, drowning out the approaching voices.

Caine must have sensed her panic, because he reached out and squeezed her shoulder once. Then he shifted and the coiled tension emanating from him seemed to fill the enclosed space.

Her arm curled around the still-sleeping Ana, hovering over her protectively, and she waited for someone to rip the cover off their hiding place. But after a few minutes the voices stopped abruptly, and immediately the plane began to move.

Lexie collapsed against the side of the crate, exhausted and trembling. Caine didn't move. He waited, crouching still and silent, for a long time. Finally, though, when he felt the plane lift into the air, he sat back down. Lexie heard the whisper of metal against leather as he sheathed his knife.

He slid over next to her and put his arm around her again, and she could feel the tension that still hummed through his body. "What was that—" she started to say, but he covered her mouth with his hand.

"Not yet," he murmured into her ear. "Wait."

Unease trickled through her as she realized that he wasn't sure all the danger was behind them. She stared in his direction, trying to figure out what he was worried about. He pulled her close again and dropped a kiss on her hair, whispering, "Don't worry. I think everything's fine."

But he wasn't sure, and that was why he didn't let himself relax. She leaned against his shoulder, letting his warmth seep into her frozen muscles, and swallowed hard. The terror of the darkness in the enclosed crate had been replaced by a fear of what waited outside.

It seemed as if hours had passed when she heard someone prying the nails out of the lid of the box. Caine reached for his knife and she pulled Ana closer. When the lid moved slowly sideways, letting dim light into their hiding place, Caine leaped up from a crouching position, holding the knife in one hand.

"Take it easy, buddy," she heard a laughing voice say. "I'm one of the good guys."

The lid slid completely off the box, and a young, blond-haired stranger extended a hand in her direction. "Welcome aboard, Mrs. Smith," he said, smiling. "Come on out."

She watched as Caine slowly slid his knife back into his boot and turned to her. Ignoring the young man's extended hand, he reached down and pulled her to her feet. "It's okay, honey," he said. "He's on our side."

Slowly Lexie stood, blinking in the light, stretching the kinks out of her legs and looking around. They were surrounded by cargo of all kinds, piled halfway to the ceiling of the silver plane. Behind the blond man she could see an open door that looked as if it led to the cockpit.

"What happened back there?" Caine demanded, and the young stranger stopped smiling.

"Trouble," he said bluntly. "Those rebel soldiers wanted to check all our cargo. I don't know if they knew you were on board or if they were checking everyone. I came down hard on them at first, but I didn't want to make them suspicious so I finally just gave them a bribe. I acted like I figured that was what they were after all along."

"And they went along with that?" Caine asked. Lexie could hear the doubt in his voice.

The blond man shrugged. "Hell if I know. I didn't wait to find out. I shoved them out the door and started the engine. I thought I heard them shouting as I started to roll, but I ignored it. I figured once we were in the air they couldn't stop us." He grinned at them again. "I waited until we were out of San Rafael airspace to let you out, though."

Lexie could see Caine finally relax. "Thanks, Dan. If anyone else had been flying, we'd probably still be sitting on the runway back in Limores." His mouth curved up in a ghost of a smile. "Jones said you were the best, and I guess he was right."

Dan shrugged as he turned back to the cockpit. "I aim to please. Sit back and enjoy the ride. It'll be three hours or so before we get there."

As he disappeared into the cockpit, Lexie said, "Where are we going, Ca—"

Before she could finish his name he'd plastered his hand over her mouth. "Don't use my name. As far as Dan knows, we're Mr. and Mrs. Smith. He doesn't want to know the truth any more than I want him to."

She looked toward the cockpit, where the door was slightly ajar. "Who is he?"

"He owns a charter company in the States and one of his customers is the U.S. government. He does the odd job for us every now and then, but it's less awkward for everyone if it's kept anonymous."

Nodding, she glanced once more toward the front of the plane, where she could hear someone whistling off-key. Then she looked back at Caine. "You didn't answer my other question. Where are we going?"

He leaned down to pick up the canteen that still stood in the corner of the crate. "We're going to my ranch," he said, his voice casual. "It's in Montana. You can stay there for as long as you like."

She started to ask him where in Montana it was, but Ana awakened and began to cry. Reaching for her, she scooped the baby out of the shawl and began to unbutton her blouse.

Caine bent down to arrange a pillow against the side of the crate. "I'm afraid this is the only place to sit," he said, his voice apologetic.

She gave him a wan smile. "I've sat in worse places to nurse. This is fine."

Her pack was just out of reach and as she leaned over to get it, Caine asked, "What do you need?"

"A diaper. She's eating so fast that I'm afraid she might burp some of it back up."

He stuck his hand inside her pack and brought out a fistful of diapers. As he tried to disentangle them, a brown manila envelope fell onto the floor.

Caine froze, staring at the innocuous-looking envelope. Without taking his eyes off it he handed Lexie one of the diapers, then shoved the rest back into her pack. Finally he looked up at Lexie.

"Can I look at the pictures?"

She nodded, watching him, but didn't say a word. It looked like she was scarcely breathing.

It was hard for him to catch his own breath. Something had his chest in its grip, squeezing so hard that his blood pounded in his ears. *Put it back,* a voice inside him pleaded. *Once you look, it'll be too late.*

But somehow he found himself reaching out, taking the flat package in his hands. The envelope crinkled, the paper stiff and rough against his suddenly sensitive fingers. He looked at Lexie again, but he couldn't read her expression.

In spite of the warnings screaming in his head he couldn't stop himself from looking down at the envelope again. The feel of it burned into him, but he turned it over, examining it for the first time. He recognized Lexie's handwriting. On the front she had scrawled "Santa Ysabel." Farther down, in a different ink, she had written "Ana."

Slowly he straightened the metal prongs holding the envelope closed. The voice inside him warned that things would never be the same if he looked inside, but he couldn't stop himself. Suddenly he was consumed with the need to know what his daughter looked like when she was born, to see how she had changed in the last two months.

The pictures spilled out into his lap. The one on top was of Lexie, looking radiant but exhausted, holding a tightly wrapped bundle. She sat propped up in a bed, grinning weakly at the camera.

His heart ached. "Who took these pictures?" he asked, his voice hoarse and unfamiliar.

"Maria," she answered in a soft voice. "She's the local midwife. Ana was born in her house."

Slowly he laid that picture aside and picked up another one. As he reached for it he noticed that his hand was trembling. "She looks different," he said after he'd studied it for a while. "Like she's not fully formed yet."

"She was only two days old. I guess that's the way new-borns look."

He looked over at Lexie, but she'd put the baby on her shoulder and was murmuring to her. When she glanced over at him, he thought he saw a sheen of moisture in her eyes. She looked away so quickly, he couldn't be sure.

He looked through all the pictures, feeling his heart expand in his chest until he was afraid it would burst. Right in front of his eyes he'd seen the kid change. Finally he looked up at Lexie again. "She's so different now. I had no idea so much happened in two months."

Lexie gave him a smile tinged with sadness. "She changes every day. That's why I wanted those pictures. It's already hard to remember what she looked like back then." She lowered her head to look down at the baby in her arms and her hair swung over her face. "You can have the pictures if you want them."

Something exquisitely beautiful and equally painful moved inside him at her words. He closed his eyes and struggled for control before he spoke. "Thank you. I couldn't take your pictures." He swallowed and, trying to sound nonchalant, added, "Maybe I'll make copies of them, though."

"I'll send you copies," she whispered. She kept her head bent over the baby, but he thought he saw something wet fall onto the shawl. He wanted to reach for her, but instead he forced himself to gather the pictures back into a neat stack.

He'd picked up the envelope to replace them when he stopped. One of the other pictures was a group shot of what he assumed were some of the villagers of Santa Ysabel.

"Do you mind if I look through the rest of these pictures?"

She shook her head. "Be my guest."

He stuffed the baby pictures back into the envelope, his hand lingering on them as he slid them out of sight. Then, forcing himself to put them out of his mind, he spread the other photos in a semicircle in front of him.

There were group shots of people from the village, and photos of individual people. Occasionally there was a picture of a couple, or of a group of three or four. Staring at the smiling faces looking back at him, an idea stirred. He looked over at

Lexie, who was changing the baby's diaper. "Do you know who all of these people are?"

"Most of them," she said without looking up.

"Would you mind looking through them and telling me if there's anyone you don't recognize?"

She raised her head sharply then. "Why? What are you thinking?"

He handed her the stack of pictures and leaned back against the wooden crate, watching her. "It's a long shot, but suppose you have a picture there of someone who'd rather not be photographed. That might be one reason why El Cuchillo is so eager to catch you."

Thumbing through the pictures, studying each one, she said, "But why would they have let me take a picture of them in the first place? And why would they wait until now to try and get it back?"

"Who knows?" He shrugged. "Maybe circumstances have changed since the picture was taken. Maybe he just remembered that you had it. We may never know."

He stared at her as she slowly and methodically looked at each picture, then set it down. "Everyone familiar?" he asked softly.

"So far." She didn't look up, just kept on examining the photos.

Suddenly she froze, staring at one picture. Caine had to stop himself from grabbing for it.

"I'd forgotten all about this," she whispered.

"About what?" His voice was too sharp, but he didn't care. Sliding over next to her, he looked at the picture she held in her hand. She handed it to him.

"About Pedro." She stared at the picture again, a stricken look on her face. "Five or six months ago, one of the young men from the village came home with some friends of his. Pedro is one of Santa Ysabel's success stories. He goes to the university in Limores, and everyone expects big things from him. His friends were men he'd met at school."

"But," Caine prompted. He could see from her eyes that there was more to the story.

"But these men made the rest of the villagers uneasy. They all whispered that Pedro had gotten in with a bad group. They were only there for a few days, then they left and we never saw them again. The next time Pedro came home, he was alone. When someone asked him about his friends, he said only that he had been mistaken in their character. We never heard anything else about them. Then when Pedro went back to school, he disappeared. No one's heard from him for three months."

He could feel her eyes on him as she asked, "Do you recognize any of the people in the picture?"

"No, but that doesn't mean anything." He looked at the photo again, then up at her. "May I keep this one? There are people who might recognize some of these men."

"Of course," she said immediately. She watched as he tucked it carefully into his pack, then asked, "Do you really think that picture is the reason El Cuchillo wanted to catch me?"

"There has to be some reason," he answered, his voice grim. "And this makes as much sense as anything else."

He watched her jerky movements as she settled the baby into the shawl and realized she was frightened again. Sliding over next to her, he wrapped one arm around her and said, "Hey, it doesn't matter anymore. We're out of Limores and we're safe. All you have to do now is lean back and enjoy the ride."

She gave him a shaky smile and snuggled closer to him. Desire flared inside him at her unconscious gesture of trust, but he fought against it. This wasn't the time or place. "Why don't you try to sleep? It'll be a while before we get there."

"I spent the whole day sleeping," she protested, but she laid her head against his shoulder. In a few minutes, both mother and daughter were asleep.

Lexie awoke with a start when she felt the bump. Sitting up and looking around wildly, she realized she'd been asleep, lying in Caine's lap. The nightmare of their trip out of Limores came flooding back, and she glanced around warily.

"It's okay." Caine's voice was soft and reassuring. "We've just landed."

She looked over at him, and saw that he was holding Ana. When he saw the direction of her gaze, his face reddened slightly and he held the baby out to her. As she took Ana, he said, "She looked uncomfortable and I was afraid you might roll over on her if she was still in the shawl."

"Thank you for taking care of her," she murmured, her heart singing. He couldn't be as indifferent to Ana as he'd wanted her to believe if he'd held her all the way from Limores to Montana.

"No problem," he answered, his voice gruff. Without looking at her, he began gathering their things and shoving them into the backpacks.

The plane slowed down and came to a stop. Lexie snuggled Ana into her shawl and climbed out of the crate. She headed for the door of the plane, but suddenly stopped and turned around.

"I never asked you, is it warm enough in Montana this time of year to be dressed like this? Will I need something else to cover Ana?"

"Lexie," he began, looking uncomfortable. "There's something I should tell you."

She waited for him to continue, but before he could speak, Dan the pilot strolled out of the cockpit and opened the door of the plane.

"The weather is a balmy sixty-five degrees here in Washington tonight. It'll probably feel like the Arctic after San Rafael, but there it is. I radioed ahead and there'll be a car waiting for you, but I'm sure you know the routine. Thanks for flying CharterAir." With a wave of his hand he jumped onto the asphalt and disappeared into the night.

Lexie turned to Caine. "What did he mean, the weather here in Washington? We're supposed to be in Montana."

Caine stooped to grab his pack, then stood and slung it on his back. He didn't look at her. "We can go to Montana in a few days and stay there for as long as you like. But we had to come here to Washington first."

"You promised me, Caine," she whispered. She stared at him as her heart broke into little pieces. "You promised me we wouldn't come to Washington. Why did you lie to me?"

"I'm sorry, Lexie. You don't know how sorry I am. The last thing I ever wanted to do was lie to you. But we had to come here. It's the only place where I could make reasonably certain that you and the kid would be safe until this situation with El Cuchillo is resolved. And now it's the only place where I would have the facilities to deal with that picture.''

"It was just a job to you all along, wasn't it?'' She felt her eyes filling with tears and blinked them furiously away. She refused to allow herself to cry in front of him. "You were simply following orders again. My father told you to find me and bring me back, and that's what you did. My wishes didn't make a damn bit of difference.''

"That's not the way it is, and I think you know it. I'm trying to do what's best for you and the kid.''

"And don't call her that again.'' Lexie heard her voice rising, but she didn't care. Something broke inside her as pain tore at her from every direction. "She has a name, and it's Ana. Call her by her name, dammit!''

His gaze flickered to her shawl, then snapped back to her face. "You have every right to be upset with me.'' His face was pale, but he looked her in the eye. "I admit it. I lied to you when I told you I wouldn't bring you back to Washington, but don't you see that I had to? Especially now. El Cuchillo's soldiers know where this plane was headed. What if they try to come after you? I can protect you far better here than I could on my ranch in Montana. It should only take a few days to resolve this, then we can go there. You don't even have to see your father if you don't want to.''

"So there really is a ranch in Montana? I thought maybe that was a lie, too.'' She stared at Caine for a moment, until she felt her lip quivering. Then she spun around and stared out the window of the cockpit at the twinkling lights of the airport.

"Yes, there's really a ranch in Montana.'' There was no expression in his voice. "I've already handed in my resignation. When this job is finished I'm moving there for good.''

This job. Her heart shriveled into a small, aching mass. "What about everything else that happened on this trip? Was that a lie, too?'' she asked softly.

She felt him start toward her, then stop. "I think you know the answer to that,'' he said gently. "I knew when I decided we had to come to Washington that you might not forgive me for tricking you and bringing you back here, but I had to do it anyway. It was a choice between having you alive and having you mad at me. Which would you have chosen?''

Before she could reply, another man came out of the cockpit. "This is the end of the line, folks," he said in a cheerful voice, as if he hadn't heard any of their argument. "Hop out. I have to pull up to customs now."

Lexie's face burned as she turned away from him and stumbled toward the door of the plane. It was bad enough to have to face Caine's betrayal. To have a witness on top of it was almost too humiliating to think about.

Caine somehow managed to get to the door of the plane before she did. She ignored his outstretched hand, but he picked her up and swung her down onto the asphalt anyway. When she moved away he let his hand drop, but he stayed close to her side.

"There's the car," he said in a neutral voice.

She had no other choice but to get in the car, and she knew it. Without a word she stalked to the nondescript dark sedan and yanked open the back door. Caine slid in beside her, then leaned forward to say a few quiet words to the driver.

He settled back against the seat next to her, and in a few minutes they were on the expressway and heading out of the city. Neither of them spoke for a long time.

As the lights flickered past the car, becoming fewer and fewer as they drove along, she looked down at Ana, lying on the seat beside her with a seat belt wrapped around her. All her dreams tasted like dust in her mouth. Propelled by her pain, she found herself saying, "I hope my father appreciates your loyalty."

"What do you mean?"

"There can't be too many men who would obey their boss so blindly. Especially in personal matters."

"This isn't exactly just personal, Lexie. And even if it was, I still would have brought you here. This is where you'll be the safest."

She heard the pain in his voice, pain that he tried to hide, and for a moment she wavered. But she forced herself to think of what had happened eleven months before. "I suppose it wasn't 'personal' when my father ordered you to leave the country and you didn't even bother to say goodbye to me? It wasn't 'personal' when I woke up in your apartment and found out you were gone?''

"I never intended to be gone for that long. I was supposed to be back in two days. I thought I could explain it to you then." His voice was carefully expressionless, but she didn't want to think about why.

"Too bad it turned out to be inconvenient for you to return then."

"Yes."

The silence in the car reverberated against her ears, heavy with tension. When she glanced over at Caine, he was staring out the window.

"Why, Caine?" she asked, unable to keep the remembered hurt and pain out of her voice. "Why didn't you ever get in touch with me?"

"Would it have made any difference if I had?"

"You know it would have. I was in—" She caught herself and stopped. "I was infatuated with you, and you knew it. I thought my father had sent you away, and you didn't care enough to get in touch with me."

At that he turned to face her. In the intermittent light from the highway she could see the lines of pain on his face. "That wasn't true, Lexie," he said in a low voice. "I would have walked through hell to get back to you. But I couldn't."

"Why not?" she asked, her voice passionate. "If it wasn't my father, what was stopping you?"

He turned away again, silent for so long she thought he wasn't going to answer. Finally he said in a low voice, "The mission your father sent me on got screwed up. The group I was supposed to contact found out who I really was and they kept me locked up for seven months. I had been home only a couple of weeks when your father told me you were in San Rafael."

"Oh, Caine!" Her anger disappeared, replaced by horror. She glanced over at his rigid profile, almost afraid to ask. "What about the rest of the time?" she whispered.

Again the silence in the car was heavy with tension. Finally he said, "I was in the hospital."

"Caine!" she said, shocked, thinking of the scars she had felt on his back, remembering his fear of medical care. Her heart twisted, wondering what he had been through. "Why didn't you tell me this earlier?"

"What was the point? At first, after I found out about the baby, I didn't care what you thought of me. Afterward, I didn't think it mattered anymore. I assumed you had figured out that I would have been with you if I could have."

She wanted to tell him that she had, that she'd assumed that all along, but she knew she couldn't do that. All along, she'd assumed the worst of him. And she was still doing it, she realized slowly. He had lied to her about coming back here, it was true, but maybe he was telling her the truth when he said he'd done it only so he could make sure she was protected.

She turned to him, knowing she didn't mean the hurtful words she'd spoken and needing to tell him so. But the car slowed down and Caine leaned forward over the seat to speak to the driver. They rolled to a stop in front of a modest-looking house on a quiet street, and Caine got out of the car and waited for her to join him.

"You'll be safe here for as long as it takes to clear this up," he said softly.

He didn't touch her as he waited for her to move. She wanted to say something, anything, but his face was as remote and closed off as she'd ever seen him. As she started toward the front door, he said, "There'll be a guard with you all the time. It's over now."

His words had a ring of finality and she stopped and turned to him, a huge weight settling on her chest, crushing her. He wasn't even looking at her. "What about you?" she asked, not even trying to hide the desperation in her voice. "You'll be here, too, won't you?"

He shot her a surprised look, as if he couldn't believe that she would want him there, then shuttered his face again. "I'll be back when I can."

Without looking at her again he opened the front door and nodded to the man who stood blocking the way. "It's okay, Tim. It's us."

The man he'd called Tim nodded and walked away, leaving them together. Caine turned to look at her, then his gaze shifted to where Ana slept in the shawl. "Take care of yourself." He reached out a hesitant hand and skimmed one finger over the top of the baby's head. "And take care of Ana."

He left without looking back. She wanted to call to him, to tell him that she was sorry, but her throat was swollen and thick and the words wouldn't come out. As she listened to the door gently closing, heavy tears welled in her eyes and slid down her cheeks. She stood there for a long time, the steady stream of her tears soaking the shawl.

Chapter 16

Lexie opened her eyes with a start and looked around. The semidarkened room was completely unfamiliar and she rolled over, looking for Ana and Caine.

Ana slept in a bassinet right next to the bed, but there was no sign of Caine. As Lexie sat up, pushing her hair out of her face, she remembered.

Caine was gone. He'd left her here, in this house, while he tried to find out more about the men in her picture. He'd promised her that she would be safe, but she felt more alone this morning than she ever had in her life.

Ana fidgeted in the white bassinet, and Lexie reached for her child, holding her cradled against her. "I bet you miss him, too, don't you?" she whispered in the baby's ear, inhaling her warm, sweet scent. "Don't worry, he'll come back eventually." *He has to,* she told herself. He wouldn't just leave them here until this was all over, then send someone else to set them free.

Why not? a quiet voice asked. *You made it pretty clear that not only didn't you trust him, but you wanted no part of him at all.* Lexie sat staring at the frame of golden sunlight that surrounded the closed blinds and remembered Caine's face the night before as he'd told her to take care of herself. And Ana.

She closed her eyes to blot out the memory of the pain she'd seen in his face. Pain that he hadn't even tried to hide. He'd called his daughter by her name, let his hand linger on her head, then turned and walked out the door without looking back.

And why would he have? the same insistent voice asked. It was the second time she'd turned away from him. Old habits were hard to break, she reminded herself bitterly. Caine, she was sure, was thinking the same thing.

The sound of Ana whimpering brought her back to reality. She held the baby clutched to her chest, and Ana was wriggling in discomfort. Forcing herself to relax, Lexie leaned back against the headboard of the bed and put Ana to her breast.

As she nursed, she looked around the unfamiliar room. It was no more personal than a motel room, although someone had attempted to make it welcoming. There were pictures hanging and the walls were covered with a delicate, floral wallpaper, but the room chilled her. It looked the way she felt—as if all the life had been drained out of it.

When Ana had finished, Lexie rolled out of bed to find that a stack of disposable diapers had been placed on top of the dresser, along with baby wipes and a couple of tubes of ointment. Laying Ana on the bed, she picked up a neat paper-and-plastic diaper.

So this was civilization, she thought as she examined the diaper. Closing her eyes, she longed for Santa Ysabel with every fiber of her being. She wanted her uncomplicated life back, where all she had to worry about was if she would get the vaccines she needed from the government of San Rafael, and whether or not she'd washed enough diapers for Ana.

Slowly she opened her eyes and smoothed out the paper diaper. If she were back in Santa Ysabel, she wouldn't have found Caine again, she reminded herself. And even if she never saw him again, she wouldn't trade their time together for anything in the world. Not even for her old life in the village. She treasured every moment of those few days they'd spent together, and she would guard their memory in her heart for the rest of her life.

"Come on, sweetheart, let's get one of these contraptions on you," she muttered to Ana. They couldn't stay in this room forever.

Fifteen minutes later, dressed and hungry, she opened the door of her room. She found herself at the top of a staircase, and at the bottom, sitting in a chair in the living room, she saw a man put down a newspaper and smile up at her.

"Good morning, Ms. Hollister. Did you sleep well?"

She nodded as she walked down the stairs. "Yes, thank you." She paused, feeling her face redden. "I'm sorry, I don't remember your name. I know...Caine...introduced us last night, but I've forgotten." Her face got even redder when she stumbled over Caine's name, but the man at the bottom of the stairs didn't seem to notice.

"My name's Tim," he said easily. "And don't worry about it. You were awfully tired last night."

"You're very diplomatic," she replied, giving him a tiny smile as she stepped off the stairs. "Thanks, Tim, for being here like this." She gestured to the room. "For guarding me, I mean."

"Hey, it's my job." He grinned at her. "But it doesn't always come with such cute packages."

For a minute Lexie thought he was referring to her, and she squirmed with discomfort. Then she saw he was staring at Ana, and she felt herself relax as her heart expanded. "Thank you," she said, her voice soft.

"How old is she?" Tim stood on tiptoe, trying to peer over the blanket that covered the baby.

"Two months."

Tim flashed her a grin. "Is she smiling yet?"

Completely disarmed, Lexie moved into the living room and sat down on one of the chairs. "She sure is." Looking over at the man opposite her, seeing the yearning on his face, she said impulsively, "Would you like to hold her?"

"I'd love to." He held out his arms, and Lexie handed him the baby.

As she watched him for a while, she couldn't help but think of Caine. Would he ever be half as eager to hold his daughter?

Would he ever even see his daughter again? Blinking back tears, she forced herself to talk to Tim.

"You must have kids of your own."

He looked up at her and nodded. "A daughter who's two and a half, and a son who's six months. It's hard to be away from them when I'm on a job like this."

"How long are you going to be here?" she asked, unable to keep the eagerness out of her voice. Maybe he would know if Caine was coming back.

Shrugging, he handed Ana back to her. "We never know. As long as it takes. It could be days or weeks." He looked at Ana one last time, his longing for his own children naked in his eyes, then glanced up at Lexie. "There's some cereal and other breakfast stuff in the kitchen, and coffee's already made. Help yourself. After you're done, we can talk about the rules here."

"Okay." She was famished, she realized. When she'd dressed that morning, in clothes that had been washed and ironed, she'd found that everything hung too loosely on her frame. She'd lost weight during their trek through the jungle, and now she could hardly wait to eat.

A half hour later, Ana lay on a blanket on the floor and Tim was quietly telling her what she could and couldn't do. When he was certain that she wouldn't pull back the blinds, use the telephone or open either of the doors, he went back to his paper and she stared at Ana, happily gurgling on the floor.

The day stretched in front of her, empty and lonely. What was wrong with her? she wondered as she went into the kitchen to get another cup of coffee. She'd never had a day free of responsibilities, when she could do nothing but enjoy Ana and relax. And now that she did, all she could think about was Caine.

Where was he? And what was he doing? She stared sightlessly at the white kitchen cabinets as he filled her mind. Was he thinking about her at all? Or was he too busy trying to figure out why the rebel leader El Cuchillo was so anxious to capture her? Would she ever know?

She'd never even told Caine that she loved him. The kitchen cabinet blurred in front of her burning eyes. Now, maybe she would never get the chance.

She heard a noise behind her, and she spun around. Tim stood in the doorway to the kitchen, leaning against the wall. "Why don't you watch some television?" he suggested gently. "Or there's a bunch of books in the extra bedroom. We probably won't hear anything today."

"Do you think he'll come back tomorrow?" She couldn't disguise the eagerness in her voice.

Tim didn't even pretend not to understand. "I don't know, Ms. Hollister. I got the impression that he had a lot to do."

The faint trace of pity she saw in his eyes made her turn around and fumble with her coffee cup. "It's just hard to wait, not knowing anything," she said in a low voice. She hoped that he wouldn't notice how her voice trembled.

"I know." The sympathy in his words made her throat tighten. "But worrying about it isn't going to make the time pass any more quickly. Why don't I turn on one of the talk shows? I'll bet you didn't see much of those down in San Rafael."

"All right." Slowly, trying to control the shaking of her hand, she poured cream into her coffee. "I'll be right out."

Two hours later she laid Ana in her bassinet for a nap and wandered into the third bedroom, looking for a book. She'd found the television talk shows annoying and too loud, and had turned them off abruptly when she'd found herself longing again for the peace and simplicity of Santa Ysabel. Looking over the books stacked in the bookshelf, she selected a mystery and headed down the stairs. Tim looked up and smiled as she sat down.

"That's a good one. I think you'll enjoy it," he said, nodding at the book in her hand.

She forced herself to smile back at him. "I hope so."

By the next evening she felt like a captive tiger, pacing back and forth in her cage, desperate for a way out. There hadn't been a word from Caine, although the phone had rung several times and Tim had held long, whispered conversations. When she'd asked him what they were about, he'd smiled and told her they were just routine checks.

Even Ana had been cranky today, and Lexie had breathed a sigh of relief when she'd finally fallen asleep an hour earlier. The mystery she'd selected to read couldn't hold her attention, and neither could any of the programs on television. She longed with all her soul for Caine.

But apparently he didn't feel the same way. It had been almost forty-eight hours since he'd left her at this house—the longest two days of her life. He still hadn't called, and worry for him was beginning to coalesce into a thick lump of despair in her chest. He was perfectly capable of disappearing from her life without a word, especially if he'd decided that it would be the best thing he could do. And after what he'd told her in Limores, she was desperately afraid that was exactly what he'd decided.

She wandered into the kitchen to make herself a cup of tea. Tim still sat in the living room, reading a book. She turned around to ask him if he wanted some tea, but froze before she could get the words out.

As she watched, he dropped the book on the floor and stood in one fluid motion, pulling his gun out of his shoulder holster. He started for the door, but before he could get there it flew open and Lexie heard a muffled spitting sound.

She watched in horror as Tim slowly crumpled to the floor, bright red blood oozing from his chest. She must have cried out, because two figures stepped around his body and filled the doorway of the kitchen.

She didn't recognize either of them, but from their appearance she knew they had to be from San Rafael. One of them pointed a gun at her. It had a long tube on the end of it, which she realized must be a silencer. Somehow the evidence of their planning terrified her even more than the gun.

"Don't move," the one holding the gun said in a guttural voice.

Lexie beat down the gurgle of hysterical laughter that threatened to bubble out of her throat. Didn't they know she was incapable of moving a muscle right now?

"Where is it?" the other man asked.

She licked her dry lips. "Where's what?" she managed to whisper.

"Don't play games," the first man warned. "You know what we're looking for."

Lexie's hands clenched on the counter behind her. When a drawer began to open she jumped, then slid her hand inside. "I don't know," she insisted. If she played dumb, maybe she could buy some time. She couldn't look at Tim, lying on the floor behind the two men, his life seeping out of him. Tim couldn't afford any time, but it was all she had to bargain with for her and Ana's lives.

"We know you took it with you." The man with the gun spoke again, shifting restlessly. "Give it to us, and we will not hurt you."

She saw the lie in his eyes even as he spoke, and fear paralyzed her again. Then she thought of Ana, asleep upstairs in the white basket, and she straightened. Speaking in a louder voice, to disguise the sound of her hand rummaging in the partially open drawer, she said, "I have no idea what you're talking about. We only took food and clothes with us when we left Santa Ysabel. If you tell me what you want, maybe I can help you."

The man holding the gun stepped closer, and she shrank back against the counter until the drawer cut into her fingers. "We want the pictures and the other information," he hissed.

"Pictures? And other information?" She didn't have to fake her confusion. "What information? I have no idea what you're talking about." She tried to banish the image of the manila envelope from her mind, afraid they would somehow see the knowledge in her face.

The man swore at her in the language of San Rafael, his dialect a mixture of Spanish and Indian. She pretended not to understand.

"The pictures from your house, *señorita*," he said through clenched teeth. "The ones you took with you before you left. And all the other information you collected for your father the spy, James Hollister."

If she told him that Caine had the pictures, he would kill both her and Ana. She knew it with a cold-blooded certainty. So she shook her head and focused on the demands about her father. "You are mistaken. We left in a hurry and didn't have time to take anything as sentimental as pictures. They are all still in my house in Santa Ysabel.'' She lifted her chin. ''And my father has nothing to do with this. He didn't even know where I was.''

''Don't lie to me!'' he answered savagely. ''Of course, your father sent you to Santa Ysabel to spy on El Cuchillo. He is a friend of the yellow dog who is our president, after all. The pictures you took are proof of his interference in our country. And don't you think we searched your house from top to bottom?'' His voice was scathing. ''The pictures weren't there.''

She couldn't afford to think about her father. The pain and anger wouldn't help her right now. She had to focus on the pictures, and convince these men she didn't have them. ''Then someone else must have taken my pictures, although they were only scenes from the village. My father had nothing to do with them.'' Her hand closed around the handle of a knife, and she slowly pulled it from the drawer. Trying to distract the men, she nodded toward a corner of the kitchen. ''There's my backpack. I haven't touched it since we got here the day before yesterday. Go ahead and check it if you want.''

''Toss it to me.''

She moved away from the counter and pretended to stumble. ''I . . . I can't.'' She stared at him, letting all her fear show in her eyes. ''I'm too scared.''

''Go search upstairs,'' the man with the gun told his silent partner. ''I'll get the pack.''

''No!'' Lexie cried, watching the other man turn away. ''This is all I have, right here. There's nothing upstairs.''

The man with the gun gave her an evil smile. ''She's very anxious for you not to go up there. Go see what she's trying to hide.''

Nausea roiled in her stomach as the silent man turned and disappeared up the stairs. The man with the gun looked at her, then walked over to where her pack was propped against the wall. He threw all her dirty clothes and Ana's clean diapers onto the floor, then turned to her. ''They are not here.''

''I told you I don't have them,'' she said desperately. ''I didn't bring any pictures with me.''

At that moment the other man walked back into the kitchen. ''Nothing upstairs but a baby.''

The man with the gun looked over at her and smiled again. "Bring the baby down here. Maybe we can think of a way to make her mother talk."

"*No!*" Lexie pushed herself away from the counter and charged at him, slashing him with the knife in her hand. Both men stared at her, shock on their faces. The man with the gun looked stupidly down at his upper arm, where a line of red suddenly became a thick river of blood coursing down over his elbow and dripping onto the floor.

"*Madre de Dios,* she cut you." The silent man spoke, staring at his partner.

The man with the gun turned slowly and looked at her. His black eyes glittered with pain and hatred. He tried to lift his gun with his injured arm, but it dangled helplessly in his hand. Cursing at her, he reached for it with his other hand.

Lexie leaped again, aiming the knife at his face and closing her eyes as she slashed at him. *He was going to hurt Ana.* The words drummed through her mind as she heard him grunt. *If she didn't stop him, he would hurt Ana.*

Suddenly his hand pushed at her chest, shoving with all its might, and she stumbled backwards. Opening her eyes, she saw that the man with the gun wasn't looking at her anymore. He'd transferred his gun into his other hand and was pointing it at Caine, who stood in the doorway. The silent man was nowhere in sight.

"Caine." His name was torn out of her with a despairing cry, and she leaped again for the man with the gun.

"Lexie, stay back," Caine shouted. She heard the muffled spitting sound of the silenced gun at the same time, and saw Caine dodge sideways. As the man turned toward her and raised his weapon, Caine came flying through the air and landed on top of him.

The struggle was silent and vicious. Lexie shifted the knife in her hand as she watched, helpless fear making her stomach churn. The two men were both moving too fast for her to be able to do anything. She was afraid that any move on her part would hurt Caine rather than his opponent, so all she could do was watch.

Both men suddenly froze. Caine had managed to wrest the gun away from the other man, and now he held it to his opponent's head. The only sound in the kitchen was the harsh breathing of the two men.

Caine looked up at Lexie as he held the gun rock steady against the other man's head. His eyes looked flat and deadly, and they made her shiver. "Are you all right? Did he hurt you?"

She shook her head. "I'm fine. He didn't touch me."

"How about Ana? Is she all right?"

Lexie paled. "I think so."

Caine said, "Go check," but she was already out of the room and running up the stairs. Out of the corner of her eye she noticed that someone knelt on the floor next to Tim, and that the second killer lay spread-eagled on the floor of the hall. Bursting into her room, she rushed over to Ana in the bassinet. She didn't look as though she'd moved since Lexie had laid her in the basket an eternity ago. Gently she turned the baby over, saw that she was still asleep, and breathed a prayer of thanks. Then she covered Ana again and closed the door behind her.

Returning to the kitchen, she said, "She's fine."

Caine glanced up at her from the floor, and some of the flatness disappeared from his eyes. "Thank God." Then he looked back down at the helpless man on the floor, and Lexie saw his finger tighten on the gun. She watched, horrified, as Caine stared at him for what seemed like forever. Then, slowly, he lowered the gun and stood.

The next moment, two uniformed police officers stepped into the kitchen. "Get this one out of my sight," Caine said. One of them clicked handcuffs on the injured man and the other read him his rights.

Caine looked over at her, then reached out and gently took the bloody knife from her hand and laid it on the counter. She hadn't even realized she was still holding it. Slowly, he pulled her into his arms.

At his touch she shuddered, then closed her eyes as hot tears began rolling down her face and onto his chest. "Caine," she whispered, burrowing deeper into his embrace and inhaling his scent, "I didn't think I'd ever see you again."

"Shh, Lexie, it's all over," he soothed. "Don't cry. We caught El Cuchillo in Limores this afternoon, and all his followers in this country besides these two. You're safe now."

Pushing out of his arms, she looked up at him. "I'm not crying because I'm scared, you idiot. I'm crying because I didn't think you were ever going to come back for me and Ana."

Something shifted in his eyes, and he looked away. "We found out all about El Cuchillo," he continued, as if he hadn't heard her. "He was one of the men in your picture. His real name is Carlos Fuertes, and he's nothing more than a sleazy drug dealer. He was originally from San Rafael, but he spent the last dozen or so years in the U.S. When things got too hot for him in this country, he went back to San Rafael and decided there might be more profit in running a country than in running drugs. He was so insistent about getting rid of Americans because he was afraid someone from his old life would recognize him and ruin the good thing he had going. And he was after you because he'd recently run into Pedro again. He didn't remember the pictures you had of him until after he'd killed Pedro. Then he apparently panicked. He knew who your father was, and thought he'd sent you to San Rafael to spy on him. That's why he was so relentless. He figured you were leaving the country with evidence against him."

"O'Roarke, have you ordered an ambulance for this man yet?" a voice barked from the hallway, and Lexie jumped away from Caine. It was her father's voice.

Caine grabbed her hand and pulled her behind him as he answered, "It's on its way."

"Damn good thing. He's not going to die, but he's lost a lot of blood, and he needs—"

Her father had walked into the kitchen and stopped dead when he saw her. He paled, then looked accusingly at Caine.

"Why didn't you tell me that my daughter was here, O'Roarke?"

"It wasn't my news to tell."

"Dammit, you let her get involved in this. She could have been killed. You had no right to bring her here."

"Where would you have suggested I bring her?"

''You could have brought her to me. That's where she lives, after all.''

Lexie squeezed Caine's hand and stepped in front of him. ''It's not Caine's fault, Daddy. This is where I wanted to come.'' She drew a deep breath and felt the anger curl through her again. When would her father stop trying to manipulate her? ''Why didn't you tell me the president of San Rafael was a friend of yours?''

As James Hollister stared at her, she could see the hardness fade from his eyes, replaced by a longing that astonished her. ''I knew if I did, you wouldn't go to San Rafael. And I wanted to be able to keep track of you,'' he said simply. ''At least he was able to tell me you'd made it safely to Santa Ysabel. Are you all right?'' When she nodded, he said, ''I've missed you, sweetheart.''

As she watched him, she felt her anger slipping away. Suddenly, with the insight she'd gained since becoming a parent, she understood that he'd done what he thought was necessary to protect her. She might not agree with his methods, but she would always be his child and he would always worry about her. She took a step toward him. ''I've missed you, too, Daddy.''

She realized with a sense of wonder that it was the truth. As she watched her father, she felt Caine's hand on her shoulder. It was as if he gently pushed away a huge weight. Reaching up to cover Caine's hand with her own, she knew that she would never be intimidated by her father again. He was trying to protect her, not control her, and she was strong enough to understand the difference. Caine and Ana had taught her that.

She truly had grown up in Santa Ysabel. Stepping away from Caine, she walked into her father's embrace.

Her father's arms tightened around her so fiercely that she could hardly breathe, then he loosened his grip and stood back. ''You look good, sweetheart,'' he said softly.

She gave him a tremulous smile. ''Santa Ysabel was good for me,'' she replied. ''And I brought something back for you.''

When her father looked at her, she glanced over at Caine. He gave her a short nod and watched her with unreadable eyes. Slowly she looked back at her father. ''I brought you back a granddaughter.''

He stared at her uncomprehendingly. "A what?"

"Caine and I have a daughter," she said gently. "Your grandchild."

"What?" He stared from one to the other, and slowly he smiled. Lexie watched, astonished. It was the last reaction she'd expected.

"It's about time the two of you saw the noses on your faces." He looked at them again, and his smile broadened. "You can tell me all about it later. Right now I have some business to attend to."

For a long time, Lexie stared at the place where her father had been, then she turned to Caine. "I had no idea it would be that simple."

"Most things are, when you think about it."

"What about us, Caine?" she asked, feeling her chest contract at the tightness in his eyes at her words. "Is that going to be just as simple?"

The pain she could see in his face tore at her. "I tried to keep it simple," he whispered. "God knows, I tried. But I couldn't leave without making sure you were safe."

Grabbing his arms, she forced him to face her. "What do you mean? Where were you planning to go?"

"It's best this way, Lexie," he said, not answering her question. He didn't meet her eyes. "You have every right to feel the way you do about me. I tricked you from the very beginning. I knew we would have to come back here all along, and I manipulated you into going along with me. I thought it would be easier for you if I just disappeared."

"You have no idea what would be easy for me, or how I feel about you," she said. "Instead of guessing, why don't you just ask?"

"You made yourself pretty clear the other day, and you were right about all of it."

"The last time I saw you I was scared and upset. I said a lot of things that I didn't mean, and a lot of things that were just plain wrong. I know that, Caine, and I suspect you do, too." Slowly she reached out and touched his face. "Ask me how I feel about you, Caine. Please."

He grabbed her hand and held her away from him as he studied her. She saw a faint spark of hope in his eyes. "How do you feel about me, Lexie?" His voice was rough.

"I love you, Caine," she whispered. "I think I have, all along. But before I went to San Rafael, I was too stubborn and spoiled to admit it. You wouldn't change to become what I thought I wanted, and I was too immature to realize that I wanted you just the way you were."

"I thought you were afraid I'm too much like your father." She saw a flicker in his eyes. "You don't want to be controlled ever again, remember?"

"Do you think I don't know you, after we walked through the jungle together? I love you," she repeated. "Even when you would have been justified in doing it, you didn't bully me. You never would."

His hands tightened on her shoulders, but he didn't pull her closer. "And what about Ana?" he asked. "Aren't you even a little concerned after what I told you?"

"I trust you with her life, Caine," she said, looking into his eyes. "You would never hurt her. You're not capable of it."

"Neither one of us knows that, Lexie."

She smiled mistily at him. "Oh, yes, I do. If you couldn't hurt that man who was trying to kill you, how could you hurt your daughter? I know you, Caine. I think I know you better than you know yourself."

"Are you sure, Lexie?" he asked, his voice urgent. "Are you very sure you're willing to take that chance?"

"I'm not taking any chances, Caine." She reached out and touched his face again.

He pulled her into his arms and buried his face in her neck. "Oh, God, Lexie, I love you." Slowly he lifted his head. "And I love Ana, too. I'll try to be a good father to her, I swear it. But I don't know anything about being a parent."

"Then we'll learn together." She linked her hands behind his neck and pulled his mouth down to hers. The other men in the room faded away, the noises around them faded away, until nothing existed but the two of them. His kiss was a pledge and a promise and a solemn oath.

He lifted his head to look down at her, and all the shadows were gone from his eyes. "You're all I've ever wanted and more than I ever dared dream of. When will you marry me?"

She smiled at him, her throat tightening, feeling as if her heart would burst. "Isn't that awfully presumptuous? Shouldn't you ask me *if* I'll marry you, first?"

"I don't think our daughter would approve of us living in sin." He brushed his lips over hers. "What do you think?"

Lexie listened for a moment, then smiled at him again. "Why don't you go ask her?"

He raised his head, and his face softened when he heard Ana's sharp cry. "I think I'll do that."

A minute later he walked back into the kitchen, holding the baby cradled in one arm. He draped his other arm over Lexie's shoulder. "Ana says that she wants us to get married tomorrow."

She looked at him, standing in front of her holding their child in his arms, and felt her throat tightening and her eyes swimming. All she had ever wanted was being offered to her, and all she had to do was reach out and take it. "I think we have a very wise child," she whispered.

Caine reached out with his other hand and drew her close to him until the three of them were standing in an unbroken circle. "I love you, Lexie."

She reached out and embraced both of them, holding them against her heart. "And I love you, Caine."

*   *   *   *   *

The collection of the year!
NEW YORK TIMES BESTSELLING AUTHORS

Linda Lael Miller
Wild About Harry

Janet Dailey
Sweet Promise

Elizabeth Lowell
Reckless Love

Penny Jordan
Love's Choices

and featuring
Nora Roberts
The Calhoun Women

This special trade-size edition features four of the wildly
popular titles in the Calhoun miniseries together in
one volume—a true collector's item!

Pick up these great authors and a chance to win
a weekend for two in New York City at the
Marriott Marquis Hotel on Broadway! We'll pay
for your flight, your hotel—even a Broadway show!

Available in December at your favorite retail outlet.

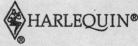

MILLION DOLLAR SWEEPSTAKES

SWP-M96

As seen on TV!
Free Gift Offer

With a Free Gift proof-of-purchase from any Silhouette® book,
you can receive a beautiful cubic zirconia pendant.

This gorgeous marquise-shaped stone is a genuine cubic
zirconia—accented by an 18" gold tone necklace.

(Approximate retail value $19.95)

Send for yours today...
compliments of *Silhouette*®

To receive your free gift, a cubic zirconia pendant, send us one original proof-of-
purchase, photocopies not accepted, from the back of any Silhouette Romance™,
Silhouette Desire®, Silhouette Special Edition®, Silhouette Intimate Moments®
or Silhouette Yours Truly™ title available in August, September, October, November and
December at your favorite retail outlet, together with the Free Gift Certificate, plus a
check or money order for $1.65 U.S./$2.15 CAN. (do not send cash) to cover postage and
handling, payable to Silhouette Free Gift Offer. We will send you the specified gift. Allow
6 to 8 weeks for delivery. Offer good until December 31, 1996 or while quantities last.
Offer valid in the U.S. and Canada only.

Free Gift Certificate

Name: _____

Address: _____

City: _____ State/Province: _____ Zip/Postal Code: _____

Mail this certificate, one proof-of-purchase and a check or money order for postage
and handling to: SILHOUETTE FREE GIFT OFFER 1996. In the U.S.: 3010 Walden
Avenue, P.O. Box 9077, Buffalo NY 14269-9077. In Canada: P.O. Box 613, Fort Erie,
Ontario L2Z 5X3.

FREE GIFT OFFER   084-KMD
ONE PROOF-OF-PURCHASE
To collect your fabulous FREE GIFT, a cubic zirconia pendant, you must include this
original proof-of-purchase for each gift with the properly completed Free Gift Certificate.

084-KMD-R

SILHOUETTE... Where Passion Lives

Order these Silhouette favorites today!

Now you can receive a discount by ordering two or more titles!

SD#05890	TWO HEARTS, SLIGHTLY USED by Dixie Browning	$2.99 U.S. ☐ /$3.50 CAN. ☐	
SD#05899	DARK INTENTIONS by Carole Buck	$2.99 U.S. ☐ /$3.50 CAN. ☐	
IM#07604	FUGITIVE FATHER by Carla Cassidy	$3.50 U.S. ☐ /$3.99 CAN. ☐	
IM#07673	THE LONER by Linda Turner	$3.75 U.S. ☐ /$4.25 CAN. ☐	
SSE#09934	THE ADVENTURER by Diana Whitney	$3.50 U.S. ☐ /$3.99 CAN. ☐	
SSE#09867	WHEN STARS COLLIDE by Patricia Coughlin	$3.50 U.S. ☐	
SR#19079	THIS MAN AND THIS WOMAN by Lucy Gordon	$2.99 U.S. ☐ /$3.50 CAN. ☐	
SR#19060	FATHER IN THE MIDDLE by Phyllis Halldorson	$2.99 U.S. ☐ /$3.50 CAN. ☐	
YT#52001	WANTED: PERFECT PARTNER by Debbie Macomber	$3.50 U.S. ☐ /$3.99 CAN. ☐	
YT#52008	HUSBANDS DON'T GROW ON TREES by Kasey Michaels	$3.50 U.S. ☐ /$3.99 CAN. ☐	

(Limited quantities available on certain titles.)

TOTAL AMOUNT	$_____
DEDUCT: 10% DISCOUNT FOR 2+ BOOKS	$_____
POSTAGE & HANDLING	$_____
($1.00 for one book, 50¢ for each additional)	
APPLICABLE TAXES*	$_____
TOTAL PAYABLE	$_____
(check or money order—please do not send cash)	

To order, complete this form and send it, along with a check or money order for the total above, payable to Silhouette Books, to: **In the U.S.:** 3010 Walden Avenue, P.O. Box 9077, Buffalo, NY 14269-9077; **In Canada:** P.O. Box 636, Fort Erie, Ontario, L2A 5X3.

Name:_____

Address:_____ City:_____

State/Prov.:_____ Zip/Postal Code:_____

*New York residents remit applicable sales taxes.
Canadian residents remit applicable GST and provincial taxes.

Silhouette®

SBACK-SN3

You're About to Become a

Privileged Woman

Reap the rewards of fabulous free gifts and benefits with proofs-of-purchase from Silhouette and Harlequin books

Pages & Privileges™

It's our way of thanking you for buying our books at your favorite retail stores.

PROOF OF PURCHASE
SIM-PP19
Offer expires March 31, 1997

**Harlequin and Silhouette—
the most privileged readers in the world!**

For more information about Harlequin and Silhouette's PAGES & PRIVILEGES program call the Pages & Privileges Benefits Desk: 1-503-794-2499

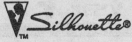
Silhouette®

SIM-PP19